D0934223

GCLS

Gloucester County
Library System

389 Wolfert Station Road
Mullica Hill, NJ 08062
(609) 223-6000

AN EVANS NOVEL OF THE WEST

BILL BRAGG AND R.C. HOUSE

DRUMM'S WAR

M. EVANS & COMPANY, INC. NEW YORK

GLOUCESTER
COUNTY LIBRARY

Library of Congress Cataloging-in-Publication Data

House, R.C.
Drumm's War / R.C. House
p.   cm.—(An Evans novel of the West)
ISBN 0-87131-695-1 : $16.95
I. Title   II. Series.
PS3552.R262D78   1992
813,54—dc20   92-28138
CIP

Copyright © 1992 by R.C. House

All rights reserved. No part of this book
may be reproduced or transmitted in any form
or by any means without the written
permission of the publisher.

M. Evans and Company, Inc.
216 East 49th Street
New York, New York 10017

Typesetting by AeroType, Inc.

Manufactured in the United States of America

9 8 7 6 5 4 3 2 1

Dedicated to the memory of
BILL BRAGG

In late 1987, his days numbered in his fight against cancer, Bill Bragg—my Western Writers of America pal of ten years—asked me to enhance and embellish one of his last manuscripts. Somehow he respected that talent in me. He did not live to learn of its acceptance for publication. Somewhere, I'm sure he's aware.

—R.C. House, 1992.

"A pal's last need is a thing to heed, so I swore I would not fail . . . "
—Robert W. Service, "The Cremation of Sam McGee"

Foreword

"Sure enough," Von Holder exclaimed to Drumm. "The Republic of Texas, annexed by the United States on July 4, within the boundaries agreed upon at 42 degrees north latitude and 106 degrees west longitude." He hummed. "We should cross into a part of the State of Texas in three days' time, or about August 4." (page 90)

(Morella) studied Drumm contemptuously. "What brings you into Mexico, Capitano Gringo?"

"Mexico!" Drumm laughed. He looked at Peagram. "He's been gone so long from Santa Fe he hasn't heard this is now the State of Texas, annexed by the United States on July 4, 1845. It's my turn, Captain. What the hell are you and your men doing in the American State of Texas?" (Page 114)

Co-author's note: Much of the *Drumm's War* story depends on a little-known fluke of history. When Texas was annexed, its famous "Panhandle" had a western boundary based on 106 degrees west longitude and would have included all of what is now the eastern half of New Mexico and Colorado. The 42-degree latitude line—the "top" of Texas—crossed present-day Wyoming slightly north of Cheyenne. Thus it was possible for Drumm's army to get from extreme northwest Colorado to Texas (quoting August Von Holder) "in three days' time . . . " RCH

Prologue

When Hard Winter Davis couldn't find Captain Drumm at the Johnson House Hotel, he soon learned why. The Drumm woman and her infant son had died of cholera early in March.

"Fact is," the desk clerk whispered to the weathered giant in dirt-glazed buckskins pushing against the tall counter, "the cemetery is the fastest growing business in St. Louis this spring." The clerk cocked an eye knowingly. "Nearly 5,000 died before they could leave on the Oregon Trail, poor souls."

Davis pondered a moment, sifting that information before asking the clerk the way to the burying ground. He spun lightly for a man his size and went to find his horse.

It sure looked busy, Davis mused a few minutes later as he walked his mount through the hilly cemetery, a somber place under spreading oaks. It wasn't long before Davis saw him, his head hung in grief, sitting at the end of a mound, holding the reins of his horse.

Davis drew up. He stared at the seamed, agonized face of Andrew Jackson Drumm, Captain, U.S. Topographical Corps. No mistake. Grief couldn't hide the dark, handsome features and deep blue eyes under straight, black eyebrows. A noble beak of nose matched prominent cheekbones.

Davis pondered the long, livid scar that began above Drumm's left ear, running along the jaw—a pink and proud relic of a recent wound. He remembered the day it happened.

Drumm became aware of Davis like a man coming out of sleep.

1

"They're dead, you know, Hard Winter." Drumm drew himself up to his full six feet plus, brushing dirt and twigs from his breeches. Trembling in grief, Drumm leaned against his horse. "My God, Hard Winter. What am I going to do?" Anguish thickened his speech and twisted his face as he gripped the saddle. "I wasn't even here! She and the babe died by themselves!"

Davis arced a leg and swung out of the saddle. He threw an angular arm across his best friend's shoulders. "Ahh, Andy. Ya cain't blame yourself now. You was in Washington on official business. We both was. An' you know it." He patted Drumm's shoulder, a timid but sincere gesture alien to men who had fought and caroused together. "And Amy wouldn't have had it any other way."

He stepped back, done with the awkward chore of comforting. "Now. Come on back to the hotel. We'll send Amy's belongings back home to her folks."

Drumm stared into Davis's eyes, then blinked and nodded reluctantly. An hour later they had piled everything left over into a trunk and saw it off to Alexandria, Virginia. Then Drumm asked to be alone.

The next day, with Drumm acting more himself, the two haggled with a round-gutted, ill-kempt man at the livery yard over forty head of big mules.

"Big, strong and young," Hard Winter observed to Drumm. "No bridle-worn lips is a good sign. They'll do in a pinch, I'll allow. They never can get enough water to kill their thirst where I'm goin'. When I water 'em, it may be their last sip for three or four days."

Drumm managed a grin at Davis's words. "You ought to feel honored," he told the liveryman. "That's the longest speech I ever heard that old man make."

"Waugh!" Davis snorted. "Anythin' to take your mind off your woes."

They parted the next morning in the dusty street in front of the hotel. "I'll see you north of Fort Bridger at South Pass the first of July, give or take a couple of days," Davis said.

"Keep your powder dry and your hair out of the smoke, Hard Winter. I'll see you then."

Davis slapped Drumm affectionately on the rump, a fatherly gesture. "You'll be all right, Andy. Mournin' don't help any of us. Take care yourself."

Drumm watched Davis's mule cavalcade out of sight before taking one last look at St. Louis. He thoughtfully levered himself into the saddle and swung the horse's head toward Fort Leavenworth. There, as a topographical officer, he would take command of a small unit attached to the five-company squadron of the United States Second Dragoons marching to Fort Laramie, on to South Pass, and back. The commanding officer would be Colonel Stephen Watts Kearny, and second in command would be Captain Philip St. George Cooke.

Along with his commander, Colonel James Abert, U.S. Topographical Corps, and Colonel Kearny, Drumm had received his orders directly from Secretary of War Marcy in Washington in February, 1845.

Drumm had taken the keen old mountain man to the conference. Hard Winter Davis, the Secretary had learned, was a legend among Indians and mountain men from the Pacific to the Missouri and from Mexico to the Yellowstone. Marcy had enthusiastically agreed that Davis would be Drumm's strong right arm from now on in everything—in everything except grief. The young officer bottled up his sorrow during his time with Davis. But when Drumm left St. Louis for Leavenworth, he was overwhelmed with despair. Visions of Amy haunted him waking and sleeping; he went without food. He grew so sick that he dismounted at one point, hugged the earth and wept.

Finally, after days of torture, Drumm decided to try and pull his life together. One evening, while the dying sun painted tendrils of clouds with glory, he made a small fire and had some coffee and ate a piece of hardtack. He remembered the gala supper and ball he and Kearny and Abert had attended at Secretary Marcy's handsome Washington home.

Drumm found himself dinner companion of a quiet and beautiful Englishwoman, Lady Diana Abney, sister of Lord Parton, Sir Hardwig Abney, special envoy to America. Kearny whispered, behind his hand, that the Abneys were in Washington to see if the United States intended to support its citizens crowding the Oregon

3

Trail into Mexican Territory in California and into British Territory in Oregon.

At Lady Diana's inquiry about his scar, Drumm explained that he had taken a head blow from an Indian war chief. She next wondered aloud if America was going to continue to usurp territory from other countries by allowing its citizens to squat on land they didn't own.

Drumm kept his tone level. "Land occupied or owned by absentee landlords usually gets settled one way or another. Sometimes the owner tries to coerce loyalty from people who don't feel they owe it," he said.

His meaning was not lost on her brother. "Surely you don't think we would require that of your settlers," her brother asked, dabbing beads of consommé from his lips. Andy, knowing he was drifting into deep diplomatic waters, said, "It is beyond my comprehension, Sir Hardwig. I'm just a simple soldier."

The meal over and the musicians tuning up, Drumm stood, offering his arm, and led the ash-blond beauty onto the dance floor. "For the time being, let's have music, a dance, and peace."Diana smiled.

"All right, Captain Drumm. But some day I'd like to debate you on those unoccupied lands and people being coerced."

Little did she realize that, four months later, she would have the opportunity to debate Drumm on those very subjects.

The memory faded and Drumm, still sick at heart, drifted into a fitful slumber. The next morning, he made his weary way to Fort Leavenworth.

Chapter One

"Bugler! Play me a tune!"

"Sir?"

"'Boots and Saddles!'"

Squaring his shoulders and tipping back his head, Trumpeter Gates brought his short brass bugle to his lips in an exaggerated military jerk, sun glinting in its slow curves. The bugle's stirring staccato shrilled on the dawn breeze and carried nearly half a mile down the valley. Alerted, a squadron of the Second Regiment of the United States Dragoons mounted and wheeled their horses into a regimental front.

Watching his squadron with a practiced eye, Colonel Stephen Watts Kearny observed their precision with satisfaction, scanning them with his short telescope. He spoke to the bugler again.

"Bugler. Squadrons." The colonel waited until the notes cleared the bell of the horn before ordering the command of execution.

"By the fours. Right about. March!"

The three men on the barren pass looking down on the horse soldiers, saw the squadron ride out, swing into columns of four, and begin its long march home, baggage trains lumbering in the rear, their canvas tops puffing and swaying with motion.

Kearny spoke to the middle-aged officer, proud and erect beside him. "A brave sight, eh, Cooke?"

Captain Philip St. George Cooke, Kearny's second in command, allowed it was indeed a brave sight. He laughed. "They all know

5

they're headin' for Leavenworth, too. Makes for a right happy crowd this mornin', sir.''

Kearny, his eye still focused through the telescope, nodded as the mass of riders in blue nudged their horses up the long incline of South Pass on the Continental Divide.

''It helps. Been a long haul since we left in April. Home sounds good to them.''

Kearny loosened the chin strap holding his visored kepi and ran a hand through his shock of bright red hair. ''I only hope this tour-de-force has convinced the British and the Mexicans that we can put a first-class army into the field at almost a moment's notice.''

Cooke scratched his chin. ''I'd bet a year's salary that somewhere between South Pass here, Fort Laramie, and Leavenworth that both British and Mexican spies made detailed reports about us.''

His chin strap firmly back in place, Kearny said, ''And now the second phase of this operation is about to take place. Take command of the line of march. Present my compliments to Captains Irons and Drumm. Tell them to join me here.''

Flinging a salute to Kearny, Cooke turned his big black and drove him at a gallop over to the squadron slowly laboring up the grade of the pass like a giant inchworm.

Kearny watched Cooke ride off and then gazed at the majestic chain of mountains rearing regally behind him. He had never seen anything like them. He drank in their beauty as the flat orange light of early dawn fingered its way into each yawning canyon starkly outlined on the sides of the towering range. Even though this was the last day of June, snowfields still rode safely in the mountains' deep folds, and the dawn breeze speeding past the snow and ice carried a chill. Shivering, Kearny remembered that during the entire week he had been at South Pass, where the Oregon Trail wound through a gap in the Rocky Mountains, a sheet of ice had formed on the water bucket outside his tent each morning.

And the wind was there eternally, there on the earth's backbone, tugging at a man, pushing and rushing at him from all sides.

He looked east at a distant point where the Oregon Trail dipped out of view, and even as he stared into the horizon, a white-topped prairie schooner hove into view. It was followed by another and, within minutes, more than thirty wagons were visible, toiling their way west to California or Oregon.

He motioned to Gates. "Ride over and tell the wagon boss that he needn't give way to our troops. We'll ride around. Then . . . report to Captain Cooke." He watched the young man confer with the wagon master and then ease back, passing the two captains on his way to report to him.

Captain Isaac Irons, serving his twelfth year as a dragoon officer, was a beefy man. His dark face was framed by bushy muttonchops, and his coarse black hair escaped the sides of his forage cap. Even his hands carried a heavy growth of hair. He was commanding officer of B Company, Second Dragoons, and although Kearny knew him to be competent, he also knew the man to have a vicious streak.

"Mornin', gentlemen," Kearny said as the two drew up and saluted.

Irons only nodded. Drumm said, "By your leave, sir."

Kearny assessed Drumm, liking the young man. He had all the solid maturity of a first-class officer. Kearny had only known him since March, but he had no cause for concern on the long, two-month mission that had ended here at South Pass the week before. Drumm had learned, had worked, and was well liked by men and officers. "He uses his eyes a lot and his mouth little," was the way Cooke had described Drumm to Kearny.

Irons, on the other hand, made no bones about his type of discipline, and offered no apologies for it.

Kearny undid the middle two buttons of his Dragoon shell jacket and extracted a sheaf of folded papers. Handing several to Drumm, he said, "Here are your orders, Andy. Starting tomorrow, you will take the first platoon of Company B, and your own topographical unit south into territory claimed by Mexico for a sixty-day reconnaissance patrol. Do everything you deem proper to stay out of a military action against Mexican cavalry or any Mexican troops."

Drumm nodded as Colonel Kearny verbally repeated what both men already knew was in the written orders.

"Now. Here is your commission as a captain in the Second Regiment of the Dragoons." Kearny's tone changed as he regarded Irons. "In all matters, Captain Irons, Captain Drumm is your superior officer, your commanding officer, and you and your men are to obey him.'' He paused as the countenance of Irons grew dark with pent-up outrage.

"Keep your temper under control, Irons, and if you have a challenge to the command here given to Drumm, let it be in writing, and given by your hand to mine this day.''

Irons angrily fished out a parchment and handed it to the Colonel. ''I already have. I am the senior officer, and deserve this command.''

"I quite agree, Captain Irons, and I'm sure Captain Drumm believes it unfair, too. But you must remember, the orders come from the Secretary of War, not from myself nor Mr. Drumm.''

The matter settled to Kearny's satisfaction, he had finished speaking when out of the distance, six hundred voices drifted to them on the crisp morning in a spirited marching song.

Then — Hip! Hurrah! For the prairie life!
Hip! Hurrah! For the mountain strife!
And if rifles must crack, if swords must we draw,
Our country forever! Hurrah! Hurrah!

It was Kearny's favorite, and the three men were silent as they watched the Dragoons parade by. Cooke led the black horses of A Company, followed by the half of B Company on their bays, and C Company on its grays, until all the men had moved past.

As the baggage trains waddled past on bouncing wheels, the three officers heard the last rousing refrain:

To the far, far-off Pacific sea,
Will you go, will you go, dear girl, with me?
By a gentle brook, in a lonely spot,
We'll jump from our wagon, and build a homey cot.

The halted immigrant train raised a cheer for the singing, blue-clad soldiers and, as the squadron dipped out of sight, Kearny turned his attention to the officers at his side.

"Captain Drumm, we'll expect you at Fort Laramie in mid-September. No later, eh, Drumm?''

"God willing, sir.'' Drumm said. "Do you still plan on sliding south to the Arkansas River at Bent's Fort before heading back to Leavenworth?''

"That's our hope, Andy.'' Kearny stepped his horse away from the two. "Well, gentlemen, good hunting!" Whirling his mount around, he rode off to join his beloved regiment.

Drumm broke the silence with a soft drawl. "Ahh, Irons. I know how you feel, but I know I can count on your help in the days ahead. I—" He was brusquely cut off by the irate Irons.

"Don't play word games with me, Drumm!" Irons yanked his horse around. "I am damned sore at those orders. Me, a line officer with two campaigns under my belt serving as second in command to you . . . a . . . " Irons fought for words, "a . . . damned staff officer . . . a toy soldier who ain't never heard a shot fired in anger." Irons put spurs to his horse meaning to ride off, but he sawed back on the reins. "Oh, hell! I gave my word to Kearny and Cooke. I'll take your orders, Drumm, because I am a soldier!" He glared. "But don't ask me to bow down any, or to like your orders, because sure as God made little green apples, I won't like 'em." Irons brutally spurred his horse, which half-reared in surprise, moving away from Drumm.

Drumm rammed his bigger horse over to Irons' chunky bay and continued to crowd Irons' horse until it was pinned against a granite outcropping.

His face dark with anger, Drumm leaned forward and gritted out his words.

"Since you appear to fancy such dark thoughts, Mr. Irons, I spent two years living with the Cheyenne, scouting with old Hard Winter Davis, a regular he-dog of a mountain man. That's where I got this." He fingered white scar tissue along his left jaw line.

"That was right after I got out of West Point." Drumm bit off each word. "Then I spent two years among the Seminoles in Florida while you and your regiment were ridin' back and forth between forts and towns." He paused to let it sink it, and drew a ragged breath. "That was in '38. All before I was sent to serve with the Corps of Topographical Engineers."

Drumm swallowed hard, sitting his saddle stiffly, rigid in his own fury. "Now, Mister. That may not be line duty the way you count it, but in my book it was line duty, and hard duty at that with shots fired in anger every single day for longer than I like to remember."

His bluff called, Irons sat sullenly and heard the younger man out. "Well . . . what I meant was . . . " he offered, but Drumm cut him off.

"Ah, hell, I know what you meant. I just get damned tired of hearing from you horse jockeys how damned good you are." He leaned forward and laid a heavy hand with a viselike grip on Irons' forearm.

"Well, Mister. I'm not exactly line, and I'm not exactly staff. But I am your commanding officer, so let's get one thing straight. You either cooperate with me, or by God, I'll see you shipped to Leavenworth in chains!" His eyes bored holes through Irons.

The heavier officer tried to pull back, but Drumm's grip tightened.

Drumm gritted, "You got that, Mister?" His clenched teeth gleamed white behind narrowed lips.

Nodding, Irons grunted. "You call the tune, ah, Captain, and I'll follow." Irons watched the blush of fire leave Drumm's face, and the ice soften in the blue eyes.

"Good. Glad we could part with this ill blood between us, Irons, and not before the men." Drumm eased his horse around, pointing south. "Now, Captain Irons, I'd like you to ride back to camp and ask Lieutenant Ives, First Sergeant Peagram, and Mr. Von Holder to join me on the other side of that far ridge inside the next hour."

He smiled at Irons.

"And you, sir, are invited to join our little party, too."

Chapter Two

They found Drumm sitting on a boulder alongside a gurgling brook where it bubbled its way out of a narrow canyon and meandered along a grassy floor in a long, wide valley.

Tying their horses to clumps of willows, the junior officers joined Drumm near the big rock. He tapped his shell jacket. "I've orders here to take command of the first platoon of the Second Dragoons along with my own Topographical Corps unit and to make a deep reconnaissance patrol inside Mexico. My second in command is Captain Irons."

He pointed south with a willow switch he had been whittling. "Not more than five, six miles from here is the border into Mexico. A good day's ride beyond Bridger's Fort, and then either into British Oregon, or Mexican California."

Pacing back and forth now, Drumm continued. "With nearly 5,000 Americans heading for California each year, our government needed to prove to the emigrants, and to the Mexicans and the British, that we could put an army into the field out here rapidly." He paused for effect. "That's why Colonel Kearny made this rapid march to South Pass, and right now is riding back to Leavenworth.

All along the way, whenever Indians gathered to see the soldiers, Kearny put on a show of strength by firing those two twelve-pound howitzers. We knew the Indians had seen cannon fire. But they've never seen shot that exploded farther away."

The officers and aides around him remembered the big Sioux chief at Fort Laramie calling them "the guns that talk twice." They recalled with grim satisfaction how the guns' deafening roars and the resulting blasts of the "rotten shells" that exploded near the impact point had impressed the Sioux as well as other Indian groups they encountered on the long march. The Indians had also looked with grudging respect at the splendidly equipped dragoons, decked out in new uniforms, carrying sidearms as well as sabers, and a shortened version of the issue musket called carbines.

"Altogether, the ride out has been a success because we are pretty certain spies for both British and Mexicans saw the regiment and the speed with which it could move."

Drumm studied the attentive, eager faces around him; these were men who relished adventure . . . and danger.

"Now, let's backtrack a bit." He perched on the rock once more. "In February, I was ordered to Washington to meet with Mr. Marcy, the Secretary of War, and Colonel James Abert, who commands the Corps of Topographical Engineers. Out of that meeting, I learned that Texas has been accepted for annexation effective March 1, 1845. Texas decided to dissolve its republic on July 4, 1845. That is only four days from now.

"Mr. Marcy told me that, in anticipation of that annexation, General Harney was ordered to take an army to the north side of the Nueces River where he is encamped at this very moment. If the Mexicans offer trouble to the Texans, General Harney is to come to their direct aid."

Drumm again studied the men, whose attention was fixed on his every word.

"There isn't going to be another Alamo in our history, if you know what I mean."

A low murmur rippled through the men. "Hear. Hear."

Drumm continued. "At the time all this was taking place, my orders were to gather a number of scientists who would form a unit of the topographical engineers to map and study the country as Colonel Kearny and his dragoons marched up the Oregon Trail to South Pass, the limit of the United States at this time."

Standing again, Drumm pondered his next sentences. "When Kearny made his turnaround, I was to detach my unit and add a platoon of Dragoons and head south into Mexico where the Old Spanish Trail makes a broad curve north from Santa Fe to the Colorado River, and then on to Los Angeles.

"Our job is to spend time in the vicinity of the trail, observing any extra heavy military traffic going to California or to New Mexico." Drumm quickly scratched a map in the dirt with his switch. "It doesn't take any military genius to figure just how easy it would be for Mexican cavalry to slip north of the Spanish Trail and take Bridger's Fort. The Oregon Trail would be cut in half, exposing countless emigrants, and threatening our nation with a war on the west side of the continent while we beef up our Texas friends."

Tall, blond, and burly Lieutenant Ives was about to ask a question but Drumm cut him off. "In a minute, Ives. The British would love to see us in a war with Mexico so they could leisurely build up their strength in Oregon. President Polk made no bones about how he feels about this situation. Last fall he ran on the ticket of reoccupation of Oregon and reannexation of Texas. Now . . . any questions?"

Irons shot out, "You just going to ride into Mexico with a platoon of soldiers and a gaggle of bug catchers, spending God knows how long down there, and then turn around and ride right out?" Irons snorted. "Impossible." He looked triumphantly around. "We all know what happens to gringos caught in Mexico."

Drumm paused to let his own rising ire simmer down. Out of their earlier dispute, Irons was setting himself up to be an annoying devil's advocate over the course of the whole damned patrol. "I understand your fears, Captain Irons, and under ordinary circumstances, I'd have my doubts, too. So let me answer your question. First off, why do you suppose I had you meet with me here?" He answered his question in his next breath. "Because for the next ten days we are going to be camped here, out of sight, off the Oregon Trail and still inside our own border. Here we are going to learn to be something a hell of a lot different than soldiers or surveyors."

He motioned at Lieutenant Ives. "Mr. Ives is nearly big enough to pick up one of those twelve-pound howitzers Colonel Kearny left behind. But more than that, Mr. Ives is the best young artillery officer in the United States Army. His field of expertise is the twelve pound howitzer, and he is going to help me divide all men—soldiers and scientists—into gun crews who, at the end of ten days, will be able to lay, sight, and serve either gun with deadly accuracy.''

Irons butted in again. ''Even so, how do you propose to haul those monsters along on a reconnaisance patrol? Those guns will slow us down so much that foot soldiers could easily capture us if they've a mind.''

''Good solid question, Captain,'' Drumm answered. ''Ives here knows how to take them down and mount the limbers, the wheels, barrels and ammunition aboard pack mules. We'll leave the caissons here.''

''What mules?'' Irons' brow was knit with bewilderment.

''With any kind of luck, they are due to arrive tomorrow, Captain.'' Drumm stared into the homely face of First Sergeant Peagram. ''You look like a man with a problem, Sergeant. Spit it out.''

Peagram shifted his tobacco chaw to the other side of his leathery cheeks. ''By your leave, Cap'n. Uniforms and horses, sir. We jes' going to ride right into Mexico in dragoon uniforms on bay horses all branded real pretty with the big D-2?''

''Straight thinking, Sergeant. You guessed it. One of the baggage wagons carries a large assortment of civilian clothing.'' He squinted south. ''Jim Bridger and Hard Winter Davis should come poking into camp with mules and horses tomorrow or the next day. I bought forty head of Missouri mules last spring, and Davis drove them to Fort Bridger. We also contracted with Bridger for sixty head of horses. He'll take ours and drive them back to Fort Laramie the day after we make the trade.''

Drumm turned to Von Holder. ''You all have had the opportunity to visit with Mr. Von Holder since we joined forces back at Leavenworth. He is not only a distinguished biologist, but an observer here for the Secretary of War. He can answer any other questions you might have.''

August Von Holder, a spare, middle-aged man in a slouch hat, nondescript coat, and matching trousers, siezed the opportunity given by Drumm.

''Well, I doubt I can add anything Captain Drumm hasn't already touched on. But, I do know we have a mighty big task facing us. I will need several soldiers to assist my colleagues. We hope to train them at once so they will have a clear understanding of what duties they should be performing.'' Von Holder cleared his throat. ''I'll need them to assist Mr. Killdare, the meteorologist; Mr. Collier, the mineralogist; Mr. Biltmore, the geologist; Mr. Smith, the cartographer; and Mr. Attix, the naturalist.''

Drumm interrupted. ''What Augie is saying is that in order for this unit to look like a real topo setup, all of us will have to take on extra duties assisting the scientists who will be mapping and collecting specimens. It won't be hard work. I'll expect Mr. Peagram and Captain Irons to assign men to those tasks at morning call tomorrow.''

Drumm stood up, brushing his pant legs. ''That about does it. Let's bring the troop up here and make camp. One bit of news that will be welcome is that Mr. Blanchard, the topo cook, will cook for the whole unit now. The soldiers won't have to cook their own meals.''

Chapter Three

Later that afternoon, when the unit of topographical engineers and the platoon of soldiers had moved from South Pass to their hidden valley, Drumm turned to First Sergeant Peagram at the first platoon muster roll call, "Do you mean we have three brothers in this platoon?"

"Yes, sir!"

The three Harrigans stood at attention before him like three solid casks of Irish whiskey, grinning sheepishly. Drumm noted there was a distinctive cut to their jib that marked them as Irish . . . and as brothers. He stopped at the first one, taller and obviously older than the other two."

"Your name?"

"One, sir!"

"One?"

"Yes, sir! One."

Drumm glanced over his shoulder at Peagram who nodded back with an impish twinkle in his eyes. Drumm stepped to the next brother, a freckle-faced youngster with orange-red hair. "Your name?"

"Two, sir!"

"Two?"

"Yes, sir! Two, sir!"

"Drumm stepped in front of the third brother. "Don't tell me your name is Three?"

"Three, sir! That's m'name."

Peagram spoke up. "It ain't no joke, Cap'n. One, Two, and Three is their God-given names, the names they enlisted under."

Drumm strode back to One Harrigan. "Private, is that the truth?"

"Whist, Cap'n. Our dear old Da lost track of names when we three arrived, an' as we already had six older brothers, he just named us One, Two, and Three. By your leave, sir!" One's good-humored ruddy face split with an easy grin.

Drumm couldn't hide his own grin, shaking his head in bewilderment. "Carry on, Privates One, Two and Three Harrigan."

Drumm finished his inspection and held a short meeting with Irons, Ives, Peagram, and Ordnance Sergeant Quinn. "Who is the best man with horses, Captain Irons?"

"Kincaid, and I'd guess Upton."

"Let them be in charge of all animals and serve with Farrier Sergeants Rawson and Ehler."

He asked Quinn and Ives, his artillery specialists, "Anyone suit you for help in the howitzer training?"

Lieutenant Merry Christmas Ives bit his lip thoughtfully. "While I hate to ask for him, Co'pral Doyle did serve in the artillery before joining up with the Dragoons."

Irons shook his head, still playing the fly in Drumm's ointment. "This ain't no military outfit anyhow, so take him if need be."

Drumm studied the muster roll. "Well, that leaves the three Harrigans, the bugler Miller, and Privates Getter, Kilmer, Newman, Brady, Bonnett, Smith, and Jones." He looked at Peagram. "Smith? Jones?"

"Hell, sir," Peagram said, again biting his lip. "The onliest one around that can talk their lingo is Getter. I 'spect they're Prussians, or Austrians."

"Go get Getter," Drumm said, smiling over the staccato of his words.

As the stocky, red-faced Getter rushed up and snapped to a rigid attention, breathing hard from the exertion, Drumm said, "The first sergeant tells me you are the only one who can converse with Smith and Jones. That right?"

"*Ja*. I talk. They *versteh*."

Drumm turned to Peagream. "Are they good soldiers?"

"Other than just communicatin' with 'em, I'd have to say yes."

Drumm swung back to Getter. "Did either serve in the army? Back where they came from?" He saw a sudden shadow of fear cross Getter's face. Drumm calculated to asssure Getter.

"Private Getter, I don't give a good tinker's cuss where they came from, or even if they ran away from an army in Europe. I'm trying to find out if they were good soldiers and if so, if they were foot, artillery, or horse."

Getter stood stiffer now. "Both served Austrian cannon, *Herr Hauptman* . . . I mean, Captain." He stuttered the last.

Getter was silent a few seconds as if he had more to say.

"Like many of us, sir, they serve in the army here so they can become American citizens."

Drumm laughed. "Don't worry, Getter. Smith and Jones may be the answer to our prayers." He dismissed Getter and looked at Ives. "If I were you, I'd add Smith, Getter, and Jones to my artillery teaching staff."

Drumm turned his attention to Irons. "I want Bugler Miller as my personal aide. That leaves a man to be assigned to the scientists and several to the cook." He was trying to reassure Irons that his command savvy was sorely needed. "How does that fit with your plans, Captain Irons?"

Typically, Irons saw fit to misinterpret. "Do I really have a choice?"

Drumm ignored the bitterness of Iron's pouting retort. "Well then, let's move the troops to the baggage area. By nightfall I want every soldier in civilian clothes and the uniforms bundled and stowed in the caissons Bridger will haul back to Fort Laramie."

He looked at Ives. "I want artillery teams lined up and serving those two twelve-pound beauties of yours at first light tomorrow. Time is running out. We can't afford to waste a single second."

Chapter Four

Harrigan One lifted his rosy nose like a dog hunting a scent. He caught the rich aroma of fresh-ground coffee beans brought to a merry boil. The red-headed son of a' old sod perched on the edge of his India-rubber ground cloth, drawing trousers over his skinny legs.

"'Tis a wonderful thing, Co'pral Doyle," he said. "The topo cook makes the best coffee and pan bread I ever laid lip to. Yes, sir, Mr. Hudson Blanchard gets my vote for the best cook in this world. Umm-wah!" Harrigan One smacked his lips in anticipation.

Standing off to one side, Drumm and Augie Von Holder cupped their cold hands around steaming coffee cups as they watched the thirty-man unit wake up, stamp feet into boots, and struggle into uniform. The first rays of a new day caught a murmuring, laughing crowd rolling night gear and throwing the bedrolls into the baggage wagon.

Drumm sensed a tickle of thrill tremble inside him; this bunch would shape up into a real fighting team; men to depend on. He swished the last of his coffee around his teeth. "Can't say anything worth recording for history, Augie, but I'm excited." He grinned as Augie Von Holder tried twice before lighting his first cigar of the day.

"Seriously, Andy, what are you really thinking about?"

The grin faded from Drumm's face as he gazed across the wide, windswept prairie, a naked land with only sagebrush and clumps of willow along the banks of the small stream that meandered through their camp to relieve the starkness. He saw the first streaks of dawn rob the prairie of its gloom as dawn illuminated the sky with shades of pink, salmon red, and pale yellow.

A long way off he saw a small herd of antelope turn their white rumps as they trotted away, dancing like brittle leaves driven before a crisp morning breeze.

"I don't know, Augie. I'm trying to get a handle on how long it will take to hammer this crowd—yours and mine—into capable gun crews, and turn some of my men into assistants for your topographic pursuits. The last, of course, in case anyone is watching us." He pulled off his forage cap and ran his hands through his hair past the widow's peak.

Resettling his cap he said, "Counting today, we have about sixty days to train two gun crews, train assistants for you, slip into Mexico, and then head back to Fort Laramie around the first week in September."

He grinned again. "So let's get humping, Augie. Time is burning away the day."

Within an hour the blond giant, Lieutenant Merry Christmas Ives, soon to be handed the moniker, "Guns", was holding an informal lecture on artillery as he walked around one of the howitzers.

"First, I'll show you how we are going to transport Betsy"—Ives slapped the breech of the first gun affectionately—"and Lou here."

He studied the men around him, pleased with their looks of undivided attention. "Yes, sir," he continued, "these are the only two ladies we have with us—Betsy and Lou. I guarantee you will come to love these beauties and hate them at the same time as dirty, heavy bitches that you have to hoist, heave, and haul around."

"Nothin' too tough for Drumm's Devils," Harrigan One joked. The others laughed. That, too, would become a byword.

"Hmm. Drumm's Devils it is, eh?" Ives scratched his unruly mop of silver white hair. "I guess the name fits us all right. Come on then, you Drumm's Devils, observe and learn."

Farrier Sergeants Ehler and Rawson, First Sergeant Peagram, Ordnance Sergeant Quinn, Smith, Jones, and Getter rolled up their sleeves. They tore Betsy down, separating limber from tube, removing each wheel and hanging packsaddles on the giant mules that had helped drag the guns from Fort Leavenworth to South Pass.

One packsaddle was a special cradle into which the gun barrel, or tube, fit snugly. Another special harness held the long limber, and each wagon wheel was balanced on a single mule. Special panniers handled bridles, harness, lash ropes, linch pins, traversing screws, yokes, halters, blinders, and picket pins and ropes.

The rest of the equipage was smoothly put together with little effort. Cannisters holding the grape shot, powder bags, and the ramrods were another mule's burden.

"Just so long as we don't put too big a jag on our long-eared friends, say seventy-five to a hundred pounds on each side, they will step right out and stick with you to eternity," Peagram said.

Ives gave them the reverse demonstration—off-loading Betsy, setting up the gun, using the limber to square her away at the intended target.

Ives had the men build a big pile of willow and sagebrush. After his lecture, he aimed to have the burst knock out the pile of brush. His crew swabbed, rammed, aimed, and then ignited the powder. The cannon boomed and moments later the shell burst 500 yards away. As the smoke cleared, the men saw few, if any, stray piles of willow and sagebrush where the shell had burst.

Ives stood by Drumm. Out of the corner of his mouth he said, "It was a clean burst. Anything other than that and it would have been hard to make the crew believers in the guns."

Drumm responded quietly. "Amen, Mr. Ives. Amen." Drumm watched as the eyes of the admiring men followed Ives as he started the drills and the work it would take to create gun crews.

The affair was a lark for the dragoons. They felt they had the best cook in the world and they liked the cut of Drumm and Ives. Learning to fire Ives's two pieces was routine army to them.

At noon, each man turned in his uniform and scrambled around finding the appropriate fit and style of his new civilian duds. Drumm had told them their expedition into Mexico must take on the appearance of a topographical unit. With the howitzers dismantled, no one would suspect them of being able to defend themselves from an all-out, head-on cavalry charge.

Gleefully they donned hickory shirts and jean pants, chose from beaverskin caps, flat-crowned and plug hats, and Mexican-style sombreros. Drumm watched them trade back and forth until each man had himself stylishly attired. Little clothing was left.

Drumm felt sorry for Irons, Peagram, Quinn, Ehler and Rawson. All had worn the blues so long they felt out of place as they walked around, eyeing each other and themselves dubiously. Even then, Drumm mused, it would be quite a spell before they felt comfortable.

Drumm told Peagram to fold his captain's uniform, Peagram's own and Bugler Miller's separately. "I want our Second Dragoon guidon and our national ensign to be packed with these uniforms," he said. "Just in case, Mr. Peagram. Just in case."

"You sound like your old father, Cap'n." Peagram's eyes caught Drumm's and they held.

"You knew my father?"

"I was a wee bugler lad when I served with Colonel Toyal Drumm, commanding the Light Dragoons. It were in 1814 at New Orleans when your dad and Andy Jackson whipped the lobster-backs."

"Then you were there when he was wounded?" Drumm hadn't meant it as a trick question. "Hell, First, I mean you must have been there when he—"

"Lost his leg!" Peagram grinned as he shifted his chew of tobacco. "I was there, sir. Indeed I was. No offspring of 'Toy' Drumm would ever become casualty to a lie."

Memories flooded Drumm. "I was just a boy when he came home to Pamlico Landing in North Carolina. He was a bitter, sour man. Hard to get along with. Mother died giving birth to me, so he really had only me to come home to."

Drumm squinted, remembering. "I was glad to get away, to go to West Point. He wanted me to be elegant, a cavalry officer, equally efficient in the drawing room as in cavalry action." He shrugged. "Instead I graduated first in my class and Colonel Abert took the three highest into the Topographical Corps. My father was furious, mad as hell that I didn't become a Dragoon. That's the way it is with us today."

"Well, Cap'n," Peagram drawled, "he was like a father to me, the father I never had." He quickly added, "As he was to his whole command. T'was the men first, and one and all loved him. But . . ." Peagram leaned on the word, " . . . he could hold a grudge for a long time if he thought a man did wrong. He sure would respect you now, sir."

"I'm glad we had this talk, First. This command will take a lot of nerve and some iron in all our backbones. I guess I'm saying that I'm glad you're here with us."

Both listened to Ives telling the men that he had lately returned from India where he had spent three months with the Royal Horse Artillery. "I was in the state called Punjab and there they haul cannon many times larger than Betsy or Lou on top of lumbering pachyderms—elephants, if you like." His audience was round-eyed as he described the destruction the huge howitzer created when cavalry charged.

Slapping Betsy he said, "This little lady will throw a nine-pound shell nearly nine hundred yards with accuracy. Nine hundred yards, men! That is half a mile, or about twice the distance to our brush-pile target."

He crouched, hand on its elevating screw. "If we turn this screw to a five-degree pitch, a Mexican cavalry charge would be torn apart if our two guns were reasonably serviced, aimed and fired. Inside each of these brass walled cannisters are about twenty-five lead balls, grape, or shrapnel."

He leaned against the howitzer's breech. "The first rounds at seven hundred to eight hundred yards would kill both horse and men. And—" Ives paused dramatically. "And if we are fast enough, we can fire at nine hundred yards, repeat at seven hundred, again at five hundred and finish off the charge at three hundred yards. If need be, we would depress the tube and fire point-blank."

Ives' face turned grim. "You Dragoons know what it is to ride into howitzer fire. It is devastating and most horse troops will turn at the third or fourth barrage.

"That's why every single one of you is going to learn all there is to know about these lifesavers. The pity is I've only got a few days to help you learn." Ives looked hard at his crew, "Learn and live. Simple as that."

Ives divided the men into gun crews, mixing Von Holder's

civilians with the more experienced soldiers.

"Sir," Harrigan Two asked. "When are we goin' to get a chance to shoot these lovelies?"

"The answer to that, Two, is when you can take a gun down, transport it two hundred yards, reassemble the gun, learn to aim it, then the whole business again and return here. Then we'll burn some powder." He waved at the noncommissioned officers who prodded the teams into action.

Drumm took Augie to Blanchard's woodpile. He selected a number of boards rescued from the worn-out wagon bed, explaining as they worked, "I want to set these boards up at fifty, one hundred, and two hundred yards from a firing line."

He gave Augie a wry smile. "I don't completely trust Ives and his pair of howitzers. Hard Winter Davis is hauling in twenty percussion half-stock rifles of the variety mountain men have used and found invaluable." Drumm drove a board into the ground and tied a white rag to it. "I figure if a man is properly acquainted with a rifle like that, he can fire, reload, and fire in a couple of minutes. Some accurate rifles will help Ives and his guns finish off a cavalry charge."

He stood after driving the two-hundred-yard stakes into the ground. "Think of two artillery pieces firing—one-two, one-two— at eight hundred yards, at six hundred yards, at four hundred yards, and then twenty percussion rifles joining. My guess is that nearly any outfit will have to turn or retreat."

Drumm leaned against his horse, looking across the saddle at his bewhiskered friend in the act of lighting a cheroot.

"By God, Andy," Augie allowed, slapping his thigh, "dang me if you ain't getting the maximum use of your fire power!"

Chapter Five

For three punishing days, Ives and his noncommissioned officers plus his "furriners"—as Harrigan One described Getter, Smith, and Jones—drilled relentlessly under a scorching sun. In the thin air at 8,000 feet above sea level, gun barrels grew so hot that some of the apprentice artillerists wrapped their hands in rags to handle them.

Recognizing his men were losing their body water, Ives gave them morning and afternoon breaks. The crews sopped up water from the crystal clear stream close to camp and relaxed in the shade of great cottonwoods.

Shortly after noon of the second day, Augie Von Holder and his geologist followed the stream into the small canyon. They were back by three to dump more than 100 chunky native trout into some of Blanchard's pots, and Blanchard announced a fish-fry. "Compliments of Dr. Von Holder and his crew!" The trout were delicious and everyone's feelings ran high.

Captain Irons got out his Jew's harp, Rawson played the bones, and Blanchard hummed into a comb as the three produced "Old Dan Tucker," "The Arkansas Traveler," and "The Girl I Left Behind Me." They ended with "My Old Kentucky Home." Awkward clog dancers made the packed earth resound with boot thumps.

Many of them, settling in for the night, watched the brilliant stars in the clear heavens above. "They're so close, I could reach out and take one home with me," Farrier Sergeant Rawson's deep voice boomed across the quiet camp. A coyote lifted his snout into the dark sky and howled after all the human sounds died out.

At this time of the month, the moon was only a bright horn of light against an ebony sky.

The next day, as the men prepared to get back to howitzer drill, Drumm called for a muster. "Each Dragoon is to turn in saber, pistol, and carbine. Sergeant Quinn will give each of you credit before Mr. Ives welcomes you back to Betsy and Lou."

He watched as all the men were checked off Quinn's muster roll. "First," Drumm nudged Peagram, "save out our sabers and pistols, and stash them with our uniforms." He winked. "Anything might happen."

At midday, one of the scouts, Harrigan Three, galloped into camp. "By your leave, Sir, they's wagons an' animals a-comin'."

Riding ahead of the train, Hard Winter Davis sat stiff in the saddle up to the knoll where Drumm and some of his officers waited. Eyeing the bunch critically, Davis stepped out of the saddle, braced his hands at his waist, and leaned back, bringing relief to cramped muscles.

"Hear that, Andy!" he whooped. "That's my butt bones a-groanin'." He eagerly shoved out a hand, which Drumm grasped. Davis grinned in reunion.

"It's a hell of a long haul from here to Sa'nt Louie, eh, Andy? I swan, them mules moved slow as snails on a slick log."

Drumm laughed. "Hard Winter Davis," he said, "meet Dr. August Von Holder, chief of the topographical unit. You remember him from Secretary Marcy's meeting?" Davis glanced at Von Holder with eyes bright enough to light a pipe by.

"Shore as I'm a foot high! Got some cigars for you in the wagon, Augie. Knew you'd be about out by now."

Von Holder brightened. "My compliments, Mr. Davis."

"This is Captain Irons, B Company Commander in the Second Dragoons," Drumm said. "His platoon is part of our party."

Irons made a long, sour face. "Frankly, I take a dim view of having civilians along on this stupid affair," he said, his lip curling as he took in the mountain man's ironlike leather pants, his fringed hunting shirt, his flat-crowned hat, moccasins, and his lean, unshaven face.

Davis squirted a stream of tobacco juice dangerously close to Irons's toe. "Ain't 'zactly what the Sec'tary a War told me personally in Wash'ton. He said he invited me along 'cause he didn't want any papercollared soldier boys screwing up." Davis aimed a bright eye at Irons. "You ever wear a paper collar, Captain?" His words had an accusing tone; Davis knew Irons and didn't like him.

Drumm wasn't about to let bad blood poison his mission. He spoke to Davis with forced cheerfulness. "The rifles? Did you find any?"

Davis tore himself away from Irons, whose face was growing redder by the second. "Got 'em in the big wagon there." He jerked a thumb at the wagon emerging from the cloud of dust raised by the horse and mule herd also coming into view.

Drumm ordered Peagram to build a cavvy yard, a sort of rope corral for the herd of newly arrived animals. He watched the big young Missouri mules walk into the corral and settle down. For all their legendary stamina, they were trailworn.

Davis eyed the corralled animals beside Drumm. "Good for us to have a few days to recruit them animals, Andy. They's tough as hickory, but they been drove hard."

Irons stomped up, bound to have the last word. "Where did you find those runts?" He pointed at the horses, staring at Davis for an answer. Instead, Drumm spoke. "They're Western Plains horses. Quick as cats, all pretty well broken, and if they like you, they'll carry you to eternity and back.

"Best of all, Captain Irons," he added, speaking slowly and distinctly, "these horses don't need grain or corn. They'll feed right down to the roots of the grass, which is what they're going to have to do. This mission isn't exactly going to be a Sunday School ice cream social."

Irons stomped away and Drumm muttered to Davis, "that *ought* to stop him. It won't, though. He isn't exactly happy with me. I was named his commanding officer."

Davis threw a long arm across Drumm's shoulders; they'd been a long time apart and spoke with mock formality "Should you require someone to explain the facts to Captain Irons, I'd be plumb pleased to apply for the job." Davis changed his tone. "Watch out for that man, Andy. He's yellow as mustard without the bite."

A small black man emerged out of the confusion of men and horses, rode up, and stepped lightly out of the saddle. Like Davis, he wore a powder horn and hunting pouch on a leather strap, with a fourteen-inch Bowie knife sheathed on a wide leather belt. His white teeth gleamed as he made a courtly bow, out of place in this setting, sweeping the ground with his fur hat.

His voice sounded uncommonly cultured and decidedly French. "*Bon jour, monsieur*! Claude Bochey, late of New Orleans. I am called Le Black Cat of the Swamp. At your service!"

His head had been wrapped in a long red scarf, almost a turban. when he bent forward, the whole affair slid to the ground revealing his bare skull. An ugly scar ran clear across his head, separating his hair from the skinned skull. The man had been scalped, but survived.

Hard Winter broke the silence as Bochey, with all the dignity he could muster, wrapped the scarf around his head and settled the fur cap in place. "Well, Andy, you just met your counterpart. Ol' Clauday here nearly lost all his hair to a Cheyenne couple seasons back." Davis pointed at Drumm's facial scar. "See here, Clauday—Andy ducked faster and better'n you. You two got lots in common, eh?" Davis danced a rattling jig around them, pounding his two friends on their backs. "Both of you are goin' to carry Cheyenne marks the rest of your ornery lives."

With the sixty horses and forty mules corralled, a wagon drew up and a short, swarthy man stepped down. His garb said Mexican from the tip of his fancy boots to his flat crowned hat, his thin mustache to the embroidery on his short jacket.

"This here's old Louie Vaskiss, Jim Bridger's pardner," Davis said. Drumm looked at Louis Vasquez with alarm. Davis was quick to reassure him. "Aw, hell, Andy, old Louie here is all American. If it ever comes to dyin', this here's a man knows how to take it standin' up. He only posed as a Mexican so's he could get a land grant for the post him and Bridger own."

A lean, forty-year-old mountain man showed up in the ring of men looking at Vasquez. He walked stiffly as if favoring a mess of old wounds. His eyes held a seasoned squint and his mouth was set in a grim line. His appearance almost shouted his name to Drumm.

"You Drumm?" He offered his hand in a businesslike way. "Name's Bridger, and Davis is dead right. Louie's my pardner and the only man I'd trust my life with." Bridger looked around the circle. " 'Spect that's good enough fer ya?"

The men stared at "Old Gabe" Bridger, a legend in his own time. He gazed back and smiled, then sat down against the wagon's big rear wheel and stuffed his pipe. Drumm, Davis, Bochey, Vasquez, Von Holder and Ives parked on the ground around him.

Bridger used a thick rounded glass from his possibles pouch to focus the sun into his pipe bole; in an instant he was drawing smoke. "Say, Drumm," Bridger said thickly through fresh smoke, "I killed two fat cow buff'lo about a mile south. Figured your crew can use the meat."

Drumm signalled Peagram and in a few minutes an empty wagon rattled past them for the downed buffalo. Davis looked at Drumm and Augie.

"I'm a day late. That spoil your schedule?"

Drumm ran a hand over his jawline, stroking his scar thoughtfully. "Your timing was nigh perfect, Hard Winter. Two days from tomorrow I'm planning to pull up stakes and move out. It'll take that long for my crowd to learn about mule artillery from Mr. Ives here. I've a list of supplies I'm going to need from your fort, Mr. Vasquez." Drumm had composed the list in Spanish.

"You also speak the tongue?" Vasquez said.

"Not real good, *Senor*." Drumm grinned. "Try English."

Jim Bridger coughed restlessly, seeking Drumm's attention, and changing the subject; Bridger, Drumm knew, wasn't one to let someone else hog the conversation.

"Ha, well, Cap'n Drumm, you can talk of your damned supplies. But mebbe they's fiercer business afoot." Bridger spoke with astonishing directness. "I'm married to a Snake, sort of relatives to the Utes. You savvy?" Drumm nodded.

"Well, this sort of second cousin of my squaw spent the night at my lodge a day or two ago. He was all the time blowin' off how him and a bad case renegade Ute called Bad Heart was goin' down to the Green to see some Mexican cavalry, or so he says.

I know this here Bad Heart and he's about as useless as an unstoppered powder horn.''

Bridger had a pull from a jug of whiskey Vasquez produced. No one spoke as the jug passed around the circle. It was Bridger's story.

"Well, I spent some time primin' him an' he said the Mexie cavalry was going to throw . . . '' Bridger paused to take a swig, "waugh! . . . a hell of a big party for them, give them guns, powder, lead, and whiskey. Waugh! Then they was going to raid a wagon train, er sumthin.''

Drumm leaned into his inquiry. "If he didn't tell you what the raid was about or where it was, you must have an idea or two we could use.''

Bridger cocked his head at Vasquez, giving him the opening to speak.

"Senor Capitan, I have only a mouse of a rumor.'' He held up a thumb and forefinger so they nearly touched. "A tiny hombre. Some gringos of importance are traveling from Santa Fe and Taos to Los Angeles. This raid will happen where the Verdant River joins the Colorado.'' He sighed.

"All right,'' Drumm said. "That's information we didn't have and now it's ours to deal with.'' He stood up. "Let's see if Mr. Blanchard can show you his culinary best on some buffalo hump ribs.''

The next morning, Hard Winter Davis and Bochey broke open the wooden cases of percussion rifles, powder horns, and bullet bags. A crowd gathered as each rifle was inspected by the two mountain men. Von Holder's men and the dragoons watched with mounting curiosity.

Drumm told Davis, "Go ahead. Show the men what you two can do with a percussion rifle starting at 200 yards, then 100 yards, and at 50 yards.

Each man made ready with his personal rifle. Their shots rang out the second Drumm called "Fire!''

Von Holder pulled out his turnip-sized watch, flipped back the cover, and counted aloud the seconds as the two fired, reloaded, fired, reloaded, and fired at three targets.

"One, two, three . . . " Both men calmly poured powder, seating the bullet and patch. Without a lost movement, only eyeing their targets as they loaded, they fired. "Fifteen, sixteen, seventeen . . . " a second volley tore a hole in the silence. "Thirty-one, thirty-two, thirty-three . . . " Davis fired. "Thirty-six, thirty-seven," and Bochey fired.

The men who had gathered around seemed to have been holding their breath and now let their air out. Davis looked at the crowd. "Well, let's go have a look-see if an' me and olt Clauday even hit Cap'n Drumm's targets."

Drumm stayed behind as shooters and spectators strode downrange. He knew each target carried a perfectly placed shot. When they returned, he announced, "Each of you will be given training on the use of one of those rifles. Mr. Davis and Mr. Bochey are your instructors."

He let the morning breeze fill the silence for a moment. "Everyone, Mr. Blanchard included, will be given a chance on the firing line. Mr. Davis and Mr. Bochey will spot the men to be designated as riflemen."

He slapped his pantsleg with a willow. "If you aren't destined to be a rifleman, you can be sure Mr. Ives will find a proper job for you. Some of you will carry on as riflemen, and when the time comes, you'll pitch in loading the mules. Now, Mr. Davis and Mr. Bochey require your attention."

Chapter Six

In the high-country air, trial and error, shooting matches, and manhandling the big guns as well as the rifles wore the men out at first. Mounted sentries patrolled the perimeter of the camp around the clock. Drumm wanted no curious eyes intruding on the secret training. He told Irons, "Tell your guards to shoot first. I'll take care of the questions later on."

They were not bothered. Each day Davis and Bochey slipped out with one of the better riflemen in search of choice buffalo, elk, deer, or antelope for Blanchard's spit.

Their seventh day in camp, Drumm called a council of war. "I reckon we're sitting on July 10. That gives us twenty-one days more in this month. Thirty-one days in August, and ten days in September.

Drumm leaned against Blanchard's big rear wagon wheel and nursed a cup of his cook's coffee. "The big question I need answered is simply this: Are we ready?"

He looked at Ives. "Guns, what's your situation?"

Ives' thatch of yellow hair had bleached nearly white under the burning sun. "I'm ready. Ready as we can ever be until we fire Betsy and Lou in action." He nursed a couple of bruised fingers. His unblinking clear blue eyes were true, Drumm knew. "Cap'n, Co'pral Doyle, Getter, Smith, Jones, and Quinn are first class. They can lay the guns, prepare them for firing, and shoot them. The rest—offloading, heaving, and hauling Betsy and Lou—is just damned hard work. I don't have a single slacker.''

He brushed a silver lock from his forehead. ''Yessir, Cap'n. We're ready.'' Drumm looked at Davis and Bochey. ''Are the rifles ready?''

With his Bowie knife, Hard Winter sawed off a chunk of tobacco from his pigtail plug of Mickey Twist tobacco and popped it in his mouth. ''Well, we got twenty men assigned rifles,'' Davis said around his mouthful. ''That includes Peagram, his farrier sergeants, and several of the bug catchers. But I ain't real certain how they'll act under fire.'' Davis looked at Peagram for assistance as he wallowed his chew around inside his cheek to find a comfortable resting place for it.

Peagram spoke up. ''Beggin' the Cap'n's pardon. My advice is we've got five crack shots, ten fairly good shooters, and five that can either shoot, or help load rifles, as the action dictates.''

''All right, First. Please ask Mr. Blanchard to join us.'' Drumm stood, stretching his arms to the heavens and took in a good eyeful of stars as Blanchard lumbered up.

''Mr. Blanchard, tomorrow we pull up stakes and head south. In two days we'll be close enough to send a pack outfit to Bridger's Fort to pick up the supplies you'll need.'' Drumm spoke slowly. ''Be certain you list everything. Mr. Vasquez has a list I gave him when he was here. Just to be certain, I want you to make a new list and give it to Mr. Von Holder tonight.''

He nodded to the men around him. ''Thanks. We leave at first light. As we leave, I want Captain Irons to assign this list of men to be assistants to Mr. Von Holder's scientists.'' He handed the list to Irons. ''You and Augie can work out the fine details. I just want us to look as much like a topo outfit as possible.''

Everyone was to sleep out under the huge starry sky. Biltmore and Irons complained until Ives told them all available canvas would be used to cover the mules' loads. That settled the issue as far as Ives was concerned. Irons looked up Drumm to lodge a formal complaint.

''You are the only one who has had a canvas cover since we mustered here,'' he grumbled.

''Get used to it, Irons,'' Drumm said. ''No more tents until we hit Fort Laramie, sixty days from now.''

While a stewing Irons stomped off into the dark, Drumm hunted up his own bedroll. Tucking himself in skillfully, he blew out a deep breath to ease the tension of command and let his muscles go loose as he drank in the sparkling canopy of planets, stars, and the vast Milky Way. His eyes closed, his memory-vision dwelled briefly on the awesome sky over him, and he slept.

Morning came cold and dismal. A stiff wind poured across the prairie, chilling the command. The men stiffened almost instantly as their bodies left their snug bedding to be exposed to the cold. Bugler Miller softly summoned Drumm awake. The Captain stomped into his boots, buttoned his jacket, and headed for Blanchard's coffee and sorghum-soaked bread. Around Blanchard's cooking place, the bowls of hot food sent up little clouds of vapor against the morning's chill.

Hard Winter Davis fell is step with Drumm as he walked to the breakfast fire. "Colder'n hell on the stoker's day off," Davis said.

After a slim breakfast, Drumm rolled and tied his India-rubber ground cloth around his soogans and tossed the bulky roll into the bed wagon. He was having trouble keeping his civilian hat firmly on his head.

The command was busy. Each man had a task or two after breakfast, and Drumm liked what he saw as the men began to load mules and gird for the day's march. Peagram and his covey of noncoms were everywhere helping, cursing, lending a shoulder when Betsy's tube appeared that it might tumble to the ground. Ives supervised, and helped too.

Von Holder in his long and voluminious scientist's duster, the cranky Irons, along with Drumm and the two mountain men were silent witnesses to the scramble to get ready. They watched as a pair of mules sidestepped, bolted, rolled over, or kicked trying to escape the massive iron tubes being strapped on their backs.

One big mule, his teeth bared and biting, lashed out fore and aft with deadly iron-shod hooves, trying to escape the indignity of the brutal load. Finally, Ives, Getter, and all three Harrigans got the tube lashed down. The mule sat down, and hee-hawed and brayed his anger into the whistling wind.

Davis strolled over to the miscreant mule with Peagram. The former stuck a burning stick from the campfire into the mule's flank while Davis grabbed the halter. Davis was pitched forward as the mule reacted to the hot brand. The big animal bolted up and hit the ground running. When his feet hit the sod, Bochey leaped onto his back as Davis grabbed an ear and took a big bite.

The mule's eyes rolled in surprise: fire on one end, an ear being bit on the other, and a load already on top. The mule saw the wisdom of settling down.

Davis spit out tobacco juice and a mouthful of prickly mule hair, grinning big at Peagram. "We make a damn good team, Sargeant!" Peagram's grin was twisted by his livid facial scar. Drumm thought his First Sergeant ought not to try smiling because the scar only made his face uglier.

Little Bochey cut in. "When you gentlemen needs the help of Monsieur Claude, jus' give the call." He snapped his fingers.

Patience was the order of the day as the command folded the camp and dissolved into a column of troops and two wagons. Irons champed at the bit as he rode in and out, seeing that each mule was being loaded properly. Finally, he rode over to Drumm in a rage.

"Dammit, Drumm, ain't you going to get this outfit moving?!"

Drumm nodded patronizingly. "You are doing just fine, Captain Irons. Your men are accustomed to your orders. You are second in command. It is your duty to move the column out. As you will, Captain."

Drumm waved a salute at Irons and walked his horse over to sit with Von Holder and the mountain men. Irons bit his lip, his face flushed in anger. He yanked his horse around and charged back down the line of forty mules, horses, and wagons.

"He sure is a right proper paper-collared sojer, Clauday, jus' like I said," Davis observed to Bochey.

"Oui, mon ami, le papier collier!"

When order finally rose out of the chaos, Drumm had the men mounted, facing him in one long line. "This is the order of march," he shouted for all to hear. "See who you are riding with today. He will be your mate for the rest of this reconnaissance. Riflemen! Ride out to join Mr. Bochey. Take the point!" He swiveled in his saddle. "Mr. Davis and his scouts have the flanks and the rear. Move out!"

He squared himself. My God, he thought, am I really going to attempt to take this odd assortment of civilians and soldiers into Mexico? He saw them watching as they began to move, almost eagerly, waiting for him to lead them into a country he only knew about from Davis and Bochey.

"Andy," Von Holder's call knifed into Drumm's reverie. Augie cleared his throat. "It's going to be hard to disguise your dragoons as civilians."

He's right, Drumm thought; civilian clothing couldn't hide the way a dragoon sat his saddle.

"That's your task, Augie," he said. "By day after tomorrow, this topographical outfit will appear to be under the direction of Mr. Von Holder and his —"

The clear Irish voice of one of the Harrigans carried on the morning breeze "—his bug-catchers." Grins and a few open laughs broke the tension.

"Right," Drumm said for all around him to hear. "Augie's Bug Catchers and Drumm's Devils are heading into Mexico! So, Bugler. Play me a tune!"

"Sir!," little Miller responded with spirit.

Drumm stood in the stirrups. "Column of twos!"

Miller's silver notes cut through the morning breeze.

Then, the command of execution, "Right about."

Again, Miller's bugle trilled the familiar command.

"Maa-aarch!"

In unison, the column of twos turned and stepped out, the long horse and mule column walking past its commanding officers. All Drumm could think was that as it passed was that it looked like a many-legged bug.

"Meaner lookin', by damn, than a centipede with the chilblains," Hard Winter Davis murmured from his vantage point beside Drumm.

Drumm nodded, his mind only briefly taking in Davis's homespun joke, his checking and rechecking everything as his Devils and Von Holder's Bug Catchers moved downrange, harnesses jingling, horse hooves clanging against stone, wagonwheel bearings stridently complaining as the column stretched out over the rocky high plateau, brakes squealing against the iron tires as the land pitched down.

Drumm's own private war with Mexico had begun.

It was July 11, 1845.

Chapter Seven

Twice during a mistake-laden day, Drumm ordered an action alert. He watched as animal tenders built a picket line to the rear as others unloaded all artillery equipment, and Blanchard set up a first-aid station. Drumm's eyes followed the men as they cursed, then pleaded or pushed the long-eared Missouri mules into place and unburdened them. Tubes, carriages, wheels, and limber were matched and put together until, out of the struggle between mules and men, two cannon were created.

Riflemen peeled out to defensive positions as Bochey and Davis posted scouts to protect the rear and the flanks of Betsy and Lou. Again Drumm wondered if he could get this unusual crew of men and soldiers acting as a unit. Like an energetic grasshopper, Peagram was everywhere, supervising with quiet efficiency. His mere presence made the men work with renewed effort; observing it sent a swell of pride through Drumm. He was confident they'd make out all right.

The exercise took a little over fifteen minutes the first time. Secretly, Drumm was satisfied that the men knew their jobs and were working hard to perform. Tearing the guns down, loading them, and putting the column on the trail again took no more than ten minutes. The men, safely astride their horses, looked at the silent Drumm as if expecting him to comment on their drill. His silence, as he cantered to the head of the column, rode hard on Peagram and his noncoms.

Harrigan One ventured, "Sergeant, sir! Ye dinna feel Cap'n Drumm was happy at our drill, then?"

Peagram wiped sweat off his brow with a knuckle without touching his hat brim. "When an officer is mum about your actions, that is the time you'd better buckle up and try twice as hard next time out." Peagram was obviously dissatisfied himself with the awkwardness demonstrated in the cannon drill. He kicked his horse ahead leaving Harrigan One with a knowing look in his eyes and a silent determination to do better.

The column halted at high noon but before the men were allowed to drink and eat hardtack and jerky, Farrier Sergeants Ehler and Rawson had them water the horses and mules, lighten their loads, and rub down the animals with empty grain sacks.

Rawson, at five-foot-five a pint-sized, bowlegged dragoon with a deep booming voice called out, "Yore best friend in all this world outside of Cap'n Drumm and First Sergeant Peagram is yore hoss and the mules yore assigned to care for. Take better care of them animals than you do yourself. Get to know and love him. Some day he may save your life!" Rawson strode up and down the picket line. "If and you don't care for your mount, I'll have you lashed to the wagon wheel and flogged. That or I'll have you walk a stretch with twenty-five pounds of rocks on your back." Now and then he or Ehler would lift a mule's or horse's foot, inspect it, pick out a pebble wedged between hoof and shoe when necessary.

The men were silent, bordering on sullen, as the sergeant inspected the picket line. They knew—at least the dragoons knew—a farrier sergeant's orders were all-powerful and, once given, a man did everything in his power to complete them.

Rawson finally reported to Drumm. "All mounts rubbed down and watered, sir. We'll feed the mules an' graze the horses."

Drumm smiled. He'd have to be tough at the outset, otherwise his force could take things for granted and become lax. "First, Sergeant! You may see to the feeding of the men!"

Clutching their rations of hardtack and jerky, the men squatted, relieved to be able to relax beside a small stream and partly fill griping bellies. The stream owed its existence to big snow fields melting on the sides of a huge mesa commonly called Oregon Buttes several miles away.

Drumm sat down to eat near Von Holder and the mountain men.

"Take six mules and head for Bridger's Fort," he told Hard Winter Davis. He looked at Von Holder. "I think you ought to go, too, Augie. A little talk over there about geology and botany will help kill any small talk or rumors about who's out here. Let's meet south of the fort on the Green River."

Drumm bellied-down over the small stream and drank his fill of the sweet, crystallike water. It was so cold, it nearly set his teeth to aching. It sat well in his stomach though, and he felt its refreshment invigorate his entire system.

Even as Davis and Von Holder and their string of six mules headed southwest, Drumm asked Irons to hold the men, once mounted. He inspected the column, halting at the halfway point. "In a few miles," he called, projecting his voice for all to hear, "we will cross the Emigrant Road or, as some call it, the Oregon Trail. We will hold up well before the trail while Mr. Bochey checks it for traffic. The last thing we want is a wagon train full of emigrants telling the whole world they saw us."

He stood in the stirrups, stretching his legs. "So, if Mr. Bochey signals us to move out, scatter out and ride like hell for cover on the other side of the trail." He turned his horse and urged it to the head of the column.

"The column is yours, Captain Irons," he said to his second in command, settling again into a crisp walk as the column with Claude Bochey at point veered south.

Within an hour, the alert little black man was back with a report that the Oregon Trail was dead ahead, and rode on. Blanchard cantered up to where Drumm rode near the head of the column.

"Captain," Blanchard said, "if you will let me take the wagons beyond your rendezvous once across the trail, I can find a likely spot to camp." The big man looked earnestly at Drumm. "That way, the evening meal will be ready when the men arrive."

Drumm considered a moment. "You have my permission, Mr. Blanchard. All we ask is that you do justice to your profession."

An hour later, Drumm ordered the second gun drill of the day. He told Blanchard to keep going. "Cross the trail and make camp when the sun goes down. That gives you five or six hours to create a good meal"—he surveyed his troop again battling balky mules and attending to the hard, physical labor of assembling the field pieces—"they're going to need it."

Blanchard's two wagons rattled on ahead, leaving the cursing, sweating men still learning how to "hoist, heave, and haul," as Ives put it. Ives and his gun captains were pleased this time as Peagram smoothly ordered his riflemen to load, shoot, and prepare their weapons for another round.

Another hour later, as the column drew near the Oregon Trail, they waited while a wagon train groaned and shrieked past them. "Gawd, listen to them axles whine," Irons said sourly. "If their trail dust and the slow crawl don't set them up as targets, then the dry axles' grinding against the hubs makes enough noise to raise the dead, not to mention the Indians."

Irons spit scornfully in their direction. "Nothing a little elbow grease and some real grease wouldn't fix. But no! Not emigrants. They're sheep!"

Drumm sized up his peer. He had to admit that Irons was a good, efficient soldier. He did his work by the manual: nothing extra. Irons's only real friend was Biltmore, the geologist. They seemed to have a lot in common. Irons like to bedevil the young bugler, James Miller. The lad couldn't tell when Irons was serious or just jobbing him as he was sent on one fool's errand after another. Only the day before, Drumm had found the boy going through the wagon where the rifles were stored looking for a left-handed rifle. Drumm told the boy he had been jobbed. Later he heard Irons reading the boy off in front of several of the dragoons.

Drumm called Irons aside and told him, "Miller is my aide. If you need him, ask my permission. In the meantime, Captain Irons, lay off the kid."

Now in the silence following Irons's sour summation of the tide of emigrants, Drumm reminded his second in command that grease on an axle in this sandy country could act as an abrasive. "It would cut right through the axle, and off goes the wheel. That's damned serious when crossing two-thousand miles of prairie and mountains."

Irons blurted, "Did you just figure that out?"

Drumm stared at the officer and quietly turned away.

Chapter Eight

Four days later, Captain Andrew Jackson Drumm, U.S. Topographical Corps, was significantly encouraged as he watched from a knoll west of the line of march, to see his command move jauntily along to the muffled clank of harness and accouterments.

Four days of back-breaking labor and action drills, and somehow the command had fused into a fine fighting unit. Hoist, heave, and haul had become familiar orders; Drumm and Peagram had rotated the men so each man learned enough of each of the skills that would make the venture successful.

Additionally, no man could complain of being unfairly treated.

Even Irons grudgingly admitted the men were getting the hang of Ives's "mule artillery," as Peagram called it.

From his vantage point on the knoll, with a fitful breeze shoving at his back like a gentle hand, Drumm noted that the land was changing as they continued south. The constant high wind was left behind as were the high, cool prairies. Now, hills and valley were dotted liberally with juniper and cottonwood, and a profusion of aspens and willows. Grass—lots of grass—provided excellent forage for mules and horses.

Bochey had come upon Von Holder and Hard Winter Davis, back from Bridger's Fort and right on schedule. Bochey rode back to report. *"Mon capitaine,"* he called a short distance from where Drumm and Irons followed Bochey up a small hill overlooking a placid Green River.

Carcasses of two mule deer rested on spits over a large pit of coals. "We figured the men would like to try Green River venison for supper tonight, hey?"

Blanchard was happy with the well-cooked deer meat and especially pleased when he unpacked his Fort Bridger supplies. After the men had eaten, Drumm had Peagram issue each of them a cup of Bridger's forty rod whiskey.

"Forty rods?" Von Holder was incredulous.

"It means you drink that cup right down and you'll run forty rods before you stop," Hard Winter said. "Tastes like galvanized sin pumped straight up from Hell, and jus' one sip'll clear out your pipes and make your eyes water. But, by damn, your spirit'll get some starch, I'm here to tell ya. Makes a man cozy as a toad under a cabbage leaf."

Drumm stared at Davis with amusement; leave it to Hard Winter to come up with colorful lingo.

A couple of sips had already gotten to Peagram who leaped up to the bed of one of Blanchard's wagons for all to see. "Drinks compliments of Cap'n Drumm. The outfit ain't an outfit no more." He paused for a long moment, a bright, but faraway gleam in his eyes. "It's a command. A gawdam command! Drumm's Devils and Augie's Bug Catchers!" Drumm's "command" hurrahed happily.

That evening Davis and Von Holder reported to Drumm on their visit to Bridger's Fort. "Must have been sixty, seventy emigrant wagons roundabout," Von Holder said. "I doubt if we raised any eyebrows. There was so much commotion and confusion with everyone trying to buy time on one of Bridger's two forges. You know, to repair wagon wheels, and the like."

"How about you, Hard Winter," Drumm asked. "anything to add to that?"

The mountain man squinted at Bochey. "Clauday, you recollect old Bad Gotia?"

Bochey's mouth fell open; when he closed it, his teeth clicked. *"Oui, mon ami."*

Davis's words were a knowing drawl. "Bridger's cousin of a cousin is the son of Bad Gotia, only this critter's knowed as Bad Heart." Davis's eyes roved the men around the fire ring. "For your information, the second season I was trappin' out here—he pursed his lips and shut his eyes in deep thought—"long about 1834, weren't it, Clauday?"

Bochey had wiped his scarred skull with some grease; the barren knob glowed like a billiard ball. *"Oui, c'est le Septembre!"*

"Shore was September, hoss," Davis agreed. "Me and Clauday was trapping for old Etienne Provost and he got us all invited to a big Ute powwow at Chief Bad Gotia's medicine lodge. Goin' to be peaceful, the chief says, so leave your shootin' iron outside as a pure sign of good faith, miserable skunk."

Davis angrily squirted a stream of brown juice into the fire where it sizzled. "Bad Gotia an' his men nigh killed all of us, for they had their hatchets on 'em. Provost not only lost an ear, but four men before he got outta that lodge. Olt Clauday there slit the lodgeskins with his Bowie, and him and me commenced making far-apart tracks."

"So," broke in Irons, "what in tarnation has that exaggerated tale have to do with us?"

Hard Winter regarded Irons with contempt. "Gabe said Bad Heart is Bad Gotia's kid. Said Bad Heart took his band of renegades south to do some raiding along the Spanish Trail." He cocked his head like a wise bird, his eyes as bright. "I'm of a mind that it'd be right peart for me an' Clauday to take us a sashay down that way, too."

"For what purpose?" Irons grunted. "What's a couple of skinny Injuns got to do with our mission?"

Before Hard Winter could respond, Drumm spoke up. "Good idea. The sooner you leave the better. We'll just keep following the Green, so we won't be hard to find." Drumm stood up, brushing twigs and grass from his trousers. He offered his hand to Davis and Bochey, wishing them good hunting. Irons glowered.

"Time to turn in, eh?" Drumm said. He spoke softly to Irons and Ives, asking them to stick around.

"So, what's that all about," Irons demanded after the others had left.

Drumm nodded at Ives. "Bear witness, Guns." He faced Irons. "You, sir, are failing this command. The Secretary of War has given us a specific mission which you are ignoring—and undermining—every way that you can."

Irons tried to interrupt with an angry "Well, I . . ." but Drumm snapped his words faster.

"Now just why, Captain Irons, do you suppose a Ute renegade with his band of cutthroats is heading south?"

Irons opened his mouth as if to speak, but no words came out. Drumm was relentless. "It was as clear as a bell to Mr. Ives and First Sergeant Peagram, and to Dr. Von Holder, and to those two dirty, ignorant mountain men you despise so freely." His eyes crawled over Irons from head to foot and back.

"I am at a loss with you, Irons. Give me an answer. You sure as hell have been free with your criticism, and your questioning of orders!" he stepped up close to Irons, facing him. "I'm waiting for an answer!" Damn, he thought, I'm losing control. He felt his legs trembling and he was sucking air, almost shuddering.

Drumm turned, waving at Davis and Bochey riding out of camp. "Lieutenant Ives! Please inform the Captain why *Mr.* Davis and *Mr.* Bochey are leaving camp." He watched the piglike eyes smolder deep in Irons' face.

When Ives spoke, there was no apology in his voice for being invited into an argument between superior officers. "Captain, those two men know the renegade Indians can raid at will along the Oregon Trail. Therefore, whatever is causing them to shift south to the Green River valley must be powerful bait indeed. Plus, we have heard that these renegades plan a raid on an important wagon train."

Drumm spoke again, hearing nothing from Irons. "In the beginning, Irons, I thought we had come to an agreement. But now all I can say is that you've given this whole command a bellyache." Drumm rammed ahead. "I cannot believe that an officer of the dragoons with your record would work so hard at causing trouble."

Irons stalked closer to Drumm, fists balled and menacing. Drumm stood his ground. "Mr. Ives," he said through gritted teeth, "make certain you record the events that follow."

He stepped around the wagon where the three of them were hidden from prying eyes.

"All right, Irons. If it's a fight you want, then let's give it a go." He began to remove his coat when the shorter but heavier man bowled into him, both fists hammering, hoping to end the fight fast.

Half expecting such a trick from Irons, Drumm sidestepped with a rolling motion and clouted Irons with a solid left hook just above the ear.

The chunky officer rocked for a moment, his ears ringing as he lunged at Drumm. Drumm ducked a wild swing, catching Irons defenseless and slamming him with two brutal punches, one to the head, the other into a paunch hard as leather. Again, Irons whirled to face Drumm; he hurt and a murderous rage was printed in his eyes.

With a growl, Irons bore in with clubbing fists. Drumm couldn't escape Irons' clutching embrace, which lifted him off the ground. Thinking he had Drumm, Irons gloated, "Now, damn your eyes . . ." Drumm yanked his right arm free and clubbed Irons at close range—once, twice, three times—before Irons let go his stranglehold.

His breath rattling in his throat, Irons waded in at Drumm once more, but this time Drumm staggered the beefy officer with a stiff left into Irons's eyes. He followed with a savage uppercut into the jowls.

Irons' legs buckled as he gamely tried to keep his body erect, but the uppercut had finished him. His eyes rolling and glazed, he folded and fell senseless to the ground.

Drumm stood over him, his chest heaving and blood seeping from both nostrils. Peagram unexpectedly stepped out of the dark with a bucket of water, which he threw onto Irons.

Ives helped Drumm into his jacket and the three men walked slowly and silently back to camp, leaving a drenched Irons to collect himself alone. Peagram spoke slowly to Drumm. "No one saw you fighting, sir. No, sir. No one saw you beat the living' hell out of Cap'n Irons, though he's been askin' for it for fifteen years."

He stopped. "I'm glad I lived long enough to see Irons whipped, sir, if you'll forgive a sergeant for sayin' it."

Drumm stared, astonished to see the entire command standing around some distance away in the dark; every man was softly clapping and smiling.

"No, sir," Peagram said. "Nobody saw a thing. But stric'ly speakin', sir, that was the best goddam uppercut I ever saw!"

Chapter Nine

Hard Winter Davis and Claude Bochey had ridden all night.

Dawn found them far down the Green River. They rested their horses in the tall grass under the early morning shade of an aspen grove and munched on jerky and hardtack. Each napped while the other stood guard.

Keeping to the fringe of timber skirting the streams and valleys that joined the bigger river, the two ghosted their way over rock-strewn mountains whose sides were a series of rims and ledges.

"Easy to git rimrocked here, Clauday," Hard Winter said softly. "Let's mosey along this rim till dark."

The ledge was high over the Green which twisting below them like a tormented serpent. Here and there the rim slanted out, a flat strata of red rock where gnarled cedar and sweet-smelling juniper crowned the hills.

Taking their time, they poked along, letting their horses find the trail. No words were exchanged until, a long way south in the deepening twilight, they saw a red eye, the smallest glimpse of a fire.

Davis grabbed his partner's arm in an iron grip. "Be damned careful, Clauday," he whispered.

Walking the horses, Davis and Bochey split up, keeping about thirty yards apart. Their glide was noiseless and effortless as they slid forward through trees and rocks, always headed for the twinkling spark of fire.

It was tedious business and they moved at a snail's pace. Yet both were schooled in the ways of stalking four-legged game. They had been both the hunter and the hunted. They kept their senses alert and their eyes suspicious of the slightest movement.

Davis edged to Bochey. "Hold my pony, Clauday," he hissed. "I'll go on down for a look-see. I'll be back 'fore dawn."

Bochey held on to Davis's arm, putting his lips close to Hard Winter's ear. "The trap, *mon ami*. Beware."

A bleached horn of moon had climbed the summer sky, bathing the land in a sort of silvery half-light that enabled Hard Winter to slip into and out of shadows with ease. He abruptly froze as he spotted a sentinel, back to a rock, one leg revealed in the wan light of the moon. Steering clear of the guard, the mountain man moved with extra care, expecting to find a second guard, maybe, he thought, even a third.

As he edged closer to the odd fire which leaped and then fell from sight, he found himself a silent spectator on the rim of a sort of bowl where the ground had fallen, leaving rimrock nearly all the way around it.

In reality, the fire was large, and it sent tongues of flame shooting ten to thirty feet into the air. Huh, Hard Winter murmurred in his mind. Cussed redhides! Ought to know better. So much for a small fire. That ain't a dancin' fire or a medicine fire. He drew careful breaths as he sought a safe place to observe.

As he drew closer, the roar of noise assaulted his ears; it was bottled up in the bowl and rose straight for the heavens, muffled by trees and branches from the sides. Around the fire, in an almost perfect circle, nearly a hundred braves whooped, chanted, and drank. A Mexican soldier, to one side on the edge of a stand of timber, was making certain every Indian had all he wanted to drink. He recognized the uniform. Judas tripes, I seen plenty of them hombres in Taos and Santy Fay, he told himself. A second soldier, obviously an officer, appeared with an Indian wearing a full war bonnet.

Hmm, Hard Winter mused from his vantage point safe in the inky darkness. There's old Bad Heart. The Indian leader brandished a firearm over his head, firing it with one hand in the general direction of the thin, crescent moon. The gun's roar was almost lost in the din around him.

He tossed the rifle into the grasping hands of one of his followers. The crowd of sweating, excited braves surged forward. The officer and the Indian shoved out a half-dozen crates which they broke open, producing more half-stocked percussion rifles which were distributed among the drunken braves to a chorus of approving howls.

The mountain man's eyes narrowed as he studied the flat black hat, the shell jacket with waist to chest brass buttons up each side, and the white belts crisscrossing the uniform. The military man wore white, skin-tight trousers tucked into knee-high boots.

Again, he thought to himself, Sure as hell! That's the regular cavalry outta Santy Fay. His mind whirled back to a time he and Bochey wintered in Santa Fe, spending their season's fur money on Taos whiskey and senoritas.

They had been welcome as the flowers in May until their money ran out. Then bozos like the one happily handing out the guns below him rode into their camp and ran them out of town, poking them with lances to hurry them along.

Hard Winter Davis watched a long time from the rimrock, seeing the Indians drink themselves into a frenzy, then stagger off into the night while others collapsed and lay as though dead.

Lord, they's noisier'n a jackass in a tin barn! Sure don't take much coffin varnish to get them redskins drunk, he thought to himself. They'll have sore heads come mornin', sure. They'll be on the peck and primed for huntin' hair.

As he watched, the Mexican soldiers mounted up, and amid cheering and firing of guns, rode off into the dark, headed south. Soon after, the camp fell silent.

He was about to ease up and make his way back to Bochey when two Indians walked along the ledge scant inches above him. They stopped, laughing and talking softly. He thought they must be new guards. He made himself as small as possible against his shelf of rimrock. The two stopped, nearly on top of him. He stopped breathing, knowing now these were the relief for two guards. But I only saw one guard. Must be they's another roundabout som'ers. Doggies, I must've walked nigh over him.

So he knew it was lay still as could be, or fight four Indians and risk rousing the others. The odds were too great. Besides, he thought smugly, if these two missed me, I'm well hidden. Ain't nothin' can penetrate my concealment, less I give it away myself.

He felt hot drops and spray sprinkling his hands as the Indians stood beside his rock, belching and urinating. His first impulse was to rear up and kill both with his bare hands. Still he remained proud of his restraint as the two Indians, both loose with booze, stumbled away into the dark.

Whee-ew! Coulda lost my topknot in this 'un if I'd of moved off too soon. They'd a-settled this child's hash for all time and then some.

It was a pepper-hot Davis who found Bochey at first light. "I'll tell you later what I seen. Just now I'm headin' for the creek."

As soon as he spotted a sufficiently deep hollow of water, he plunged into it, clothes and all, letting the plummeting water from a spillover slam his body. He scoured his urine-burned hands with a mixture of mud and sand, rubbing until he nearly wore off the top skin.

Bochey, watching him, was mystified. About the only liquid Hard Winter Davis allowed himself near was powerful and came out of a jug. And he knew Hard Winter well enough to keep his questions to himself for the time being.

Davis sat in the light of a sun growing hot, his drying buckskins hardening to the consistency of iron. He knew if he took his clothes off, they'd shrink. Waiting there, his clean hands and face gleaming, he told Bochey of his close call.

Bochey laughed hard with the telling, holding his sides and gasping. Davis took it as no joke, and regarded his companion sourly.

Bochey gasped out his word. "Ah, *mon ami*, you 'ave been, shall we say, baptised with the *eau de cologne du* Ute Indian, eh?" He broke off into gales of laughter again. Davis squinted at his companion rolling in the dirt and howling. Davis's forehead was ribbed in temporary anger, knowing it would be foolish to lodge pole the cackling little bastard.

Davis's displeasure was fleeting. He broke out a smile. "Clauday, your ear is better at furriner lingo. Listen up. I memorized one sentence the Mexican tol' Bad Heart."

Bochey came alert, his glee forgotten, all ears now and solemn as a barn full of owls. He cocked his ear to Hard Winter's recitation. "*En cinco dias mia brava soldars* . . . something, something . . . *el rio verde cruce.* Mean anythin', Clauday?"

Bochey muddled on it only a moment. "It means, *mon ami*, the Green River crossing is in five days, and he would be there with his brave Mexican soldiers to join with Bad Heart."

Both thought on the evidence for a moment, and almost simultaneously, the two jerked alert. "Hell, yes!," Hard Winter roared. "Them Utes is supposed to meet the Mexie sojers where the Spanish Trail crosses the Green!" Bochey's head bobbed in agreement.

"Listen here, *mon ami* Clauday, you hike back to Andy and don't let no sunlight between you and that saddle. Tell him what we know. I'll keep doggin' them pissin' Indians." He grinned and offered a hand for good luck. "Git goin', Clauday."

Watching his friend gallop out of sight, Hard Winter shed his shirt and pants, and scrubbed himself again under the battering waterfall. "Damn my eyes," he said as he returned to his rock in the sun. "Don't reckon I'll ever get shed of that smell. Worse, by God than a skunk!"

Dressed again, he stepped up on his roan and carefully picked his way back to the now-abandoned camp he'd watched during the night. The fire smoldered and cracked jugs and the droppings of man and horse alike littered the camp.

"One thing I know right well," he thought, his eye collecting what information was in their leavings, "a lot of big heads and short fuses are in that bunch 'day!"

He rode on a bit, following the easy trail of their departure. "Sure wish we could stampede 'em this mornin'; they'd skallyhoot like hell in ever' direction."

Chapter Ten

As he'd been bid, Bochey didn't slow up once. He rode all day, and at dusk he rested his horse and took a nap. He went to sleep, head parked on his saddle, studying the sky that was showing part of the day and part of the night. Above him, the sun floated over a rim of mountains and a stillness came on the land, lulling him to sleep.

Rested, he nibbled a piece of elk and hardtack and mounted again. He hoped to raise Drumm's command at dawn.

Calculating Drumm would have covered many miles, shortening the distance between them, the little mountain man's heels drummed his horse into a steady trot, a mile-eating pace. Picking his way along at night, aided by the same sliver of moon he and Davis had used the night before, Bochey felt good. He enjoyed the creamy night breeze after his hot dry ride during the day. It was no surprise when he was abruptly challenged by one of Drumm's sentries at daybreak.

"Eat first, we'll hear your report after," Drumm said, then turned to Irons. "Continue to load and prepare to move out."

Still sporting a yellow and purple eye plus a split lip, Captain Irons passed the order to Peagram and was about to join Drumm in his interrogation of Bochey when Drumm turned on him. "Captain, I specifically told you to carry out that order. Now, get about it, mister!"

Irons started to answer, thought better of it, and clumped angrily off to oversee the loading out of the command.

Wolfing down hot bread and warmed-over stew, washed down with piping hot coffee gave Bochey a new lease on life. He imitated Davis's sneak to the Indian fire, what he saw, and their conclusions and concerns. Davis, he told Drumm, was still on the prowl. He wisely held back telling about Davis being peed on. Hard Winter would never live it down with the troop.

To make sure he had it right, Drumm repeated what Bochey had told him. He waited until Irons had completed his duties, and included him in on the Bochey report. Then Drumm asked all his officers and noncoms to help him with advice. He heard them out, thanked them, and dismissed them.

Von Holder stayed. Drumm looked at him, wondering. "What do you think, Augie?"

"Don't confuse the issue by asking me, Andy. Since we've been together I can find nothing you've done to criticize, including teaching our mutual friend, Captain Irons, the fine art of fisticuffs."

"All that may be true, Augie, but now do we hustle on down to meet with Davis, or play the prudent, cautious hand and continue to enjoy our turtlelike trip south?"

"Sounds like your mind's made up as it is," Von Holder said.

"Yes, sir, I have that. So we move posthaste. It's about time to tell your men and mine that there's no more posing as a topo outfit. Something's brewing, and I have a hunch Drumm's Devils had best gird up to be in the thick of it."

He walked to his horse, levered himself into the saddle, and guided the animal with slow deliberation to where the command was making ready for the trail.

"Men, it would appear the fat's in the fire. Mr. Davis and Mr. Bochey have made contact with a large armed group of Indians and Mexicans. We believe they are going to attack a wagon train, without doubt containing American civilians." He paused, letting his words sink in. Again he raised his voice. "No more playing topographical engineers. I want all dragoons to draw a saber. From here on out, despite your civilian clothes, you're army, all soldiers." He nodded toward Irons. "Carry on, Captain Irons!"

Sabers were quickly issued and buckled on, the latigo knots dancing from the hilts. They looked strange against the assorted brown wool and buckskin attire.

To the Dragoons at least, the prospect of freedom from pounding stakes or breaking rocks for specimens was happy language, easily and enjoyably understood.

As they pulled out, Bochey tied his horse to the bedroll wagon, climbed in and promptly fell into a dead sleep. Doyle and Harrigan One took the point, with Rawson and Newman following well behind at drag.

The day warmed almost uncomfortably as they dropped off the high plateau and Continental Divide country. Overhead, the sky stretched deep and far, broken only by a circling eagle or a gliding hawk. At noon, Bochey was up, refreshed and in the lead, ranging far ahead of the column. On the second day they passed through the Ute encampment littered with kegs and broken jugs, battered cups, and the stench of the leavings of a hundred head of horses and as many humans.

Peagram wrinkled his nose. "The place smells of foul keep. I'd as leave we get movin' on."

"My God," Harrigan Two groused at Blanchard. "I was told the redman was noble, and the royal monarch of the plains." He sniffed, his eyebrows raised in disdain. "So much for nobility. I could never stomach 'em."

"Considerable whiffy on the leeside," was Blanchard's laconic observation. Two days later, Hard Winter Davis stepped out from behind a sandstone ledge. He looked bad, bags under his eyes, and gaunt from scant rations. His horse looked worse.

He rode to report to Drumm. "You look like you been rode hard and put away wet, Hard Winter."

"But I know more'n I did, Andy. There's a hell of a swarm of Mex cavalry about twelve miles south of the crossing, all horns and rattles. A couple of 'em has already met with ol' Bad Heart and his collection of renegades." He pushed away a cup of coffee. "Later," he told Blanchard.

"That bunch of Mexicans seen to it ever' Injun got him a gun." Drumm began to interrupt but was stopped by Davis's wave. "Andy, I got to git this off my chest." Davis leaned against a wagon wheel and got out his Bowie and his Mickey Twist and prepared to cut off a cud. He held them ready, but went on with his report.

"Sure looks like there's a big wagon train headin' west on the Spanish Trail with a big cavalry escort. I got close enough to see a white couple and lots of Mexican families, includin' old folks, women, and kids. Fifteen to twenty wagons."

His tired eyes stared at Drumm. "I've got this real bad feeling, Andy. The wagon train is going to be turned loose from its escort, and then them blood-minded, river-rat renegades is going to hit 'em where it hurts worst."

Now he accepted a bowl of stew and some bread, and laid his knife and tobacco aside. "How in infernal hell do you keep coffee so hot when you ain't got sign one of a fire?" he asked Blanchard.

"Easy," Blanchard said, grinning. "I always keep a pot full of coals ready to heat up coffee, anytime."

Davis rolled his eyes. "Dog bite me for a bone! I declare. That's still the best by-God coffee this yap has ever swallowed."

Drumm had Davis repeat his findings to his staff, and asked them their opinions of the action to be taken. Drumm wasn't pleased with their failure to grasp the seriousness of what he felt lay ahead.

"Let's get the column moving, Captain Irons. We're wasting light."

Mounted, he rode by the bedroll wagon to see Davis before he got in some much-needed sleep. "I 'spect, Andy, them Mexies is up to one sort of shenanigan or t'other, and them poor settler folks, well, I sure pity 'em."

"Get some rest," Drumm advised. "You and Bochey have done a hell of a job."

He spurred his horse ahead to where Von Holder waited. "We are picking up the pace, Augie, even if I am disobeying orders."

Von Holder's look was thoughtful. "It may turn out that you are in reality following orders, Andy."

Drumm stared at the scientist, plumbing the depth of the remark. He nodded at Von Holder. "Yep."

Signalling Irons, Drumm commanded, "Short rations tonight. Jerky, hardtack, and water. Maybe Blanchard can produce some of his magic coffee. We march until 10 P.M."

He turned to Peagram. "Give me a report on the condition of the men and animals."

56

"By your leave, Cap'n. The horses thrive on hard use. As for the men, sir, they will follow you to hell." Peagram snapped a first-class salute and rode off, dust billowing in his wake.

Wonderment crossed Drumm's face. "What was that all about, Augie?"

Von Holder grinned. "If you don't know, then I guess I'll have to say that your men like you." He winked at Drumm who still wore the fruits of his fight, seen in a puffed eye and a rosy, swollen cheek. "Most of all, they respect you for having put Irons in his place."

"And I asked that only Ives and Peagram witnessed it!"

"Ah, Andy," Von Holder chuckled, "when the word of the impending fight went around, the entire command sneaked up to see you bash Irons about. We all thoroughly enjoyed the whole business. In fact, if the men grow weary of routine, let's have another fight."

Drumm smiled ruefully. "That Irons packs a wallop. If we do have another fight, count me out!"

Chapter Eleven

On cue, at the crack of dawn, Blanchard was a welcome sight with his coffee, pan bread, and molasses, along with some stew from the previous night. "Take extra," he warned them. "We've a long way to go and the extra will keep you going." As the men took him up on the offer, Blanchard noted with satisfaction that there were few finicky eaters among Drumm's Devils.

Captain Drumm witnessed the morning's meal with a warm feeling "I don't know how you do it, Mr. Blanchard, but speaking for the entire command, I have to say you're the best field cook I've ever seen." Drumm tipped two fingers to the brim of his visored cap in a semisalute before walking away.

Harrigan Three cooed, "The good Cap'n must have sprung straight from County Cork, him bein' able to recognize the great artist that you are, Mr. Blanchard dear."

The burly cook laid a beefy but friendly hand on Three's youthful back. "Son, I just cook. Nothing special. Just cook it on time, and serve it hot. Do that, and much will be forgiven a humble pot walloper."

"La! Don't be beggin' off your mighty gift, Mr. Blanchard."

Walking away from the queue of eager patrons for Blanchard's hearty morning fare, Drumm mused that Davis was far ahead, and Bochey scouting between the column head and Hard Winter.

Having breakfasted, the command reassembled and moved out, strung out about a thousand feet from head to rear. Gunny sacks were wrapped around everything as a precaution to soften any noise. Drumm was aware they were moving as cautiously as possible; his gnawing concern was the pall of dust billowing up from the dry trail as animals and wagons pulverized the trail grit and whipped it into a terra-cotta colored haze.

"It ain't just dust, Andy," Von Holder called through a scarf wound around to shield his face from the dust, leaving only his eyes uncovered. "It's a scorcher. At least a hundred degrees. I'd give a box of fancy cheroots for a brisk breeze."

Agreeing, Drumm pulled off the trail with Augie. "What worries me is that cloud of dust in our wake. I hope it doesn't give us away."

Throughout the day, the reconnaissance column aimed deeper by the hour into Mexico. A small stream offered an opportunity to water the stock and the men. Drumm allowed only a half hour for the halt.

At twilight, before marching the men on into the soft summer night, and with the heat abating just a bit, Drumm called his officers and noncoms together. As he did, the sun let itself down behind a bank of clouds, and began painting with eye-popping pinks, reds, and purples as though the sky was dressing itself in a cloak of many colors.

"Herd your men along," he instructed. "Help them. It's been a long day and we need another twenty miles before we call it a night."

As the column moved off into deepening dark, Drumm told Von Holder, "It's July 23. I wonder how the Mexicans are taking the annexation of Texas?"

Von Holder lit a cigar and savored the fresh smoke for a long minute. "I'd say that's the least of our problems now."

It was tough going. The moon was waxing now, and helped the men manage the horses and mules. Drumm was riding nearby as Blanchard and Harrigan Three crawled into the bedroll wagon away from the moonbright land for a catnap. Dawn will come soon enough for those two, Drumm thought. Somehow Blanchard would turn out something good to eat and the coffee would be hot.

Bochey and Hard Winter emerged out of the mists of dawn, dogged out and famished. A fresh breeze skipped in the grass around them, dissolving the pall of night. "The Injuns is stashed all along a small valley 'bout two miles ahead, Andy," Davis reported. He held up a hand. "No need to fret. They ain't got a soul lookin' back for anybody likely campin' on their trail. But they sure as hell are paintin' for war at the crossin'." He finished some grub Blanchard had ladeled out on a tin plate. "I figure the redskins want to hit the wagon train while they's fordin' the river."

Eager to get back to his duties, Hard Winter saddled a fresh horse and took Drumm along with Ives, Miller, Peagram, and Von Holder for a "look-see." Leaving Miller to hold the horses, the remaining five inched softly to the crown of a well-timbered hill overlooking the crossing of the Green River, less than a half-mile below them. Davis waved their attention to the Indians infesting the long ridge that looked like a Roman nose, its start being a high ridge, and then losing ground all the way down to within a couple hundred yards of the river's edge. Careful not to show themselves, the Indians were scattered behind the natural fortifications offered by the tilted rimrock.

"When that wagon train comes out of those hills," Davis said, pointing out the trail to the crossing, "they will cross right in front of the Indians. Old Bad Heart is goin' to have a field day. By God, Andy, it appears to me we're close enough to hell to smell smoke!"

Drumm borrowed Von Holder's telescope, a sea captain's glass, Augie called it. Drumm muttered as his eyes roamed the area through the spyglass. "Ives is going to set Betsy and Lou up on that rim, about 600 yards from the crossing." He shifted the glass. "And Davis and Bochey with three good sharpshooters will set up on the left flank of Ives and pick off Indians at random after my First Sergeant and I hit the Indian attack on the wagon train."

Drumm rolled onto his back. Looking at the blue sky and the towering morning clouds, he handed the telescope to Ives. Then Peagram and Von Holder scanned the area with the glass.

"Here's how we hit the Indians," Drumm said softly. "First of all, the dragoons are riding along with Ives to help him dismount and lay his guns." Ives nodded. He said nothing, but his eyes danced with excitement.

"Think you can roll up the Indians when we drive them off the wagon train, Guns?"

"Yes, sir!" There was emphasis in Ives' whisper.

"We'll be counting on your accuracy because from what I see in front of us, the dragoons will be hitting an enemy who outnumbers us nearly ten to one."

He winked at Davis. "Of course, Mr. Davis and the trusty Bochey along with their three crackshots should claim at least twenty Indians." He chewed a blade of grass. "Once the Indians break and run, Mr. Ives, I want you to hit them, and hit them again. That ought to take the starch out of their sails, eh?"

The party eased down off the ridge, and Drumm sent Miller back to hurry the rest of the command along.

"I make it about 9 o'clock, Augie," Drumm said, shielding his eyes against the sun.

"Twenty minutes early, Andy." Von Holder plopped his watch case closed.

"Say, why don't you lend that telescope to Mr. Ives. It would help him, sort of keep him posted." Drumm watched Ives and Von Holder check the fine points of the spyglass. He turned to Peagram.

"Well, First, how many men can we afford to use on an all-out cavalry charge?"

"A good baker's dozen, sir. But all tried and true."

Within an hour the command was assembled in a nearby woods and screened from sight of the enemy by a pair of ridges. Ives pulled out his mule string and, together with the dragoons, moved into the position he and Drumm had agreed upon. The men worked fast and efficiently, taking great care to screen their movements. In what seemed no time, two field pieces and their bases had been born of hoist, heave, and haul.

"Drumm! Drumm!" The voice of Irons knifed into his reverie. "Judas," Drumm thought, "what sort of fly is he going to toss into the ointment now?"

"With your permission, sir," Irons said. "My place is here. Mr. Von Holder can handle the rear guard." Drumm was relieved.

"Hold the center, Captain, and glad we are to have you with us." Irons threw Drumm a hand salute and edged into position between Rawson and Ehler.

Everything turned quiet, the silence ominous. Lull before the storm, Drumm thought, looking at the tense men around him. Grim looking, he thought, but they had grit. "Chock full a' sand an' tallow," was the way he'd heard Hard Winter Davis put it. Drumm could feel the seconds ticking away with the pulsebeat in his temples.

It seemed an eternity. His hands were slick with sweat; he nervously wiped his palms on his pants. He looked down the line at Peagram on the left flank, with all the Harrigans with him. That's three. Davis took three of the scientists. Ives had Corporal Doyle, Getter, Smith, and Jones. That leaves me with Irons and Peagram, Quinn, Rawson, Ehler, Newman, Bonnett, Kilmer, Kincaid, Miller, Brady, and Upton. Peagram's baker's dozen.

Anxiety cramped his bowels. Thirteen men armed with heavy cavalry sabers, sharp-pointed but dull-edged to hack a man to his knees. Thirteen men waiting for the first gunshot and the bugle command.

Drumm thought he heard the faint report of a round being fired. Miller's clear bugle notes lifted on the midmorning breeze, the stirring "Boots and Saddles." Drumm dug spurs into his horse's flank. "We're off!"

All he could think of as he raced forward over the uneven ground was his command bunched in a column of twos forward; Miller's bugle repeated the familiar call again and again.

Drumm's meager platoon rode out into full view as their eyes registered a wagon train caught up in a full-fledged Indian attack. A third of the wagons were still midstream while the balance valiantly tried to maneuver into a defensive circle.

With a raise of his arm, his column skidded to a halt behind him. He ordered them into a single company front as Miller blasted his call to charge. The line leaped forward, each man with his saber at the ready for a thrust or slash as they rode yelling and roaring straight at the Indians. All other concerns were forgotten in the charge; Drumm sensed the true and deep exhilaration of command and combat, his chest swelling with it to the point that his breath came with difficulty.

Around him as he rode, dragoons in civilian clothes charged yard by yard to close the gap between themselves and the marauding Indians, hard-charging riders intent on ending the mayhem and murder before them.

Abruptly, the Indians saw Drumm's Devils riding them down. Astonished but defiant, some knelt to lay rifle fire or arrows into the charging rank. The line of determined horsemen appeared impervious to wounds as they stood in the stirrups, leaning forward with sabers outstretched seeking enemy flesh. Sunlight shimmered along the hungry blades, further disorienting an Indian horde which had expected no opposition.

At first the Indians held their ground, but as the wild eyed, yelling dragoons plunged into them, sabers thrusting and slashing, many turned and fled away from the wagon train, heading west into the trap set by Drumm and Ives.

Bad Heart, holding a chief's position on a ridge overlooking the quarry that had promised to be an easy, valuable target, had no stomach for a pitched fight with the white horsemen. He waved his coup stick, signaling his men back, only to see them tumble from their ponies, victims of gun fire from positions he couldn't see.

By now the strange-looking cavalry had gained the advantage at the wagon train. At least twenty of Bad Heart's horde were down, wounded or dead. He drew the remnants around him, still unable to locate the annoying riflemen. Then his quick eye picked up movement and, shouting at his men—now around eighty—directed them to eliminate the devastating fire Davis and his crew were laying down.

Ives, in position and ready for fight, saw the Indians retreat and, knowing Drumm was in command at the wagon train, aimed Betsy and Lou at Bad Heart's group as they scurried toward the position of Davis's crew.

Ives personally aimed and fired both guns. He saw the shells hit the Indians, wiping out a half-dozen with one blast. Another group was destroyed with the impact of Lou's round. Ives watched with grim satisfaction as confusion overwhelmed the Indians; nothing in their experience prepared them for the likes of the two death-dealing explosions smack-dab in their midst.

It was enough for Bad Heart. He quit. His followers raced headlong after him as Davis and his hidden sharpshooters knocked several more off their horses as they frantically scratched and scrambled to get the hell away from death's door.

With the roar subsiding, Ives' crew swabbed the guns, and began preparing them for another burst, but he held up his hand. "We did our job; the Indians are on the run." Ives was elated as he walked around shaking hands and clapping men on the back.

Chapter Twelve

Once the hard riding but outnumbered line of dragoons broke into the Indian attack on the train, they found themselves in a melee of slashing and hacking the Indians, who tried vainly to isolate and then overpower the American horsemen.

Drumm found himself parrying the thrust of a stone-tipped lance held by a charging brave on horseback. As the redskin bore in, trying to bring the deadly lance up for the fatal strike, Drumm dealt him a powerful thrust with his saber, killing the man instantly. As the Indian was swept off his horse, Drumm became aware of two Indians afoot on either side of him, moving to the attack. One arced a huge stone hammer on a long handle while the other lunged at Drumm with his scalping knife.

Time became an agonizingly slow dimension as Drumm's powerful saber splintered the hammer's handle, the shock of the blow momentarily paralyzing the Indian's arm and staggering him. In the periphery of vision, Drumm sensed the man on the other side bearing down on him with a great, glistening Bowie blade. As he moved to fend off the second Indian, a hot searing flash of agony invaded his thigh. The long, two-inch-wide blade penetrated muscle, glancing off bone. The brutal force of the Indian's thrust imbedded the knife-tip in the wood of Drumm's saddletree, pinning him.

The shock waves of pain from the wound jarred Drumm to the farthest fibers of his soul. Momentarily both he and the Indian cooperated in trying to pull the knife from its fixed position; Drumm to frantically rid himself of the searing pain, the Indian to retrieve the blade for a second attack.

Drumm gave up. Grasping his saber in both hands and raising the gleaming steel sword high, he brought it down with a vicious chop on the savage's skull. Even in death, the Indian clung to the terrible knife and Drumm, swaying in pain, pried the dead man's grip from the knife handle; each movement sent spears of agony through Drumm's body.

The Indian fell away from Drumm's prancing horse. Drumm struggled to remove the knife, consciously feeling the strength flowing from his body. Peagram, his face a bloody mask, rode up frantically beside Drumm, calmed his horse and with a great heave, jerked the giant blade free. He slid out of the saddle, slit Drumm's pantsleg to the wound with the same offending and bloody Bowie. Drumm slumped, his knuckles white as he clutched the saddle horn for dear life.

"Oh, God!" Drumm muttered through teeth gnashing against the pain.

Peagram yanked off his saber strap and tucked it under Drumm's leg above the wound. He snatched up the short length of splintered handle from the Ute war axe, stuck it under the latigo strap and took a turn.

"Tourniquet, eh, First?," Drumm hissed through his misery.

"Yes, sir," Peagram gasped. "Let the blood run a bit first, then we shut it off. That'll do till I can get you back to Blanchard, sir."

Peagram looked past the two dead Indians on either side of Drumm's horse. The savages were in frantic retreat. Peagram swiped with the back at his hand at blood around his eyes, causing him to blink; he had a shallow forehead wound. A huge burst of cannon fire sent shock waves through the air around them.

Drumm raised his head, forgetting his pain for a moment. "Good for Ives," he said, louder than was necessary. "He's right on time." His head dropped again.

A second cannon shell burst, panicking any remaining Indians in the nearby field of action to scatter in terrified flight. Concern was printed in the bloody lines of Peagram's face.

"You all right, Cap'n?"

Drumm slowly raised his head, almost accustomed now to the bone-searing pain. His eyes and mind took in the chaos and destruction caused first by the Indian attack, and by his dragoons' counterattack. We got here with no time to spare, he thought, as he viewed the bloody mess the Indians created with their devastating assault of the civilian train of hapless and helpless Mexicans.

Irons charged up, waving a United States army uniform at Drumm. "Where'd that come from?," Drumm asked.

Two more men rode in brandishing U.S. blue shell jackets. "Infantry, I'd say," Irons said. "This issue was replaced in 1840." He looked at Drumm. "We peeled 'em off three dead Mexicans. I don't know about those two, but I personally killed the Mexican wearing this one."

Irons lifted the jacket on his saber tip for all to see where his sword had claimed a Mexican life. "By his actions, I'd guess he was a real soldier—not ours—Mexican."

Drumm, still trying to absorb the shock of his wound, grunted, "Somebody sure tried to pin this attack on us."

The knot of men were a few yards away from a badly damaged wagon whose canvas top was partly gone. Screams and groans of pain issued from the wagon's occupants, then were muffled as someone tried to smother the sound. Drumm was closest and, despite his pain, swung his horse toward the wagon's rear to investigate. He yanked at a torn and dangling shroud of wagon cover.

He looked straight into the grey eyes of Lady Diana Abney. She was comforting her brother, Lord Parton, Sir Hardwig Abney whose white shirt was scarlet from a gaping shoulder wound spewing blood.

Drumm was stunned, as were Irons, Peagram, Miller, and Harrigan One, all witnessing the astonishing spectacle. Drumm fumbled for words only to have Lady Diana blurt out, "Well, Mr. American, I should hope you are proud of your actions today murdering defenseless Mexicans and damned near killing my brother!"

All Drumm could think was, my God, she sure is angry, mad clear through and so damned beautiful. Her beauty transfixed him; he couldn't blink an eye or even breathe.

She stood up now, stamping a booted foot on the wagon bed when a clear look of recognition swept over her. "You! You're the Captain I met in Washington in March!" She jabbed an accusing finger in Drumm's direction.

He nodded dumbly, his tongue cleaving to the roof of his mouth in astonishment. Forgetting his wound, he stepped out of the saddle and made several steps in her direction. His leg buckled and Captain Andrew Jackson Drumm fell into a big, black hole where, thankfully, he knew no pain. He could hear, though, as Peagram said, "Beggin' your pardon, ma'am. It was the Mexicans and Injuns who . . . "

It seemed only moments later but the sun said hours had passed when Drumm's consciousness returned. Pain wracked his injured thigh with every jarring jounce of the wagon he lay in; he grit his teeth and resolved to rise above the agony. The welfare of Drumm's Devils was in his hands, complicated now by the presence of Lady Diana and her brother, and the other survivors of the intended Indian massacre. He could not give in to pain.

His mouth was dry and sticky and sick-tasting. He tried to raise up, his vision was blocked by Lady Diana. The sun behind her created a shining aura around the ash-blond hair cascading over her shoulders, making her seem a fantastic creature made of gold. In Drumm's borderline delirium he thought of the paradox of all that beauty in this land of dismal, wholesale carnage.

"Oh, Captain Drumm!," she said, seeing he was awake, and restraining his movements with a firm hand. "You must rest." She was smiling.

Drumm turned his head to regard the only other occupant of the wagon box, stretched out beside him. The face of the man beside him was a chalk mask, drawn and seamed in pain. "It's your brother," he said and at once he realized how stupid he sounded.

Diana rocked with the wagon's careering motion. "Dear Hardy is not in the best of shape. At least his wound has ceased to bleed."

She examined Drumm's leg wound. "Your wound also stopped bleeding an hour ago when Mr. Blanchard devised that bandage." She pinched her nose. "I must say, it certainly is strong smelling. I wonder what Hardy will say when he wakes smelling like a barnyard." Drumm realized that Blanchard had come up with some form of local remedy, and foul-smelling it was.

He knew she was right as the odor of manure engulfed him, too. He tried, with excruciating pain, to raise his leg. Somehow in his resolve to stay in control and not favor his infirmity, agony strengthened him, rather than turning him feeble.

Through the oval of canvas cover at the wagon's front, he saw Harrigan Three's burly Irish back at the reins. "Halt, Three!" he yelled, and the vehicle ground to a stop. Von Holder and Irons, who'd been riding together, appeared at the wagon's tailboard.

"How long have I been in this wagon?"

Irons answered, "Since the skirmish ended this morning. It was the best we could do for you."

Drumm thanked them. "Bring my horse. I'm good enough to sit a saddle."

By now, Blanchard had made an appearance. Standing at the rear wheel, he offered, "Captain, if you move now, the bleeding will start again. Give it two, three days and you can ride in the wagon seat." Blanchard looked at Peagram who along with Davis had joined the concerned group at the back of the wagon.

"Don't fret none, Andy," Hard Winter chimed in. "You ain't lost your command. You just goin' to give orders from a wagon, not from top of a hoss." Davis gave Drumm a wry grin.

Drumm knew he was defeated; the growing pain was helping his decision. "All right." He looked at Irons. "Please return to your duties, Captain. Would you ask Mr. Ives to report."

Diana watched Drumm gingerly inch his body to a sitting position. Blanchard came back with two mugs of his life-giving coffee, offering the woman one and handing the other to the dragoon captain. Drumm was back in command, and she liked the easy way he did it.

She knew now it was Mexican treachery that nearly killed her and her brother: it was a cold-blooded trick. The Mexicans would have claimed the British diplomat and his sister had been murdered by American soldiers. She shuddered at her close call with death.

Before Drumm regained consciousness, she had told Von Holder, "Our deaths could have caused an international incident. Your country would have been the unwitting scapegoat and Hardy and I would have been dead, innocent victims of Mexican treachery."

Then she told the friendly scientist how they had met with Mexican ministers at Vera Cruz. Hardy had wanted to take a ship to Oregon, but an important Mexican persuaded them to take the more beautiful route from Santa Fe to Los Angeles on the Old Spanish Trail. "We could easily find a ship at Los Angeles, they said."

Von Holder was a diplomat. He smiled, saying nothing as they rode along in the back of the bedroll wagon. "I thought the Turks were crafty," she added, "but I must admit, the Mexicans really used us."

She looked at Drumm's aquiline features as he lay on a bedroll still unconscious. Her eyes skipped from his sharp nose to his firm lips, the blood drained from them as a result of his injury; they were slightly parted, showing his startling white teeth. Her eyes followed the angry weal of scar up his jawline where it vanished into his dark hair.

Impulsively she brushed back an unruly shock of hair which fell over his forehead. She blushed, knowing Von Holder was watching.

"Quite a man, our Andy," Von Holder murmured.

She started to protest, but he went on, telling her that after Drumm left Washington he discovered that his young wife and six-month-old son had died of cholera.

"It was with a heavy heart that Andy joined Kearny's column at Fort Leavenworth." The scientist absently stroked his chin whiskers.

Diana's mouth formed a small circle of recollection. "Oh, I remember you now." She frowned and brushed an errant lock of hair from her face. "You were at Secretary of War Marcy's dinner party when I met Captain Drumm."

Von Holder smiled. "I can still hear you telling Drumm you would like to debate him in the future."

Diana smiled with the memory. "You know, he told me he got this scar from an Indian chief." She ran her fingers lightly up the scar tissue.

She squared her shoulders and looked deeply into his eyes, her own eyes deadly serious under dark eyebrows. "Was he telling the truth?"

Before Von Holder could answer, Hard Winter and Bochey rode

up with some mossy roots and soil. The concoction smelled terrible. "This here's what Blanchard is usin' to make your brother an' Andy better." Davis looked down from his horse. "He is better, ain't 'e?"

"Oh my, yes." Diana pointed at Blanchard in the wagon ahead. "Better give that, ah, poultice to Mr. Blanchard."

Davis leaned on the wagon sideboard. "I know your brother ain't well neither, an' I know you'll take as good care of old Andy as you can." He wagged his bushy eyebrows. "Andy's my best friend, ah, more like a younger brother, you mind." He tipped his floppy brimmed hat in respect and left as Bochey gallantly bowed from the waist purring "*Porty-vous bien.*"

Diana watched them ride ahead. "You were saying, Dr. Von Holder?"

"His description of the scar fell short of what actually happened." He pulled out a cigar, looking at the girl who gave her silent permission. He fired a lucifer on his boot sole and puffed the cigar to life.

"That mountain man, Davis, and Andy were on a government scout a couple of years ago. Davis got ambushed and Andy tracked him down to a northern Cheyenne encampment." He paused. "Let's see. That would be on the North Platte River about six or seven hundred miles north of here.

"When Andy found his partner, Davis was staked out and the squaws were poking him with sharp sticks."

Von Holder shifted his seat. "Old Hard Winter told me that Andy just rode straight into the enemy camp, proud as you please. Showing dignity and spunk, attitudes Indian warriors really respect, got Andy into the camp. He jerked a war lance from the hands of a warrior, and without so much as a go-to-hell." Augie paused. "Pardon, ma'am."

Diana signalled her eagerness. "Please. Go on with your story."

"Davis told me most of the braves stepped to the doorways of their lodges, waiting to see what the whiteface would do next."

"Long Lance, war chief of the Hmi-sis, a tribe of the northern Cheyenne, was the he-dog of all the men there. Andy knew instinctively who the head man was and he rode right up to him and jammed the war lance at the chief's feet meaning, of course, he challenged Long Lance to a hand-to-hand individual fight.''

He cocked a wise eye at the Englishwoman. "Like knights of yore where you come from, flinging their gauntlets down in a challenge to a trial by mortal combat.''

Diana was caught up in the telling. "What did the chief do?''

"What else could he do? His honor was as stake. It was his choice of weapons and he took his war-hatchet and mounted his best horse. The village was filled with noise, everyone yelling and shrieking, betting on the outcome. Then the battle area was measured off.''

He flicked a long ash from his cheroot. "Andy got to Davis and had him propped up so he could see the fight. Davis talked to Long Lance and told him if Andy won, his only request was that both men be allowed safe passage out of camp.''

"Did Mr. Davis tell you about the fight?''

Von Holder nodded. "When the fight started, the chief nearly won with the first blow. It knocked Andy off his horse, nearly tore half his face off, but there's a lot of fight in that man. He kept his saber at the ready and for the next ten minutes he dueled the chief, parrying his mighty swipes of the deadly hatchet. Each time the mounted Indian tried to ride him down, Andy slashed and thrust with the saber so the Cheyenne was bleeding freely from saber wounds on both legs.

"The chief made a last charge on Andy who staggered as he faced the chief. Ducking under the wild swing of the hatchet, Andy thrust the saber deep into the Indian's hip, causing him to fall to the ground. Before he knew it, Andy was kneeling on the chief's shoulders, his hands gripping the saber, the tip just touching the region of the Indian's vitals.

"Davis said you could have heard a needle drop in that camp. The silence was broken only by Andy's deep, labored breathing as he looked deep into the chief's eyes. The chief looked up into Andy's eyes, gleaming with murderous intent, the blood from Andy's face dripping into his own.

"'Tell him, Hard Winter,' he called, 'Tell him to give up or I'll kill him!' Davis called out and the chief turned his head away in surrender. When he stood he told Davis to take this madman and leave before Drumm turned his warriors against him.''

"And that's why Mr. Davis is so concerned about him, isn't it?''

A deep voice boomed, silencing their conversation. "Pardon, miss." It was Farrier Sergeant Rawson with two cups. He was on horseback and had dropped his reins.

"Here's a bit of sour mash whiskey mixed with cold branch water and some mashed sprigs of wild mint." He lifted one to his nose which was nearly lost in the forest of his huge, drooping black mustache. "Ahh, a smell fit for royalty, and t'will do the wounded no harm."

Diana graciously accepted the cups, handing one to Von Holder. "I'll be proud to tell them you gave us these mint juleps, ah . . ." She searched for a name.

"Farrier Sergeant Edgar Rawson, ma'am. Them drinks is from all the lads wishin' the Cap'n gets well real soon." He tipped two fingers to his hat brim, held up, and let the wagon pass.

Augie sipped from his cup, nodding to Diana to do the same. "Neither of them can manage this now, and damned if I'm going to let the closest thing to a mint julep out here stagnate. Salute!"

She found her sip of drink cool and invigorating. "Did Captain Drumm save Sergeant Rawson's life, too?"

Augie finished off his drink with gusto. "No, I suppose not. Not in that sense. Only that his magnificent command saved a lot of soldiers' lives in the fracas we just came through. I'd wager most of the men would follow Andy to eternity, if only he'd ask."

"Surely they can't have served under him that long."

"True." Augie looked at the young officer, sleeping peacefully despite the wagon's bone-jarring bounce. "Some men are natural-born leaders. They instinctively do the right thing even in the face of great odds." He added softly. "Or when orders direct otherwise, as in your own case."

She looked at him sharply. "You mean you didn't even know we were a part of that wagon train?"

"Not even a vague hint. Fact is, Andy's orders were to mount a deep reconnaissance into Mexico, a sort of probing patrol to see if the Mexican cavalry, or anyone, might figure it would be to their benefit to raid north to the Oregon Trail, destroy Bridger's Fort, and force America into a war on two, maybe three, fronts." He gave her a fatherly smile. "No, my dear. Andy counterattacked because a mangy force of renegades was killing innocent people.

We found the American uniforms on Mexicans and then we found you and your brother.

"Andy instinctively does the right thing at the right time. And he holds the welfare of the men of his command as just about his first priority. That, my dear lady, is leadership."

Diana studied the sleeping Drumm again, her respect and affection growing. She touched the stray lock on his forehead again, brushing it back.

Augie Von Holder smiled, thinking that she instinctively does the right thing, too.

Chapter Thirteen

When Ives appeared at the wagon, awkwardly astride a Missouri mule the size of a Percheron, Drumm stifled a grin and motioned. "Stay aboard your friend, Guns. Ain't enough room in here for you, anyway." Ives was accompanied by Peagram.

He tried to sit up and Diana propped another bedroll behind his back. He looked at Peagram. "Report, First!"

Peagram dug in his jaw with a grimy finger and tossed a soggy tobacco cud overboard. "Skirmish finished off. Mopping up action produced four more U.S. Army uniforms, old style, 1840 issue, worn by Mexicans."

"Any survivors from the wagon train?"

No, sir. Well, only your British friends. What Indians and Mexicans didn't go down got away scot-free. We regrouped and Cap'n Irons took charge—" he coughed. "—In your absence, Cap'n."

"Casualties, First?"

Harrigan One caught an arrow in his left arm. Mr. Killdare strained himself bad hoistin' Mr. Ives' guns."

"Looks like you, too, forgot to duck, First." Drumm stared at the crimson slice above Peagram's eyebrows.

Peagram rubbed the scar at the corner of his mouth. "Sure don't need no more scars, do I? I'm gettin' to be uglier than a mud fence." He looked out the corner of his eye at Diana.

She smiled. "But your scars, Mr. Peagram, are marks of honor and do not have to be shielded."

Drumm studied Peagram's blush turning his cheeks nearly the same crimson as the forehead abrasion. The man might fight with a tiger's ferocity when the enemy was engaged, but where a handsome woman of high breeding was concerned, he demonstrated all the timidity of a newborn kitten.

Peagram, Drumm mused, old enough, almost, to be Drumm's father, was all soldier and a yard wide.

"Horses and mules, First?"

He waited as the momentary blush drained from Peagram's cheeks. "Ahem, sir. Three horses down. Had to shoot 'em."

"What will we do for replacements?"

Peagram grinned, his sky-blue eyes a-twinkle. "I reckon you'd say we inherited twenty pretty good Indian ponies. Not bad stock neither, sir."

"Useable?"

"Yes, sir." Peagram snapped out his words in military style. "After Ehler and Rawson have a talk with 'em, those horses will do just fine.

"Carry on, Peagram," Drumm called. "Mr. Ives. Did you fire more than once?"

"No sir. That is, one time each for Betsy and Lou." He looked a little worried at the question. "We would have fired again, but the Indians skedaddled out of range."

"Exactly, Mr. Ives. Outnumbered as the dragoon line was, I sure counted on you to persuade the redskins that retreat was the better part of valor." He grinned at Ives. "Guns, pass my compliments to your party. I trust Mr. Killdare is well enough to sit his saddle."

"He hurts. l know that. But Mr. Killdare is bent on becoming a gunnery sergeant."

"That's a sign he's all right." Drumm turned to see Hard Winter watching him. "I've heard the men say you and Mr. Bochey stung the Indians with great accuracy."

"Ain't that the way you ordered it, Andy?"

"I hoped it would work to our advantage, yes."

"We took about a dozen or more o' them savages right outta their saddles."

"Between you and Mr. Ives, the tide turned in our favor."

Drumm shaded his eyes with a hand; the wagon had turned and he was blinded by the late afternoon sun. "What happened after I blacked out?"

"Cap'n Irons took command, him bein' next after you, sir," Peagram offered. He swallowed hard, his Adam's apple jerking up and down in his corded neck. "But he only took command after Mr. Davis had the good sense to get us movin'."

Drumm raised his eyebrows as he looked at Davis, who was studying Diana curiously. "Women of her breeding," Davis said, "is about as scarce out here as sunflowers on a Christmas tree. Anyway, Lady Diana told us that two, mebbe three days before the attack, their military escort turned around." Hard Winter wrinkled his forehead in thought. "Then she said the escort was a hull squadron of cavalry and I sort of felt they was a hell of a lot closer to that ambush than we know."

"Then?" Drumm pumped Davis for more.

"I told that paper-collared Cap'n I guessed the Mexicans might could overtake us while we stood around gabbin' an' lickin' our wounds." He smiled. "Your man Irons listened real careful when I tol' him, Mr. Ives, and Sergeant Peagram that we'd best be skallyhootin' across the Green River, then hightail it upriver to the Yampa."

"Where does that river come from."

"I ain't never been to its source, but I can tell ya it's right on your way to Laramie, seein's how you got all the evidence you need. The Yampa runs in a canyon. On the other side it forks with the Little Snake. That's our way home."

Drumm looked at Von Holder. "Then we've already crossed the Green River?"

"No, and we won't if we have to take on a deep ford on the Green or the Colorado."

"They's a way out, Augie," Davis said. "We got to keep humpin' though because our friends, the Mexicans, are only a day or so behind. As we foller upriver, she gets smaller, *sabe*? Then we cross. Up there!" His face wrinkled in a friendly smile and he patted Von Holder's knee.

"That settles it," Drumm said. "Irons remains in charge. I want to have a little chat with him, Peagram. Before you leave, let it be common knowledge that our task has been completed. It's apparent that the Mexicans set up the assassination attempt on Lord Parton and his sister. Be it pure luck or chance or divine intervention, we caught them in that treachery, and found the Mexicans impersonating Americans in the ambush."

He ran a hand across his face. "I figure about now those Mexicans are fit to be tied. They'll be hot on our trail. They've got to finish what they started and we've got to get Parton and his sister and this command to Fort Laramie. Let's keep up our pace. Keep the column moving." Drumm met Peagram's eyes.

He motioned for Ives' attention. "Guns, no gun drills. Your crew has been bloodied now, so the only time we unpack is to rest the mules or prepare for action."

Drumm wasn't through. "Hard Winter! Scout ahead. Make sure nothing delays this command. And send Bochey to the rear. I want him to slip back to the crossing and keep his eyes on the direction and movement the Mexicans make."

His pitiful reserve of energy suddenly spent, Drumm leaned back against the bedroll. "Thank you, gentlemen." He finished his mug of coffee and lay back exhausted, his face drained of blood.

Irons rode up and looked over the wagon sideboard as Drumm slowly opened his eyes.

"Ah, Captain Irons." He struggled up with Diana helping prop him in a sitting position. "My compliments, Captain. I know it goes against your grain to take orders from an old mountain man like Davis. But I believe, from all reports, you made an intelligent choice."

Irons looked away. "I'm still not certain of him," he said. "He and his black partner are damned efficient scouts and expert riflemen." He turned back to Drumm. "If I have to take advice on this contrary expedition, I guess it's just as good from him or Bochey."

Drumm studied Irons' eyes. "We've learned a great deal on this patrol, and it isn't even the first of August." Irons looked back, and Drumm smiled. "Carry on, Captain! You wanted the command. It's yours until I get stronger. Good luck."

Irons hesitated, then cracked out a snappy salute. "With your permission, sir." He jerked his horse around and rode to the head of the column.

In the silence that followed, Von Holder observed, "Better watch out, Andy. That man may get to like you yet."

"I'll tell you one thing . . . "

"What's that?"

"I'll be damned glad when Irons and Peagram decide to make camp. This wagon is no holiday with leg feeling like there's a hot poker stuck in it."

Drumm heard a voice beside him. "My God, Drumm. I thought we saw the last of you in Washington." Lord Parton's voice was harsh and husky.

"Hardy! Oh, Hardy!" Lady Diana poured all her love into those few words as she buried her head in his shoulder. Parton tried to help himself up, but the pain hit as he jarred his wounded shoulder. He groaned and shifted his weight, leaning forward as Diana propped bedrolls behind him.

He was a ruddy-complexioned man with arching eyebrows, fine features, a long jaw and, from the length of his legs, would stand well over six feet. He viewed his position stoically.

"I played possum, Captain Drumm." He glanced at his sister. "That way I knew I'd hear the unvarnished truth."

"And?"

"Couldn't have handled the situation better myself." He felt his left shoulder. "I say, did that savage do all this to me with a bloody hatchet?"

"Your collar bone is broken, maybe a bone in your shoulder too, although I'm inclined to stop at the clavical, and there's a deep wound." Von Holder paused. "Terrible weapon, Sir Hardwig. The hatchet, I mean."

Parton focused on Von Holder. "You're the scientific fellow I met at Marcy's dinner. Von something."

"August Von Holder," Auggie offered.

"Ah, yes." Parton settled back. "My feelings are in tune with yours, Captain Drumm. I also wish this infernal wagon would halt. Each jar sets my teeth on edge." He winced through clenched jaws as the wagon banged over a rut.

"Get used to the wagon, brother dear, because you may have to spend a month on your backside while your topside gets well."

Diana gave her brother an impish grin, leaned over, and kissed him on the forehead. "Besides, I'm convinced Captain Drumm and Dr. Von Holder are our friends. At least we don't have to try our Spanish out on them."

Parton grew serious. "Has she told you that our escort under the command of Coronel Manuela Ortiz and Capitano Francisco Morella was two squadrons of the famed Mexican Seventh Regular Cavalry?" He snorted. "Humpf! A nasty looking lot. All dressed up like a gaggle of French Hussars, clear down to white belts across their chests and clumsy wooden saddles."

Drumm studied Lord Parton; here was the possible source of some excellent military intelligence.

"What of their strength?"

"See here, Drumm. I don't believe their two squadrons are more than a day or so behind us." The Englishman cocked his head. "Their platoons are forty men each. Mmm, that's four platoons to a squadron, or nearly two hundred men counting dog robbers, cooks, scribes, and the like."

Auggie broke in. "Ever serve, Sir Hardwig?"

"Cavalry once."

"Nonsense!," Diana huffed. "He was a colonel commanding the right wing of the Fifteenth Hussars at Waterloo!" She hooted. "'I was in the cavalry once,' ha! He spent fifteen years fighting in Spain, Belgium, Prussia, and Austria."

Hard Winter had pulled up by the jolting wagon. He squinted at Parton. "Dog bite me for a bone, Sir Hardwig, but you sure look like an Englishman I knew on the upper Green ten, fifteen years back."

"And his name? What might his name be?"

"I sure enough remember. Called himself Cap'n Sir William Drummond Stewart. But we mostly called him Sir Cap'n." He cocked a crafty smile at Parton. "You're like him enough to be cut from the same leather. In looks if not in savvy and the way your stick floats."

Lord Parton gave Hard Winter a sly look. "Exactly! Stewart's mother and mine were Drummond sisters from Aberdeenshire. He was with me in the Hussars and together we fought old Nappy at many places. He's home now in the family castle at Murthly, a gloomy bit of architecture."

"Well, bust my gizzard!" Hard Winter showed all his teeth in a wide grin. "Your cousin was a first-rate man. A prime man of gumption. Everybody, Utes, Snakes, Nez Percé, Flatheads, an' all kinds o' trappers pegged Sir Cap'n as a damn good mountain man."

Chapter Fourteen

Two days later the command struck the Yampa River as it plunged out of a yawning canyon making wagon traffic almost impossible. Davis scouted deep into the canyon to see if Blanchard and his ambulance could navigate it. While he was gone, Bochey caught up with the column and gave his report.

"For two days I hide out and late that last afternoon over a hundred mounted soldiers stop at the river crossing." The little imp of a man told his tale between gulps of hot coffee and sorghum-soaked pan bread. He also put away a giant bowl of Blanchard's stew.

"Do they have supply wagons?" Drumm asked.

"Oui, deux." Bochey held up two fingers. "Imbecile wagons, ah, *mon ami*. Donkeys pull wagons." He gratefully scraped out the last of the stew as Irons and Drumm watched him in the flickering firelight.

Hard Winter Davis materialized into the firelight out of a night black as the inside of a boot. Drumm smiled grimly; the old hivernant could have your scalp before you knew he was in camp.

Almost snatching the words from Drumm's brain, Hard Winter scowled at Irons, "I could have killed all your sentries."

Irons bristled. "How many were there?"

Davis squirted tobacco juice into the fire, where it sizzled. "Five. All dead men, 'cept I left 'em living. Better teach them not to sleep."

Casting a look of disdain at Irons, he turned to study Drumm. Ives, Peagram, and Diana joined the ring around the campfire. Davis looked tired and it was clear he wasn't in a jovial mood. The rangy mountain man took a long drink of coffee and ate some bread. He continued regarding Drumm.

"Ain't good." His ominous tone rattled Drumm's gut. "Be hard as hell to haul the wagons and make any time. You got a month. We can do it, but I don't reckon we got that much time to burn."

Drumm listened, mentally accepting and discarding ideas. "Is there any kind of trail a mounted column could follow?"

"Right along the south rim."

Drumm flexed his injured leg. He winced, but realized that if he took it easy he could take a few steps before it buckled under him; being in the saddle might be easier. As a commander, he knew that stern situations required stern measures.

"Captain Irons, I'm taking command. You've done a good job. Don't take old Hard Winter's remarks personally. Even if I were in charge, he'd be ragging me about the inept guard force about now. We all thank you."

Irons was about to object; he saw the faces measuring him around the fire and accepted Drumm's decision.

"First Sergeant!"

"Sir!"

"If we dumped Blanchard's pots and pans and supplies and emptied the bedroll wagon, could we shift everything on the horses we captured?"

"I don't see why not, Cap'n. We might have to cull out some of Blanchard's extra gear, but my guess is, yes, sir. First thing tomorrow morning." Peagram gave Blanchard a grim look.

"Well, Mr. Blanchard," Drumm asked. "How does the prospect of a pack outfit instead of a wagon sound?"

"All I need is Sergeant Peagram's help and . . . " he smiled shyly "a big mule for me to ride."

"Yes to both questions," Peagram said.

Drumm looked at Parton. "Your shoulder feel up to riding in a saddle, or shall we make a travois for you?"

"Perish the thought, old boy! I gather you plan on sitting a saddle?"

"That or a travois, and a travois bumping along makes a wagon ride a picnic."

"Well, then, Captain Drumm, we both ride, and Diana can ride with the best of them." He looked at her.

"Sidesaddle, ma'am?," Peagram said. "Only we ain't got a sidesaddle."

"Do you have any more of those clothes?" She pointed at Peagram.

"Sure thing. Mr. Blanchard's got a whole pile of cast-off outfits."

Diana spoke up bravely. "Then I'll just find some pants, a shirt, hat, and jacket. I'll do just fine, Sergeant, since I'll be riding astride."

"By jove, Sergeant," Parton chimed in. "It's the truth, s' help me. She learned to ride astride, scorns the dastardly sidesaddle. Ha, ha! Sis is going to show all of you a thing or two, believe you me!"

"All right." Drumm was all business now. "At dawn, Mr. Blanchard loads out, and he will be in charge of that detail." He told Peagram to have Farrier Sergeant Rawson report.

Rawson appeared in the firelight, his expression one of eagerness and willingness. Drumm admired him. "You and Mr. Davis will drive both wagons as far up that canyon as you can. Hook up a pair of those Indian horses captured at the crossing." He grinned. "I know they aren't broken to harness, but knowing you, I believe the horses will listen to your brand of reason."

"No trouble, Andy," Hard Winter said. "We'll just abandon the rigs and try to climb a canyon wall to find you."

"That's the drill. We want you to delay the gang following us into the canyon. I'm hoping they think we've got a wounded Parton and his sister while we hightail it for parts unknown."

"Hell," Irons muttered. "Those are seasoned soldiers, Drumm. They won't fall for such a childish maneuver." His voice dripped with scorn.

Before Parton could defend Drumm's decision, Drumm spoke. "Those are my orders, Captain Irons. I'm counting on the Mexicans believing Lord Parton and his sister are with the wagons because that's exactly what the Mexicans would do if they were in our situation!"

He gave Irons a sinister look. "You can bet your bottom dollar they have orders to kill Parton and his sister. Think, man!" He drove his right hand into his left palm. "What was their objective at the river crossing ambush? To kill the Englishman and his sister and pin the blame on Americans!"

He studied Irons, oblivious to the faces watching him. He wanted Irons to see what he saw. "They know Parton was badly wounded. They know where he goes, so goes his sister. These two members of the British aristocracy are living witness to the awful treachery of the Mexican government." He drew in a deep breath. "So come on, Irons. Join the party. We have to save these two people." He let his statement ride in the silence.

"Now . . . post your sentries. Try to keep them awake. Dismissed!"

Drumm turned to Davis. "You were saying?"

"I sure hope our wagon tracks keep the Mexicans off your trail, Andy."

"That's the general idea, Hard Winter."

Dawn saw the camp alive with activity, the first being Davis and Rawson putting on a sideshow as their Indian horses resisted wearing any kind of harness, let alone pulling a wagon. At length the will and the savvy of the two seasoned horsemen prevailed and their wagons rattled off on the mission to bewilder the enemy.

Drumm gingerly stepped into the saddle, noting the bloodstained gash in the leathers. He winced as his hip wound sent streaks of pain shooting through his system. As the pain subsided, he felt no warm dampness that would come from the reopening of the wound. He began noting everything going on around the camp.

He watched Parton take his horse to the downed timber, then hand the reins to Diana as he stepped up on a giant log. As she led the horse near, he slid smoothly into the saddle.

His sister held the reins but Drumm knew as he watched that the jar of sitting down caused a wave of pain to wash over Parton. The plucky Britisher slowly brought his head up through his pain, a courageous smile wreathing his face as he took the reins.

Diana was a slim figure in her jury-rigged outfit. She had found some pants that fit, he saw; they fit only too well. Her hair was piled on top of her head and held in place by a sailing master's cap with a small visor. He hadn't realized how small she was. "Supple and svelte" were words he hadn't thought of for a long time. Diana was captivating and that was plain enough as one dragoon after another was always at her elbow, giving advice, bringing a cool drink, or helping her on her horse.

Despite the grinding pain in his thigh, a surge of need welled through Drumm; he realized it had been a long, long time. He mentally thumbed back the calendar; a precious farewell tryst at bedtime with his beloved wife. His desire for Diana suddenly disappeared as a pang of grief surged back into his mind.

He shook his head. "What's the matter with me? I'm a widower not six months." Still the small voice came back to whisper, "But she is beautiful, golden." Her presence made his throat tight. He felt clumsy, unworthy and foolish around this woman.

He wheeled his horse, feeling her eyes on him. They stared at each other. It hurt, fast movement did. He'd be more calm in a minute, he assured himself, and he switched his gaze to watch Rawson fighting his team.

Davis had "sweet-talked" his outfit which was racing and lurching madly into the dark maw of a cavernous ravine. He was nearly out of sight. Meanwhile Rawson was having no easy time of it. "Naw, I don't need no help," his voice boomed in the morning air to his sidekick, Farrier Sergeant Ehler. It had now become a matter of pride. Davis had either tricked him by picking out his team first, or he was the better man with a span of horses.

Rawson got gunny sacks over the eyes of his team and was talking softly to them as he gently pulled them forward. Drumm, joined by Diana and Parton, watched Rawson walk his team into the canyon and drop from sight.

"I say, Drumm?"

"Yes, Lord Parton."

"Oh, don't bother the Lord and Sir stuff. Call me Hardy. All my friends call me that, eh Sis?"

Drumm dared to look at her as her voice, like silver chimes, giggled. "Yes, Captain Drumm. It's Hardy for him and Di for me . . ." She looked at him warmly and he could have swallowed his tongue, "Please, Captain?"

She sure as hell was astride, he thought, his eyes devouring her boyish looks, her eyes teasing him, whether or not she intended it that way.

"Gawd, Sis. Turn off the charm. Tend to your poor wounded brother," Parton snorted.

Her face flushed as she pushed her horse to watch Blanchard finish off. His last pot packed, he wiped his forehead and stuck a big boot into a stirrup and swung onto the largest mule in the column. The mule laid his ears back but Blanchard pulled its head around and popped some sugar into the animal's mouth. The friendship sealed between these two, Peagram and Irons began moving the column along the trail Bochey had pointed out.

Parton joined Drumm on the march. "I say, Andy, is this horse the kind my cousin rode out here?"

Diana rode with them. Drumm was determined to keep his senses. "You bet. They don't look like much, so let me warn you they can stop—bang—and turn so fast you might topple out of the saddle. Good animals. Spirited. Damn awful quick on the getaway."

He sized Parton up, his extra long legs using every inch of stirrup leather, wincing now and then with a wound even more painful than his, but never whimpering.

Drumm looked at Diana; she smiled, saying nothing.

Drumm couldn't help himself. "I have to say, Di, you and your brother are, in my opinion . . ." he fumbled for a congratulatory expression. " . . . are damn all-real Dragoons. We are, every single one of us, proud to have you in our command."

Drumm leaned forward. "Hardy. Don't spur your horse too quickly. You will get piled and, since we have no wagons, I'd hate to have you ride a travois." He touched his cap and rode forward to join Peagram and Irons.

"I say, Di, what do you suppose got into Drumm?" Lord Parton rode along. As she was silent, he spoke again, "A dotty sort of statement, though I know he meant well." She remained silent and Parton's face lit with sudden realization. "I'd bet my only pair of knickers young Drumm is attracted to you, eh, Sis?"

She smiled at him, put a shushing finger to her lips, and stepped her horse to join Von Holder, leaving Parton to join ranks with Ives, who rode alone nearby.

As the command headed out in a column of twos, each dragoon had accepted a laden mule or horse as his personal responsibility. At the end, Ives and his mule artillery plodded along, eating the powderlike dust rising from the trail.

Ives had a silk handkerchief over his nose and mouth. He leaned over to help Parton stretch a neck scarf over his lower face. Conversation was nearly impossible, so the two rode in silence.

Just ahead of them, Blanchard's kitchen was spread out among a dozen mules and horses. Miller and Harrigans Two and Three helped Blanchard over the rough trail as it edged along the rim of the deep canyon.

Quickly disgusted with eating dust, Parton urged his horse to the head of the column, joining Drumm. He pulled the dusty scarf from his face and a clean demarcation line showed across his nose; his cheeks and forehead were tinged with terra-cotta dust.

"There is some justice being head of the column at that." Parton laughed. "I say, Andy, that cookfellow, Blanchard, is being fussed over like a queen in a hive."

"I'm happy with Blanchard," Drumm responded. "He is living proof that an army travels on its stomach."

"Now, old lad," Parton said. "It was that old blighter, Napoleon, who said, 'An army *marches* on its stomach.' If you are bound to use a quote now and then, let it be right, eh?"

Both wounded men held up as the long winding column climbed higher until looking down into the canyon was a challenge to all but the bravest. The trail led past barren ridges, sharp draws, and the only vegetation was the gnarled juniper and towering tree-sized sagebrush.

By noon the heat was oppressive; men, horses, and mules grew hot, tired, and impatient. Diana pointed to a pair of eagles casting huge lazy shadows as they hitched rides on the thermals rising from the desert landscape. At times the great birds rose so high Diana nearly lost sight of them.

"How cool those champions of the air must be," she said.

"Careful," Drumm chided in jest. "Remember you are talking about the American bald eagle, our national symbol." His lips nearly split with the friendly smile he directed at the vivacious and captivating boyish-looking girl at his side.

"Oh, you always want to drag me into a political argument." She studied him out of the corner of her grey eyes. "People taking over unoccupied land. Blather!"

He rode beside Diana and her drowsing brother. When Drumm didn't answer, she chattered on, completely ensnaring him. In spite of the weeds of mourning, he thought to himself. He looked skyward. The eagles still circled, light as feathers, not moving their wings, but just tilting round and round with the wind.

She pointed to the carnival of colors of the land, as Von Holder came up to join them on the trail. "The orange, tan, brown, purple, grey . . . oh, ever so many streaks in the soil!," she said.

Parton, rising to the occasion, said, "Colorful as it is, we are a little spare on water, I'd say." He swept his hat in a circle. "Reminds me of one tour of duty I put in under Wellington in Spain. Ah, the Peninsular Campaign, I believe they called it. Spain and Portugal, you know."

Von Holder struggled. "Those colors in the soil are the product of minerals at work." He took out a cigar and looked at it thoughtfully. "Some day we will use some of this soil for purposes yet undefined."

"I say, old man," Parton said. "Do you really believe that?"

"You can place a bet on it, Lord Parton. For instance, some of that white soil is heavy with sodium bicarbonate. Mix it with a cup of water, the right amount of course, and presto!, your headache is soothed." Von Holder grinned through his spadelike beard. "Taken in large doses it might well physic you, beggin' your pardon, ma'am."

"By God, I'll remember that. Why not start 'Parton's Physick Factory' as soon as we've dealt with those Mexican miscreants?"

Drumm pulled off from the column and waited until he, Von Holder, and the others caught up. "I've got an interesting question, Augie. I can't really answer it, but I expect you can offer a solution."

Bending forward to shield his unlit cigar while he touched a match to it, Von Holder sat up, puffing until he was certain his stogie would perform. He said around the cigar, "Fire away,

Andy."

"I recall Mr. Marcy in Washington telling us the latitude and longitude of that part of Mexico the Texans called the Republic of Texas. We both know that on July 4 this year, Texas allowed itself to be annexed as a state in the union. Correct so far?"

"You are on firm ground."

Drumm half-stood in the stirrups, favoring his aching thigh. "What were the lines, Auggie, and aren't we inside them now?"

Von Holder snapped back, "Why in tarnation didn't I think of that? It could save our lives, you know." Drumm nodded knowingly. "I'll look up the records and I'll get Biltmore. We'll shoot the sun and have an answer before dark."

Drumm watched as Von Holder and Biltmore checked log books, and then pulled off to one side to shoot the sun with their sextant. Von Holder told Drumm, "As a topographical engineer, you know all about this. Damn," he muttered. "I should have raised this question earlier."

Biltmore gave his notes to Von Holder. "Sure enough," Von Holder exclaimed to Drumm. "The Republic of Texas, annexed by the United States on July 4, within the boundaries agreed upon at 42 degrees north latitude and 106 degrees west longitude." He hummed. "We should cross into a part of the State of Texas in three days' time, or about August 4."

"Thanks, Auggie. It helps to know exactly where we are. In Mexico or in the United States."

Lord Parton overheard Von Holder and Drumm. "Old laddie," he observed, "do you really believe those Mexicans know about the annexation?" He let that line of reasoning sink in. "And even if they did know, do you think that would stop them?"

It was a question no one was prepared to argue—pro or con— Drumm thought as he kneaded his aching thigh.

Chapter Fifteen

Two days later they found Davis and Rawson on the trail, their faces drawn and haggard, their horses gaunt and trail weary.

Hard Winter narrowed his eyes against the morning sun. "This here Sergeant Rawson is all man, I'm here to tell ya. He drove his wagon up and down gulleys I thought was the end of the trail." Davis hung his head, shaking it slowly back and forth. "But, bejeez, he'd figure out another route. I think I met m' match for bein' trailwise."

Drumm mentally noted Hard Winter's assessment of the man, but stuck to business. "Sergeant Rawson, your estimate of the trip into the canyon?"

"Cap'n, sir, me and Mr. Davis taken those wagons where no man had a right to go. It taken two days 'fore we abandoned 'em." Rawson was hoarse with fatigue.

Two cups of hot coffee were produced by Blanchard; Drumm wondered how he could do it with everything on packsaddles. Davis and Rawson gratefully accepted the steaming mugs.

Rawson, his voice bolstered by the coffee, spoke over the cup's rim. "We tried to bring all four horses back. But, that trail was a demon."

Davis gulped the last of his coffee. "Rawson here is part goat, a damned billy goat, all horns and rattles to boot. We crawled out of that canyon, losin' only one hoss in the whole shebang."

"Did you make contact with the Mexicans?"

"No, sir."

"Thanks for the good work. Let's hope it holds up the squadron a bit while we gain another day or so."

That evening, the three seriously wounded men—Drumm with his thigh, Parton's with shoulder, and Harrigan One nursing a wounded arm—had their dressings changed after supper. Diana helped Blanchard. "A leg, an arm, and a shoulder," she said, wrinkling her nose while bandaging more of the barnyard-smelling poultices in place.

"Ah, Lady Diana," Harrigan One drawled, "'tis the wish of this bog-trotter that I could be sick for a year, an' you my nurse!" He smiled, and tipped his hat as she shooed him away, her delight a bright gleam in her eyes and expression.

"At my age, dear Sis," Parton said, standing up, "my bones don't knit as quickly as in days of yore!" He leaned down from his six-foot-four frame and kissed her cheek. "Still this wound, 'twixt you and that ogre-sized Blanchard, is getting better all the time." He executed a little jig as he left, pain be damned.

She faced Drumm. His trouser leg had been hastily split to a dozen inches above his knee. She was suddenly silent as she tenderly bathed the gash. The edges had been drawn together with the black surgical thread of Blanchard's stitches. The fire of inflammation had receeded to a rosy line along the raw edges.

"I can't figure if I like Blanchard better as a cook, or as a seamstress," Drumm muttered through his pain.

Diana looked up at his weak joke, concern printed on her face. Drumm impulsively but slowly reached out, cupping her chin and softly kissed her. It was, he felt, a magic moment, a piece of time suspended above the dirt, the dust, the flickering fire, the murmur of voices, horses and mules quietly active away off in the dark. She didn't close her eyes, nor did he. Neither did she try to pull away.

Blanchard's voice intruded on their bliss. "Here's some more poultices, Miss Diana." Only then did the spell evaporate as she slowly allowed a soft smile to spread across her features while she accepted the terrible-smelling compress from the command's beefy cook and medic.

"Whenever or wherever I am from now on, Captain Drumm,

when I smell this awful odor, I'll remember you!'' She brushed a stray lock from her forehead as her smile became an impish grin.

"Thanks a heap," Drumm said, smiling back, and something unexplained fused between them. They both knew it.

Blanchard lumbered back to his pots and pans. Drumm put a hand on each of her shoulders as she finished winding the bandage around his thigh.

"I'll remember you, too, and not for that," he said softly, his throat constricted. His body trembled and his hands squeezed her shoulders as they faced each other.

It was a time for openness. "I was married for two years." He stumbled along. His hands fell. "Earlier this year my wife and our baby son died of cholera." His eyes were nearly black as they stared at her. "And I wasn't even there." His dark eyes locked on Diana's and turned misty.

She tried to interrupt with appropriate words, placing soft fingers to his lips. He stayed her hand with his. "No. I've got to say this, and I have to say it now." He sighed in a deep breath.

"When she died, taking the boy with her, I thought my heart would cease to function. I even felt my pulse to see if I were alive; I was that sick with grief."

His hands rose to her shoulders again. "Until I saw you in that wrecked wagon so alive, so beautiful with death and destruction all around, I never would have believed that I could love again."

He spoke fiercely, shaking her lightly. "Do you understand what I'm trying to say?"

She laid a soft hand on his arm. "Yes, dear God, yes! I know what you are saying." Her hand went to the jawline scar which she traced to his lips. "And my heart is speeding so fast, I fear it may choke me." She smiled, her lips parting as she leaned forward to softly kiss him again.

Drumm took both her hands in his. "Another thing. I can't say everything to you that is in my heart. I've got to finish off this reconnaissance patrol. And I can't—won't—play with your emotions and mine in front of the men." He paused. "Or in front of your brother."

She giggled. "Hardy already knows. I told him I had set my cap for you today." She gave him a mischievous smile that reached in and pinched his heart, or swelled it to the point of popping. He wasn't sure which.

Hard Winter stepped into the circle of firelight. "Andy, I sure as hell hate to bother you two, but old Clauday just rode in. The news ain't the best."

It seemed like everyone gathered when scout reports were given to him, Drumm thought, as he limped to see Bochey wolfing down some stew and coffee, his black face agleam with sweat.

Not that I mind, Drumm continued to muse, but, ah, hell, you're getting as stuffy as old Irons, God forbid.

Bochey described the Mexicans dividing up, one company of forty men riding into the canyon, the other going into camp to await their return. "This *capitaine*—he's in charge now—is a very, very nervous man. He waited one day only. Then all men mount and follow the canyon trail. The other company will follow."

"How far, in terms of days, behind?"

"Three, mebbe four days." He waited, thinking. "The good news is they try to haul at least two supply wagons. It may add one more day, *mon ami*."

"Terrific scout, Bochey," Drumm said. He turned to the faces around the fire. "Nothing we can do but load, execute your work with dispatch. When we gain a minute, we gain a life."

Four days later Davis pointed across a huge valley shimmering in the midmorning sun. "That's the Little Snake joining up with the Yampa. Three days up that water, over Bridger's Pass, and we can give ourselves relief on the banks of the North Platte. She's beautiful, Andy, that water. By such a river a man forgets he will ever be tired or old. You'll knit your wounds there, I'm here to tell you."

Each day Drumm grew stronger; it wasn't long before pain was little more than a bad memory.

Von Holder drew up beside him. "I'm learning, Andy. I'm learning."

"Learning what?"

"Well, it was beyond me why you made men and horses and mules change every day." They sat their horses watching the command descend into the Yampa Valley.

"So?"

"A change in weight, or duty, keeps the animals alert, in shape. Men too. They look good and we haven't had a horse holiday since South Pass. Let's see, today's August 10 and that makes it forty-one days." Augie puffed his cheroot. "We have to be at Fort Laramie September tenth to fifteenth." He eyed Drumm. "Think we'll do it?"

"Damn it, Augie. It could be December for all I care. Our job now is to protect Parton and Diana. The Mexicans are hot on our trail. That's what's bothering me." He pounded his saddle. "I've got about thirty-one men, counting Parton. If what Bochey says is true, we're facing two companies of seasoned veterans totaling at least eighty to ninety men." He squinted at Von Holder. "That sounds like three to one to me, Augie."

They made camp well up the Little Snake River that night. Few fires were used. Blanchard cooked over *bois de vache*. When the men walked to rest their horses, they picked up the brittle dried buffalo chips, the firewood of the plains. Blanchard had told Drumm, "No smoke, and a hot fire." Drumm was beginning to understand how Blanchard could always come up with hot coffee at the precise moment it was needed most. The man was a godsend to frazzled troops at day's end.

Long after midnight, Davis tapped the light-sleeping Drumm on the shoulder. He touched a finger to Drumm's lips and in a hoarse whisper said, "The Mexicans is moving fast. They left their wagons back down the trail. My guess is they're but three or four days behind and moving fast."

Drumm was instantly awake. "What do you think, Hard Winter?"

"Was I you, Andy, an' the moon shinin' like it is, I'd load up and get over Bridger's Pass pronto. Good flat valley off yonder. If them tamales is goin' to fight, let it be on your terms with the good Mr. Ives' hellacious big-talkin' smokepoles and their rotten shells backin' your play."

Chapter Sixteen

It was just like Hard Winter had said. Bridger's Pass was no trouble for the fast-moving column when they came to it. Once through the pass, they dropped down into the lush valley of the Upper North Platte River.

There the column halted. They had left the harsh country—dry desert trails, bone-dry regions forever tagged with the hot breath of the constant southwest wind. Now they saw an entirely different region spread out before them, almost too grand to comprehend, strangely beautiful and full of distance.

Tall lush grass grew everywhere, and the valley held herd upon herd of grazing mule deer, antelope, elk, and buffalo. All around them were flowers of every hue.

"I say," Parton breathed out. " 'Tis a bloody zoo." He looked at Drumm. "Damned little powder has been burned here."

Drumm silently agreed. His concern was not hunting, but being hunted. He signalled the column forward but held up himself as he saw Bochey, a long way from him, booting his horse home, he thought, like a jockey at a horse race.

Behind Drumm and to the east, the river valley was guarded by towering snow-clad peaks of granite. Davis called them the Medicine Bow Mountains. No matter what the name was, he thought, they were majestic. Great pine forests grew on those granite shoulders, giving the range an almost mantled effect, like a royal robe upon a king's shoulders.

Diana pulled up beside him. "Oh, Andy, taste that air!" She drew in a huge breath, and let it out slowly. "It's sweet as pure honey. Makes me heady, it's so rich." She swept off her visored Dutch-boy sailor cap, a shake of her head causing the hair to cascade over her shoulders. She's like a queen, Drumm thought, and her hair was her crown.

Bochey pulled up. "*Mon ami*, the Mexicans are now two, mebbe three day behind us. And as Hard Winter say, 'mad as bear with two cubs and ze sick tail.'"

Drumm grinned as he signalled the column forward. "Hard Winter, you know what kind of camp we need. Water, grass, and good meat." He watched the mountain man step his horse into a jog and he was soon out of sight.

Within an hour, Davis waved his arms, guiding them to a perfect camp. Blanchard was the center of attention as the men helped him set up his field kitchen. Bochey brought in two fat mule deer, and all three Harrigans dressed them out. Drumm thought how like wolves they were, their flashing knives doing the same work he had seen done by wolves' dripping fangs.

Rawson and Ehler, joined by Doyle, Quinn, and Peagram were in their element seeing that each horse and mule got a good rub-down, hooves checked, their legs washed. The animals were turned loose to snort, roll, and romp their exhilaration at freedom from saddles and harness. Rawson even fed the horses a bit of grain. "A treat," he said, talking to the horses who knew his voice and his gentle hands.

"By God, Drumm," Parton said. "Look at that man! They love him." He looked at Diana. "I've got to have that man. I'll offer him a wage he can't decline."

Ehler came to Drumm. "Cap'n, sir. It wouldn't hurt if you was to give us . . . ah, ahem . . . a half a horse holiday." His honest face and keen brown button eyes pled his case. "It could mean the animals would have, ah, ah . . ." His stutter came out as Drumm interjected, "More stamina. We'll wait until the men have eaten. But you tell Sergeant Rawson I mean to single out Sergeants Ehler and Rawson in my action report as critical to our success. You have done a right smart job with the animals." Rawson had joined Ehler and both jockey-sized bow-legged cavalrymen seemed to stand a little taller as they thanked the "Cap'n Sir" and went back to work.

In the silence that followed, only Parton spoke. "I say, Drumm. I'm not a natural eavesdropper, if you know what I mean. But what you said to those two men was bloody marvelous, eh, Sis?" He winked at Von Holder. "Keeps their knickers hitched up, good for the bloody morale, and all that." Parton was sitting on a bedroll so when he stood, it was not unlike a jackknife opening, Drumm thought.

"'Sides, Drumm, if those two were civilians, I would steal them from you and whisk them away to Epsom Downs, eh, Captain, in Surry where the Derby and other horse races are held."

He tilted his hat over an eye. "Do you favor horse racing?"

Von Holder could hold back. "Does he fancy horse racing? Why, Lord Parton, Captain Drumm's family is from Pamlico Landing in North Carolina. Their stables produce some of the best horseflesh in America."

"Do tell."

"My family raises some tobacco, some rice, some cotton, and a lot of fine horses. Fact is, Lord Parton, it was a hard decision for me. Raise horses or go to West Point." Drumm grinned. "It was never my decision anyway. My father decided for me."

Parton cocked an eyebrow. "Your father is an army man?"

"My father served with the Light Dragoons at the Battle of New Orleans in 1814." He paused in reflection, wrinkles crossing his forehead. "It was ordained, I guess. My father insisted that I follow in his footsteps."

Parton's face lit up. "Your father served with the American Light Dragoons?"

Von Holder answered. "Not only did Colonel Toyal Drumm serve, he was their commanding officer."

Parton sat down again. "Ahh, yes." Drumm was seated by the Englishman who studied him curiously. "Toy Drumm, the gallant cavalryman who turned Fraser's left at New Orleans. A delightful and well-planned maneuver." He slapped Drumm on the shoulder. "He's the chap, Sis, who has been discussed over many a glass of wine in our 15th Hussar mess." He grew serious. "When this is over, I would deem it a great honor to shake your father's hand, yes, by God, I would!'' He reflected again. "That is, if Colonel Toy Drumm's son can extract us from this mess.''

Countering, Drumm offered the hospitality of his North Carolina home. "If indeed we do bring ourselves out of this present dilemma,'' he said.

The pleasantries of the small group around Drumm suddenly halted as they heard a rising crescendo of commotion where the command had halted. Biltmore emerged from the gathered mass of dragoons and came racing to Von Holder, his eyes big as bowls, his cheeks flushed.

"Gold! Gold! There's gold all over the streambed!'' Biltmore danced around Drumm's group until he was winded. He sat down, holding out a fist, which he unclenched to reveal a half-dozen gleaming yellow nuggets of gold, nut-sized and gnarled gemlike lumps.

By now, the entire command had heard the news and, to a man, were sprinting for the stream. "Take your mess gear!,'' someone shouted. "Using a plate, anyone can pan for gold!''

Biltmore raced away back to the stream, now lined with eager, shouting men. They seemed to lose their minds along with their equilibrium as they pushed and shoved their way to the stream and began sloshing pans of gravel and small rocks around.

Alarmed, Drumm strode down to try to reason with them. As wonderful as such a find might be, they'd be sitting ducks when the Mexicans arrived. Not even Von Holder's men who he had credited with greater understanding of their physical danger, would listen. In a matter of seconds, it seemed, the entire command had totally lost control of itself.

Drumm was heard by Peagram, Ives, Rawson, Ehler, and a dripping Getter. They pulled away from the stream to join his circle, their faces reflecting the seriousness of what was going on.

It was a compelling diversion, Drumm thought, but gold would do no good to a field of dead men. "Nine of us left,'' he said, "two of us carrying wounds, and one woman.'' He saw Diana stiffen. "I'm not being critical, Diana. I'm being realistic when it comes to counting our strength.'' He frowned. "We can count on Davis and Bochey not to tumble to this gold nonsense.''

In a few minutes, Blanchard fed them as the sun let itself down and lit their faces for the last time this day, sliding behind the far hills. Blanchard kept a large pot of stew simmering for the gold miners—when and if their senses returned.

Von Holder spoke softly, but addressing the small circle of unaffected members of the command. "Gold fever is a terrible disease. Look what it's done here. Trouble is, its pumpkin-seed gold, not a rich strike. But it's gold and the fever's hit."

Drumm agreed. "Here's what we have to do. Let them have a full day of trying to get rich. Then, we pack up and head for Fort Laramie." He pointed to Getter. "Talk to Smith and Jones. Tell them gold is nothing to the value of the citizenship they're seeking."

Von Holder spoke up. "First you've got to get Doyle and Quinn to forsake this idiotic quest for gold. When and if those two Irishmen return, the three Harrigans will follow."

"I just don't know your men well enough, Augie, unless we appeal to their love of country."

He ticked off the numbers on his fingers. "One, the Mexicans still don't know about Ives and his twins, Betsy and Lou. We simply can't pack them, or lay, aim, and fire them without Doyle, Smith, Jones, and the Harrigans. Ordnance Sergeant Quinn retires this year, appeal to him to finish off his career honorably, Peagram."

"Two," Drumm continued. It was dark now and Blanchard moved around the circle refilling coffee mugs. "If we stay here two days, we are going to leave the day after tomorrow, and sure as there is a sun in the sky, we need those seven men." He stood up now, stamping his feet, aware that his wound was nearly healed.

"Mr. Bochey, will you join First Sergeant Peagram and take the first watch. I'll take the second with Mr. Von Holder, and Mr. Ives and his gunner, Getter, will finish off the third watch."

He looked around the fire. "This gold fever may have run its course by tomorrow night. Mr. Blanchard, don't deny any of them food."

Chapter Seventeen

At dawn, Drumm inspected his thin picket line. Ehler and Rawson went with him. "The stock," he said, "looks exceptionally healthy."

Rawson nodded. "We have had to change the heavy howitzer loads around, and far as we can see, sir, the animals is doing fine."

After he had eaten, Drumm saw Getter talking with Smith and Jones. He strolled over to them; the three snapped to attention. "*Herr Hauptman*, ah, Captain," Getter said, tilting his head at the two wet men. "They are ready to return. No lashes?"

The two Germans, despite their aliases, stood in a kind of downcast remorse, their clothing saturated by repeated attempts to dig up and sluice stream bottom gravel. Drumm looked at them sternly, forcing down a grin at their cold, miserable condition.

"No, Private Getter. No lashes. But tell them I understand." He turned, walked a few steps and turned back. "Thank you, Getter. We surely need Smith and Jones. Tell them that."

He didn't comprehend the German words, but there seemed emphasis in the phrase *"mach schnell!"*

By noon, Peagram lined up Corporal Doyle and the three Harrigans. Drumm heard his First Sergeant growl, "I've told the Cap'n you gold diggers is ready to assume your duties."

Drumm couldn't hear what passed between the four men and their First Sergeant, but Peagram stuck his face up close to the face of each man and Drumm guessed Peagram was assessing the personal damage they could count on if they didn't take up their duties as dragoons again.

Peagram drew up in front of Drumm. "Sir, Co'pral Doyle and the three Irish brothers have given their solemn promise to behave like the soldiers they are." He saluted. "Now, by your leave, sir. I'm going to have a gab with Ordnance Sergeant Sean Michael Quinn."

Drumm watched Peagram disappear into the willows lining the small stream. Almost as if on cue, Captain Irons shouldered his way past the willows over to Blanchard's stew pot where he filled his cup. His eyes watched Drumm as he walked to him.

"I ain't quittin', Drumm. There's riches here. Look." Irons dug out a dozen gleaming nuggets. "I've never owned this much in my whole life." He curled his lip. "I ain't got an old man and a horse farm in North Carolina to fall back on when the world turns sour. And I never went to West Point. I came from the ranks." His eyes narrowed. "Twelve years, I'm a captain. Ten years in the ranks. Twenty-two years and never a chance at the easy life." He shoved the gold back into his pocket.

"Gold is a great equalizer, Drumm. And I'm going to stay here until I've got enough to live in prosperity the rest of my life. This is my chance of a lifetime, and I ain't leaving." He looked hard at Drumm. "You don't even know what I'm talking about, do you?"

Outraged, Drumm fought to control the involuntary growl in his voice. "I know this much, Captain Irons. The Mexican cavalry is only two days behind us. So, you've got the rest of this day to fill your pockets. We pull out at first light in the morning. And you'd better be there, fit and ready for duty!"

He started off, but turned. "I thought you were smart, Irons. I can't believe you'd throw away a fine career for a fool's game. It belies your character. Remember, first light tomorrow. Spread the word. I'll exact no punishment if you and your gold diggers ride with us in the morning." He raised an eyebrow. "Stay here and you deal with the Mexicans. They'll be coming right through here. If you survive that, the dragoons will find you no matter where you hide. The army looks after its own, and cleans up its own messes. You of all people know what happens to deserters and slackers."

"The Mexicans don't want us," Irons shot back. "They want the Englishman and his sister. Besides, I heard Von Holder tell you we are in the State of Texas now, so the Mexicans won't bother us."

Drumm spun on his heel, anxious now to get away from the mutinous malcontent. "You're only kidding yourself, Irons," he said.

An hour later, a spruced-up Ordnance Sergeant Quinn braced himself straight as a ramrod. "By your leave, Cap'n. I'm still a dragoon, sir, if I may be so bold."

"I told the First Sergeant that no man gets punishment if he returns today, Quinn." Drumm made a wry mouth. "Tell me, Sergeant. How much gold did you find?"

Quinn's long face, composed of flat planes for cheeks, a long bony nose and a lantern jaw, looked morose. "None, Cap'n, sir. I just ain't got the knack for gold minin'. I believe, sir, that I'm better at soldierin'."

"And you are a damned fine ordnance sergeant, Quinn. Which will it be?"

"Ordnance, sir. Ordnance!" He snapped a crisp salute and walked back to Peagram and Ives.

Von Holder came up to watch Quinn join the others. He fired one of his cigars. "Quinn, eh? That makes the seven you wanted, Andy."

A youthful voice piped up behind them. "Cap'n Drumm!" Turning, Drumm found Miller, his polished bugle glistening at his side. "I'm a good bugler, sir. I want to be your bugler again." A worried look squeezed the sixteen-year-old's face.

Drumm laid a fond hand on the boy's shoulder. "I'm glad you want it that way, James."

Miller's face reflected surprise. "No one has called me James since I enlisted at Carlisle three years ago, sir."

"Who was it then?"

"My mother, Cap'n. My mother." His eyes filled with tears. He blinked them back before they ran down his cheeks. "I promised her I'd never do anything to make her ashamed of me." He wiped his face. "I nearly did, didn't I?"

"James, I never doubted you," Drumm said slowly. "I knew when the gold fever went away that Drumm's Devils would have their bugler again." He stepped back. "Now, Bugler Miller, join the men. We're glad to have you back."

Miller's face lit with relief. He threw a salute at Drumm, who solemnly returned it. Miller turned and ran to Quinn, Peagram, and the others.

Von Holder muffled his words behind his handkerchief. "That young man will tell that story the rest of his life." He emerged from behind the handkerchief, his eyes red. He blew his nose. "Forgiveness is also the mark of a good leader."

After evening mess, Drumm had Peagram hold a muster. "At first light, we're leaving," Drumm told his assembled force. "Our mission, so far, has been successful. But the living proof of the Mexicans' savage trickery resides with Lord Parton and Lady Diana. They lived through that terrible ambush. The Mexicans know they are alive. That's why they are hard on our heels. They'll stop at nothing."

He stood stock still in the firelight. "Their mission is to kill Lord Parton and Lady Diana. I, for one, am prepared to die in denying them that opportunity." The murmur that followed was in the affirmative.

Limping up and down, he continued. "Gold fever has clouded many of your eyes and your thoughts. I've given everyone this whole day off to come to your senses. Join us now and no punishment will be handed out. I'm talking to dragoons Irons, Upton, Kilmer, Newman, Brady, and Bonnett."

He motioned Von Holder to his side. The scientist spoke. "I'm asking my men to rejoin our assigned task—Killdare, Collier, Biltmore, Schmidt and Attix. We need you."

Drumm wound up the meeting. "You know our position. Sleep on it. I'll not speak on the subject again."

Hard Winter touched Drumm's shoulder later that night. "We got to leave at dawn, *amigo*. Them chili-eaters ain't but two days behind us, and ridin' like hell."

Chapter Eighteen

At dawn, Blanchard had the chow ready for everyone—mutineers, soldiers, and scientists alike. He loaded his gear on his pack string while Lieutenant Ives directed the hoisting of Betsy and Lou on the passive pack mules. A half-hour after breakfast by Von Holder's faithful timepiece, Drumm's Devils and Von Holder's Bug Catchers moved into a column of twos. They rode northeast and away from the scene of their rich diggings and a brief insubordination.

It was a dramatic moment as two of the holdouts, Irons and Biltmore, watched them go. "Hell, we don't need them anyway," Irons growled. "We only got one of those Davis percussion rifles, hardly an arsenal. Strictly a meat gun." He fanned his face as mosquitoes swarmed up from the brackish backwater pockets of the stream. "The Mexicans want Drumm and the Englishman and his sister. Seven men and five scientists won't make any difference to the Mexicans, even if they come. Anyway, we're sitting out here looking only like common, dirt-grubbing prospectors."

He studied Biltmore. "I like the idea you had, the twelve of us forming a company." They walked to the stream where all hands were busy panning. Even as they did, they were being watched.

Drumm, Ives, Peagram, Von Holder, and Hard Winter had hidden themselves on a timbered ridge five-hundred yards from the gold diggers. Ives watched them through Von Holder's spyglass.

Drumm was bitter. "Gold. It will be their death unless we help them." He shrugged. "I can't just leave them, unarmed for the

Mexicans to make mincemeat of.''

"You got a plan, Andy?,'' Davis asked.

"It's nearly impossible to defend them unless the Mexicans attack first. That means we gamble, but once the action is joined, we stop them.'' He held up his hand. "This is pretty tricky, but I think we can run a bluff on them if they turn ugly on Irons and Biltmore's crowd.''

Together, they laid the trap.

"First, Guns, I want Betsy and Lou laid about a hundred feet apart. That way you can personally aim and fire each one while the other is being swabbed, powder and cannister rammed, and readied for firing.''

Drumm bit his lip. "My guess is Doyle and Smith and Harrigans One and Three on Betsy. Getter, Jones, Harrigan Two, and Quinn on Lou. That leaves Rawson and Ehler to jump in at a moment's notice.'' He looked at Ives, the color riding high in his cheeks as his adrenalin pumped.

Ives's eyes lit up as he nodded. "Yes, sir! Can do!''

"Hard Winter, I want you and Bochey to tend each flank. You two are the best shots by far. On my signal, I want you two to pick out a target at random—a canteen, a hat. Don't shoot to kill, only to post notice that we can pick off anyone we want.'' He grinned at Davis.

"Just before you shoot, Guns here will deliver howitzer fire from Betsy and Lou at significant targets. If that doesn't convince the officer in charge, your long-range rifle fire will settle their hash.''

Lord Parton and Diana were silent members of the council. Drumm regarded them. "I'm sorry, Lord Parton. Mutineers or not, I can't allow the Mexicans to slaughter those men.'' He shifted his eyes to Diana. "I hope you can understand my position.''

Lord Parton looked at his sister. "I told you he wouldn't desert those men.'' He looked back at Drumm. "You know, old boy, I'm really a fair shot. Give us two of those rifles. Diana can load, and I'll shoot.''

"Thanks. We'll see about that. Peagram, break out the guidon, the colors, our uniforms, and fix Miller up too.''

Peagram made his way back to the pack outfit as Ives and Drumm picked out good sites for the big guns. Davis and Parton wandered into the heavy foliage of a screen of aspens, willows, and junipers. The rest of the men urged the pack mules into a staging area for the heavy work of dismounting the howitzers.

Through the morning, Drumm, Peagram, and Von Holder inspected their trap. The gold diggers squatted, heads down, so little movement was observed. Drumm sent Hard Winter on foot close to their original camp to see if anyone or anything had given away their presence.

Bochey came in dead tired at dusk. He had scouted the Mexican cavalry, telling Drumm he had counted about sixty men.

"*Oui, mon capitaine*, these *soldats* wear flat black *chapeaux* an'—how you say?—green pantaloons an' gray jackets."

"How far behind?"

"They arrive tomorrow, *mon ami*."

Drumm turned to Parton. "Your escort?" He answered his own question. "What difference? We are going to have to suck them into our trap."

It was a cold meal and a cold camp for all hands that night. Before they crawled into the bedrolls, Drumm called them together, except for the sentries. Drumm, Peagram, and Miller were all fitted out in Second Dragoon uniforms. All carried the U. S. model single shot percussion pistol. Their visored caps were held in place by chin straps: altogether they looked every inch what Drumm wanted the Mexicans to see.

"When those troops see Irons and the others, they are going to take out their spite on the gringos. I know that. However, we dare not jump them until they have surrounded a helpless enemy."

He studied them in the dim light, devoid of the comforting campfire. "While they are engaged in their deviltry, we will show them the colors. Miller will be stationed on the ridge playing 'To Arms, To Arms, To Arms!' Then Miller will change and give us 'Boots and Saddles' three times."

He limped to his bedroll and sat down.

"By that time, Peagram, carrying the small ensign and the Second Dragoons guidon will accompany me in a ride right into whatever Mexican melee is in progress."

"I say, old man, aren't you giving your life away rather cheaply for a show of theatrics," Parton drawled.

"I have no intention of dying," Drumm said with a smile. "The trick is to get the enemy to figure they've met their match and are about to die themselves."

Von Holder piped up. "Those Mexican soldiers are well aware that Kearny's Dragoons are abroad in these parts. Why not here?"

"Exactly," Drumm said. "My guess is that Capitano Francisco Morella is the officer in charge. He knows Kearny is hereabouts. That's why they set you and your sister up for a fake American ambush complete with Mexicans wearing our army's uniforms." He drew a deep breath. "I'm going to act like Kearny sent me to run them out of Texas. I'm going to be indignant as hell at what they are trying to do to American citizens."

Ives spoke grimly. "And, if they don't listen to reason, we are going to see that they lose their supply wagons."

"Then," Hard Winter finished, "Me and Bochey, mebbe you and your sister will join us, too, Lord Sir. It's strange chance that th'ows us together, but I have a hunch we are going to do some plain and fancy shootin' to sweeten the pot, eh, Clauday?"

Chapter Nineteen

Drumm thought he would never go to sleep, but sleep he did, and soundly. Bugler Miller had a tough time rousing him. "Cap'n, sir. Blanchard chunked up the fire and has saved you some hot water to shave with. Peagram is shaving, too."

Drumm slid into his uniform trousers as Miller rambled on. "I don't have any whiskers, Mr. Blanchard said, so I've no need to shave." Drumm, recognizing the boy's early-morning enthusiasm, clapped him on the back and walked briskly to where Blanchard fretted over his pots and pans.

"Soap, hot water, and a mirror," Blanchard said, as Drumm approached. At this ungodly hour, Parton was already up, perched near Blanchard's breakfast fire, snug and letting the last vestiges of sleep ooze away.

"A regular wizard, he is," Parton said. "A wizard. I say, Blanchard, would you care to come to England with me after Drumm finishes this war? I know a dozen happy kinds of work, ahem, professional work, you could do for me."

Blanchard acknowledged the compliments without comment.

Blanchard and Parton traded small talk as Drumm scraped off a week's beard. When he finished, he caught Peagram's eye as both of them ran fingers and palms over smooth, freshly shaved jaws and jowls. The feeling was good. There was nothing like a clean shave, Drumm thought, to put a man on top of the world.

"Feels mighty good, eh First?"

"Aye, sir."

At Blanchard's quiet signal, all hands had hot coffee and a kind of gruel Blanchard poured over hard biscuits. Parton momentarily forgot his polished British etiquette to mutter through a mouthful. "A wizard, he is. A ruddy wizard!"

At eight, according to Von Holder's turnip-sized watch, everyone was fed, had inspected the positions, and had loaded the bedrolls and Blanchard's pots and pans. Drumm looked around. Everything was in shipshape readiness, his small force ready to tackle what the day would bring. Hard Winter Davis would say they had painted for war.

As Drumm was thinking it, Davis rode in from the northeast. "Turn your spyglass up yonder." Drumm's eyes followed his pointing finger. Davis spoke softly. "They'll be here by eleven o'clock, noon at the latest." Davis handed the telescope to Ives.

"First," Drumm said, "have we covered everything? All avenues?"

"I was your paw's bugler at New Orleans, sir, and I rec'llect he asked his second in command about all avenues covered then. Captain Hardee said 'yes' then, and I say 'yes' now."

Drumm abruptly grabbed Peagram's hand. "I don't want to lose you unnecessarily, First. If you want to stay here and fight, no one will think the less of you."

Sitting by her brother on a fallen tree, Diana clearly heard the offer and Peagram's response. "I consider it an honor to serve with you, sir. You're a Drumm and that's good enough for me."

Davis took Parton and Diana down the hill into the covering screen of trees and rocks where they would be safe. Bochey took Ehler with him. As they left, Parton spoke to Drumm. "Chin up and all that, old boy. Whack them good for Sis and me."

Diana offered Drumm her hand. It was cool and soft. The intensity of her eyes staring into his spoke volumes. "Godspeed, Andrew Jackson Drumm. Please come back."

She turned to catch up with her brother and Davis, slim and boyish in her coat, cap, and trousers. Drumm watched her go with a full heart, his growing love for her charging him with even greater responsibility. Ives broke Drumm's reverie.

"Cap'n, both guns ready to fire. Only the aiming is left."

Drumm studied with satisfaction his ragtag handful of fighting men leaning against the breeches of Betsy and Lou, all watching him and Ives. They were relaxed but expectant.

"Look here, Guns," Drumm said. "I'll want the howitzer to each shoot once. Right?" Ives nodded his shock of yellow hair that no hat seemed to control.

"As you fire Betsy's first round, I want you to get her ready to for a third round after Lou sounds off. Then I want Lou disassembled and packed immediately." Ives knew the drill. If it looked like they were being overrun by swarming Mexican cavalry, they were to fire the assembled gun, spike her, and save the second gun.

"You'll give me a third command by saber if your bluff works?"

"You can count on it, Guns. I'll want both their wagons knocked out, and any third target you can find—such as the commanding officer's position."

Time was slipping away, the tension mounting. Von Holder kept his eye glued to the spyglass, observing the deserters hard at work in the stream. "They are moving right along." He singled out Irons in the knot of men below. "Irons is oblivious to the situation."

He handed the telescope to Drumm, who moved the second section to a close focus on Irons. "Not a single sentry. No one watching the horses. Damn!" He studied what he took to be the Mexicans' approach route, the trail was still silent. Any minute, enemy horsemen might boil out of that countryside yonder. "Irons deludes himself that no one will harm them." He handed the glass to Ives and rolled onto his back to regard the azure blue of sky. "The fool. The goddamned fool!"

He rolled over to look at Auggie Von Holder. "Is this what Secretary of War Marcy had in mind back in March?"

Von Holder's brow furrowed in thought. "So far, Andy we've done everything Marcy asked of us. No one here, including me, Parton, and his sister, wants to leave Irons and the rest of the men at the mercy of the Mexican cavalry."

Drumm grunted and rolled, coming to his feet. Ives motioned to him, handing him the glass. The vanguard of the Mexican force materialized in the distance and grew larger; two wagons took form out of the dust kicked up by the horses. Even at this distance,

Drumm could hear the clop of hooves and the wagons' rattling and clanking, the general noise of a military troop on the move.

Suddenly it was late morning and summer heat was building under a relentless sun. There was no breeze. Drumm was thankful his men were sheltered in the shade cast by the timber. From somewhere in the distance, his mind registered the low growl and aerial rumble of heat thunder and lightning.

The Mexicans had spotted the men at the stream and the assault was mounted. One platoon was held in reserve as the other coursed back and forth in the clumps of willow, splashing fountains of water high as they drove their horses into the small stream to ride over the pitiful band of deserters, now panicking in their surprise at being caught off guard.

Drumm's eye remained glued to the telescope as he became aware that the Mexican force was composed of highly trained, professional soldiers. No irregulars here, he thought, watching the gold diggers flushed from their potential riches by saber and hoof. The Mexicans hacked, jabbed, slashed, and thrust at the dodging, stumbling men. Some were cut and wounded by the insistent sabers.

Irons stood defiant in the center of a half-circle of men, gesturing obscenely when the leader simply rode him down. Irons staggered to his feet, only to be ridden down by another. Another slashed at Irons who ducked the blow to his head, but took it square in the back. Irons faltered, tried to stumble away, but fell heavily, face down. "That's enough," Drumm screamed. "Mount up!"

Chapter Twenty

"Bugler!" Play me a tune!" At the crown of the hill, his horse prancing and eager, Drumm bellowed the command that would start the fray that could be his undoing. As he and Peagram aimed their horses at the camp, Miller's bugle blared, "To Arms! To Arms! To Arms!"

The flag and guidon Peagram gripped in his left hand whipped smartly in a crisp wind as they drove their horses toward the astonished Mexicans who seemed paralyzed at the sight of uniformed dragoons. The bugle called "Boots and Saddles! Boots and Saddles!" again and again.

In what seemed the blink of an eye, Drumm and Peagram had charged into the middle of the camp where Irons lay face down, unmoving. The other gold seekers were either sitting or trying to bind wounds sustained as the Mexicans tried to round them up.

Drumm rode straight up to a knot of Mexican soldiers. With their fancy get-ups, it was tough to see who was in charge. Drumm growled, "Who is the Commandante here?" He had drawn his saber on the charge into the camp and now he pointed it around the ring of mounted and dismounted men he and Peagram faced.

One, obviously a sergeant made a gesture of ignorance. *"No comprehende."*

"You're the Seventh Mexican Regiment stationed at Santa Fe, and you *comprehende* all right." Drumm still ground out his words. As he spoke, a trooper made an angry gesture, started to step forward, but Peagram spit a stream of tobacco juice at the man's feet.

He grinned. "Stand easy, amigo. Stand easy." Peagram's ugly scar gleamed blood red.

Now, an elegant officer stepped out of the crowd.

"I am Capitano Francisco Morella, and these are my troops, as you say, the Seventh Regular Cavalry."

Drumm pointed at the men sitting or lying on the ground. "Then what are you doing to these Americans?"

"First, Senor Capitano, who are you?" Morella perched himself arrogantly on a folding chair just unloaded from one of the two wagons which arrived in the camp a moment or two behind Drumm.

"I am Captain Andrew Jackson Drumm and this is First Sergeant Peagram. We are American dragoons."

Morella's eyes were half hidden in angry slits as he fingered his graceful black mustache. "Well, Senor Dragoon, you are out of order and out of your country." He studied Drumm contemptuously. "What brings you into Mexico, Capitano Gringo?"

"Mexico!" Drumm laughed. He looked at Peagram. "He's been gone so long from Santa Fe he hasn't heard this is now the State of Texas, annexed by the United States on July 4, 1845. It's my turn, Captain. What the hell are you and your men doing in the American State of Texas?"

Morella jumped to his feet, drawing his saber. "Don't make the fun with me, gringo." He turned as if to give his men a command.

"You are under the guns of the Second Dragoons, Senor. One false move and I'll see to it you never see Santa Fe again."

Morella spun around, his anxious eyes searching the high country around his position. "Not a good position, Senor," Drumm growled. "Low ground, while I hold the high ground."

Morella composed himself and sank back into his chair. He laughed as he explained to his troops that the gringo captain was loco. He pointed at his head, twirling his finger around his ear. "I told my men—"

"That I was crazy," Drumm cut in. "So, I'm going to ask you to turn these Americans over to me and my colonel and quietly leave the United States. I'll accept that you were ignorant of the facts and let it stand at that."

114

"Who, I pray, is your *Coronel, Senor Capitano*?"

Drumm said it with emphasis. "Colonel Stephen Watts Kearny, commanding the regiment of the Second Dragoons."

"Aha, *senor*. My scouts and spies tell me your *Coronel* Kearny left in early July. Surely you jest with me."

"Captain Morella," Drumm said, pulling Von Holder's turnip-sized watch from his shell jacket. "I'm giving you five minutes to get out of here and on your way." He wound the watch. "Starting now."

Morella jumped to his feet in fury, but Drumm cut in again. "First Sergeant, give our Mexican friend evidence that I do not jest."

Peagram kneed his horse around, dipping the guidon and riding around one of the wagons. Then, he waved the guidon. At the same instant, the unmistakable sound of cannon fire was followed by the sighing whine of a cannon ball plowing the air.

A huge bellow of noise, flame and smoke enveloped the wagon which was shattered to kindling and twisted iron strapping and wagon tires before Morella's astonished eyes.

Drumm and Peagram calmly controlled their frightened horses. As the animals calmed, Drumm spoke again." Give the *Capitano* another sample of how loco I am, First Sergeant."

Peagram rode to the second wagon, circled it as panicked Mexicans scattered like frightened quail. As Peagram quickly urged him mount back to the safety of his position near Drumm's, their audience of thoroughly cowed Mexican troopers heard another distant explosion and the whine of cannon ball through the air. They stood transfixed in the hot sun as the howitzer shell destroyed the second supply wagon and its contents.

Morella's face was black with fury. "How dare you fire on my troops!?" He strode up and down, his feet resounding in anger on the packed earth. He looked at his troops. They didn't share his anger; they were scared to their very roots. For them it was one thing to saber whip an unarmed gringo—this was much more dangerous and they realized how exposed they were.

Drumm calmly regarded Morella. "You are in the United State of America. Not Mexico anymore. You have abused these Americans." He looked at the watch. "You have two minutes, senor, to make a run for it. The next volley will make mincemeat of your command. Get that, now!''

Morella's insane anger subsided. He spoke calmly, but with resolve. "No, I'll not go." He clapped his hat on his head. Drumm lifted his saber and the snap-crack of two rifles firing tore a hole in the silence as well as in Morella's hat which was snatched from his head.

The chair he had been sitting in fell over as a bullet hole appeared in the back as if by magic.

Drumm rode over to Morella's hat, lifted it on saber tip, and examined it, poking a finger through the bullet hole in the crown. "Next time, Morella, I'll signal my marksmen to aim to kill." He threw the hat at Morella's feet.

"Put it on and get the hell out of here before I lose my temper." Drumm walked his horse up against the boiling mad Mexican officer, rudely pushing and crowding him as he tried to mount.

"How does it feel, Morella? Suppose I used my saber on your backsides like you did to those unarmed Americans?" He pulled back, allowing Morella to swing into the saddle, shouting commands in Spanish to his troops. They fell into a column of fours.

Turning, Morella shook his fist at Drumm and Peagram, his insults lost in the thunder of his troops cantering off the way they had come.

The air was split again with cannon roar as Ives sent a third round at the limit of his range, well over eight hundred yards, further hurrying Morella's men along.

Chapter Twenty-One

"During the not-so-popular Seminole War, our War Department bought six French mountain howitzer guns, all twelve pounders."

Ives was bragging on Betsy and Lou again. "They were all bronze; not the cast-iron twelve pounder we now have. An iron twelve-pounder tube weighs about 1,200 pounds." He laid a hand on Betsy. "This tube weighs about 289 pounds. And a good, big, strong mule with a proper pack cradle can manage it. A wheel per mule, and the rest—trail, ammunition, powder bags, and rounds—divided up among the rest of the mules—gives us the ability to move rapidly. Or at least a lot faster than the iron twelve-pounders the horse artillery now uses."

Ives was telling Lord Parton and Augie Von Holder the reason Drumm really held the aces in his brush with Morella.

"Captain Drumm asked Colonel Kearny for these rarely used brass howitzers way back in March. I met him in Washington and we figured why burden the Colonel with those big modern twelve pounders." Ives whistled. "By the time you add up the gun's weight and all the gear it needs plus the caisson, you are looking at a figure approaching seven-thousand pounds."

He pointed at Betsy's tube as it was strapped down and covered under the protective shroud of an India-rubber cloth.

"Old Betsy here and everything she needs won't top twelve-hundred pounds." He slapped the tube's breech area. "That's why

Captain Drumm shocked Morella when we knocked out his two wagons. He couldn't believe we had guns when he knew full well Colonel Kearny left this area six weeks ago. Morella believed Colonel Kearny was dragging Betsy and Lou, which he brought out to South Pass."

"I say, Leftenant Ives," Parton's cultured voice intoned. "Why not use them all the time if, as you point out, they are just as good as their iron sisters?"

"Beggin' your pardon, Lord Parton. I never said they were as good. Just lighter."

"But—" Parton started.

"The brass tube is not as reliable as its, ah, as you say, its iron cousin."

While Ives and Parton supervised the loading of Betsy and Lou, Drumm saw to the rounding up of Von Holder's men and his errant gold-mining dragoons.

"Turn to. Do your work. We need every hand. If your wound needs doctoring, have Blanchard have a look at it." He sat his horse in civilian clothing again.

The gold seekers, humbled by the Mexican attack and their rescue by Drumm's tiny force, thanked him.

"Now then, you heard the Cap'n. Back to your posts." Peagram had nudged himself and his horse into the scene. He turned to Drumm. "I believe Cap'n Irons would like a word with you, sir."

Irons was strapped into a makeshift litter called a travois by the Indians and French-Canadians. Two long limbs, slender as lodgepoles, were tied to a pack saddle, heavy ends forward with the lighter ends resting on the ground on either side of the horse. Several blankets were lashed together to form a litter.

Drumm rode up and Irons opened his pain-clenched eyes. "I was a fool, Drumm. No justification for what I did."

Drumm spoke softly so only Irons would hear. "Under any other circumstances, Irons, I'd clap you in chains and submit you for court martial." He held up a hand as Irons started to respond.

"My charges would stand, and those poor dragoons you took with you would be branded for life. But I'm going to forget you placed this entire command in jeopardy. The men are taking their posts knowing their chances of ever seeing Fort Laramie again are still damned slim.'' He straightened himself in the saddle. "Your job is to rest easy for now and above all keep your mouth shut. Get well as fast as you can, and rejoin our effort. Whether I like you or not, Irons, you are still a soldier, my second in command, and we need you.''

Irons tried to speak as Drumm walked his horse to the head of the column.

"He saved your life, Captain Irons," Blanchard said, arriving to peel back part of his dressing and examine Irons' wound.

Irons grunted through his pain. "He's a good soldier, a first-rate officer. He's just about everything I always wanted to be, but never will.''

Within minutes the column of twos, once more at its original strength, moved north by northeast. It was 4 P.M., Auggie Von Holder noted, August 12. "A fine Tuesday afternoon.''

Diana asked. "What Tuesday?''

"The best kind, dear lady. This Tuesday August 12 means we are about three Tuesdays from Fort Laramie.''

"Oh, is Fort Laramie a military post?''

"No, not a military post. But it is owned by an American trading company.''

Their evening meal was a cold one, but Blanchard managed to fill each cup with hot, black coffee. Davis pulled in later and between sips of coffee related the findings of his scouting to Drumm and Peagram.

"Morella halted just out of sight as you expected, Andy. He sent two scouts after you, but old Clauday and me stopped them cold. You might say they accidentally leaned against a galena pill going past.'' He patted his Hawken rifle encased in a fringed and colorfully beaded elkhide case.

"Their damned hosses hightailed it back to their friends and an hour later, at dusk, two more scouts made a wide sashay tryin' to pick up our trail.'' He grinned wickedly. "I left Clauday keeping track of 'em. I thought you'd better keep fires and noise down to a roar if you don't want Morella sightin' down one of them fancy French musketoon carbines they are sportin'.''

Davis found his bedroll, untied it and flapped it open. "Give me a couple hours, Andy. Then I'll skallyhoot back an' relieve

Clauday." He spotted Upton, one of the mutineers. "Ain't that Upton?"

"Sure is." Peagram spoke.

"He's sure a fine shooter and a damned good rider. Can I have him?"

"He's your man," Peagram said.

"And let me have either Kilmer or Newman for old Clauday. He 'special liked 'em as shooters and riders." Davis' eyes closed and he drifted off to sleep almost as his final words were formed.

Peagram strolled to Upton and motioned Kilmer to his side. "That mountain man trusts you, Upton. Why in tarnation, I don't know. And the black man trusts you, Kilmer. Mr. Davis and Mr. Bochey are the eyes and ears of this command, as you well know."

He glared at them, his eyes showing tiny rivers of blood gained from staring into the sun-baked or snow-bright land in thirty years of soldiering. He remembered Drumm asking him why he didn't retire; "You've got your time in now."

Peagram's mouth twisted in a smile of recollection. Once during his service, early in the years after the War of 1812, he had found himself in mischief enough that he had to forfeit the year in a military stockade. He had spent the years since trying to behave properly enough to live down the black mark on his record.

He looked at Kilmer and Upton, remembering he'd once been in their shoes. "You do well, and I'll try to keep your record clean," he told them. "Now, Upton, you wake Davis in two hours. Mr. Von Holder has set his watch on that pack so you can tell when to get him up. It was me, I'd saddle his horse and yours and get some hardtack and jerky to keep you until Mr. Bochey and Kilmer relieve you."

Chapter Twenty-Two

Drumm was well aware that Morella was hounding his command. Daylight and evening reports from Davis and Bochey continued to be bad. "He's back there—maybe a couple leagues—campin' on our trail, Andy," Hard Winter informed ominously, his leathery lips pursed.

Conferring with Peagram and Ives, Drumm asked the question that burned on his mind. "Why in the hell doesn't he strike us now?"

Peagram waited for Ives to respond. Seeing the artillery officer was stumped himself, Peagram offered, "With your permission, sir?" Drumm nodded. "All I can think is hoss soldier, since that's what I've been all my life. I reckon Senor Morella thinks like me, too. He can't maneuver in these draws and ravines . . . not real well, anyway. Besides, he's got to know you got some hoss artillery. What kind, he can't be sure. But he knows we got range and accuracy on our side."

Peagram snorted into his sweeping orange-colored mustache. "Oh, he's goin' to hit us for sure. But only when the terrain is in his favor and when you least expect it. If it was me out there, coyotin' along behind, I'd hit this column as it moves, and hit her dead center, cutting you away from your guns."

Ives and Drumm nodded at one another knowingly; they were hearing real experience talking. Doffing his hat, Drumm ran a hand through his hair. It was a sign of frustration. Peagram had seen frustration in many an officer, most of whom never asked their warrant officer—because that is what a dragoon first sergeant was—for his opinion.

Many officers Peagram knew had deluded themselves into the belief that intelligence was equated with metal insignia on the collar, while ignorance wore cloth chevrons on its sleeves.

Drumm, one of the rare exceptions, looked at Peagram. "First, I'm long on fight, but short on experience."

Peagram was encouraged to continue. "As I see it, sir, our Mr. Morella has got to be taught a real lesson, one that cuts his outfit down to size. I'd let Mr. Davis scout ahead. A day or so till he finds the kind of terrain Morella would like to operate from in slicing our column in half." He signalled for permission to cut a chew—helped the thought process. Drumm acknowledged it.

"Knowing what's ahead," Peagram said, settling the cud in his cheek, "I'd send my guns out with Davis, give them cover, a decent place to fort up." His grin showed most of his fine, well-set teeth. "Then I'd play along acting as bait. When the Mexies hit the kind of terrain where a hoss sojer likes to let her out to a full gallop, Betsy and Lou, on the flanks, can eat old Morella for dinner while we pepper the few that gets through with percussion rifles."

Both officers were caught in the reverie of Peagram's word pictures. "'Course, there's a chance he might not take the bait."

"Oh, I think he'll nibble," Drumm said, enthusiastically. "Morella's itching to get even with me. He got snookered once and then to make matters worse, Davis and Bochey killed his scouts."

"Maybe after that he'll be too wary," Ives countered. "Don't get me wrong. I think Sergeant Peagram's plan is sound."

Drumm was thoughtful. "How many mules do we actually need to run ten rounds each through Betsy and Lou?" He cocked an inquiring eyebrow at Ives.

"Let's see. Four wheels, four mules. Two more for the tubes and two for the limber body. That's eight. Plus six for powder and canister. I'll need Quinn, Rawson, Ehler, Doyle, Getter, Smith, and Jones. Won't need any transportation for them or me."

Ives was writing the battle plan in his head. "We move up at night. Get set up, let one man take the horses and mules back to the column. There we can load bedrolls and the like on the mules so Morella's spies see what they see—a slow-moving column of twos, prime pickin's for a bloody charge."

"Sir, you've played an open hand with the troops so far. Are you goin' to tell 'em our plan?" Peagram asked.

"All in gcod time, First," Drumm said. "All in good time."

Drumm laid the plan out to Davis when he rode in at dusk from his daily scout. "What do you think, Hard Winter?"

Davis measured his words in recollection.

"I trapped this here territory in eighteen and forty-one with old Hank Fraeb, a cockeyed, tough little German. Pronounced his name 'Frapp,' so that's what we called him. Got into a Injun surround near here. We killed our hosses, made a fort outta their carcasses and held off a pack of howlin' banshee Injuns for two days. Frapp died sittin' up, so we jes' buried him there."

Davis gulped another mouthful of stew.

"I know a good place for what you got in mind, Andy. There's a nat'ral hot springs up yonder a day or so. 'Bout four miles farther there's some level ground which drops off into the North Platte. Le's set our trap on that plain. We can dig the guns in, hide some sharpshooters, and plain knock the tarnatious stuffin' outta ol' Morella."

Drumm raised up stiffly, brushing dirt and twigs from his trousers. In that gesture, the battle action was committed.

When the command made ready to march, Drumm called them together and explained the plan which would be triggered two days hence. He expected some glum reaction. Instead, to his surprise, men volunteered to take the mules in, help dismount the cannon, and get back to the column under cover of a faint quarter moon.

When several opted for the sharpshooters detail, Drumm waved a hand. "Much appreciated, men, but Mr. Davis and Mr. Bochey must make those choices."

He ordered his noncoms—Quinn, Ehler, Rawson, and Doyle—to pick out the healthiest for the nighttime work parties.

The command took time off the next afternoon to use the great natural hot springs. Some of them jumped in, clothing and all, scrubbing away the soil, sweat and grime collected over many days. Diana asked for shelter, which Peagram, Ehler, Rawson, and Quinn provided, shielding her with tarpaulins held behind their backs while she soaped, scrubbed, and absorbed the marvels of the wonderful water.

"Shouldn't wonder," Lord Parton observed to Von Holder, "that a spa will be located here one day. Hmm, along with Parton's Physicks, which I'll render from that fine sodium bicarbonate south of here, I may just develop these springs myself."

"It will be long after our time, my English friend," Von Holder said.

Parrying Von Holder's peek at the future, Parton said, "I say, why not haul the dear old Union Jack to the top of the flag pole here. After all, my bearded companion, the saying goes that the sun never sets on the British Empire."

"Oh, I'm sure you are right when speaking of the seven seas, but when we are discussing the American continent, you're somewhat out of order."

Parton muffled an acknowledging guffaw.

That night, under cover of darkness, Ives and his party of gunners pulled out of the command. Earlier, while others languished around camp or sported in the springs, making a pretense for the benefit of any of Morella's scouts, Ives and Davis had taken a leisurely ride beyond camp. Both saw exactly where Betsy and Lou would be positioned.

With all the silence and stealth they could muster, Drumm's select team walked the mules to clumps of willow along a small stream. Earlier Drumm and Ives had conferred on the guns' placement. Ives had looked through Von Holder's spyglass, gauging the distance, the trajectory, and the ability of his brass monsters to pour fire and death into two lines of hard-charging cavalry.

"I figure to put the two side by side. That way I'll aim each gun. We'll chew up Morella at 700 yards and drive the survivors right into our line of defense."

Drumm nodded in agreement. "I'm going to mount those who

can ride, at least twelve men, and we'll be ready to take up any slack. We'd better do some tall praying that Betsy, Lou, and the sharpshooters do the trick. If not, my little force will be sitting ducks out there.''

Chapter Twenty-Three

The ruse had worked perfectly. It worked so well, in fact, that when it was done, Drumm felt at last that he was relieved of the Morella nuisance for good and all.

Drumm sat at the base of a pine tree listening to the individual reports of his officers on the thwarting of Morella's attempted annihilation of his command. Old war horse that he was, Parton praised the action.

"By Jove, old boy, it reminded me of the maneuvering in Belgium when old Nappie sent his St. Cyr Hussars after the Coldstream Guards, who were acting as a decoy—being on foot and all that."

Parton stopped, his face growing red. "Ah . . . I really didn't mean to hog the report. But dash it, man, it was a really clever trap, Captain Drumm, and I'm going to mention it in my report!"

Drumm smiled wearily. He was dog tired. Ives was too, his face smudged with burnt black powder. Ives mustered a grin, too. "It was a good scrap, Cap'n. We sat on our guns when Morella seemed to explode out of that river bottom with the sun behind him, his men yelling like . . . " he hunted for a word, " . . . like Indian dervishes!"

Ives wiped his face with his sleeve, the powder smearing becoming more pronounced. "It seemed like an eternity before they got in range."

Von Holder spoke, holding up his pocket watch. "More like

two minutes. The battle started at 2 p.m. sharp, Sunday, August 17." He snapped the watch lid shut with a click.

Ives continued. "I still say it seemed like an eternity, Augie. Then I touched the match to Betsy and ran over to Lou. I was short by forty yards with Betsy, so I elevated Lou's muzzle a notch or two and cut the heart out of Morella's first line."

Parton couldn't stand it. "By Gad, Ives, you laid seven horses and men down with that second round!"

"To keep in range as they charged, I screwed the elevation down as we swabbed, loaded and fired Betsy and Lou." Ives pinched at tired eyes and the bridge of his nose with black-tipped fingers.

"Those poor damned horses. We mowed down at least ten or twelve with our second round."

Peagram spoke. "Eleven, sir, exactly eleven and Morella still kept coming." He coughed. "I don't like him, but by God, he didn't swerve."

"Damn but don't I know it," Ives said. "We depressed Betsy and Lou, hell, they were only two hundred yards by them. Our fire blew away both first and second ranks." Ives was beginning to mumble through his fatigue. "Men going head-first into the ground, horses torn apart, and still Morella came on." He stared at the ground.

"We fired point blank and the momentum of their charge was swept away." He shook his head and sighed in relief. "My next tack would have been to manhandle those brass beauties and fire point-blank again before they ran into the column."

Drumm leaned over and laid a hand on Ives's shoulder: the young artillery officer was still shaking.

"It's over, Guns. You did a first-rate job." A low murmur rose from the men around him. "When Blanchard fills you with his special stew and coffee, you'll be a new man."

Hard Winter spoke up. "When we seen that Ives was a-tearin' big holes in them troopers' ranks, we commence to fire at 250 yards. I knew ol' Clauday got some for there was three on Clauday's side I seen tumble off their hosses."

He grinned at his black friend, who bobbed his head and grinned, sheepishly.

"Don't rightly know, but I allow we accounted for six or seven over on our side. Pretty fair shootin', movin' targets and all, even if I do say so myself. We've turned those lads into right fine sharpshooters with their Hawkins firesticks.'' Davis beamed proudly around the circle.

Peagram took his turn. "You are a sure shot, Mr. Davis, you and Mr. Bochey and your rifle squad. We all know it." He clawed his tobacco cud from his cheek. "Permission to speak, sir?"

"You have the floor, First," Drumm said.

"Well, sir, as you know, we got the best out of them gold diggers." He grinned, but it was a grim expression. "They was a mite unhappy the way Morella and his boys used 'em back at the gold stream." He sighed through his luxuriant mustache. "When Miller tooted his tattoo on the bugle, you took right out straight at the Mexicans. I think we was the straw that busted old Morella's back. Hell, not too many of us got a lick at 'em, 'cause they turned and showed us a clean pair of heels."

Peagram paused. "I believe I speak for the whole command, Cap'n Drumm, that is was a Christian gesture letting them pick up their dead and wounded."

Drumm grinned at Peagram. "And just to show you how Christian I am, my orders are for a night march." Peagram only stared at Drumm. "Lieutenant Ives, did you load Betsy and Lou?"

"Yes, sir!," Ives responded crisply.

"Very well then. Once we've had our Blanchard stew, hardtack, and coffee, plan on moving out at seven p.m. sharp. I believe soup's on. Dismissed."

Walking to Blanchard's stew pots with Von Holder and Parton, Drumm remarked, "My guess is we probably reduced Morella by about nineteen or twenty men and horses. That may give him cause to pull back and lick his wounds, if not head for home."

Parton's eyes were narrow in speculation. "That's nearly a third! We got two men powder-burned and one man was stepped on by a horse. Ha! Old boy, clearly a victory, wouldn't you say so, my scientific friend?"

Always the realist, Von Holder said, "I don't want to appear pessimistic, but Morella is far from through. Now he's got even more smarting wounds to avenge."

"So you can understand why we've got to put some miles behind us," Drumm said. "We've a good moon and the terrain is not that bad." He stooped to fill his mug with coffee. "No one was hurt, so we can cover ground without having to favor the wounded. We were lucky. Our biggest threat now is our own fatigue and, as you suggest, Augie, a red-hot Morella."

As the column moved out under the silvery half-light of a waxing moon, Drumm sat his horse off to one side watching them march past. He looked up at the dark canopy studded with the brightest stars he'd ever seen. A soft voice beside him intruded on his thoughts.

"This is a land of magnificent contrasts." It was Diana, her hair cascading to her shoulders nearly white in the light of the soft August evening. "One day," she said, "we travel through dry, lizard-infested, tortured land whose carnival of color would test the mettle of a master artist. The next few days we ride through natural pasture not unlike County Sussex where I live." She inhaled a deep breath of the pure crystal air. "And the air is full of such vitality."

Drumm pointed the way as the column snaked past them. "All of what you say is true." He reached across and laid a palm over the back of her hand resting on the saddle horn. "I've come to love these wide, open plains. They lean forward and suddenly become mountains and towering peaks. We are just now beginning to name some of them."

He signalled at a graceful mountain to their right. "Augie says that peak is probably more than 11,000 feet above sea level."

They both gazed with rapture at the peak whose crown still glistened with snow, a stark white and ragged pyramid at the crest. "Hard Winter says mountain men call it Elk Mountain; lots of elk hereabouts, y'know."

They moved out, Diana riding easily beside him. "First Sergeant Peagram says you went from West Point into the Topographical Corps against your father's wishes," she said.

Drumm muttered. "Peagram ought to tend to his own problems."

Diana wouldn't allow him to stay out of sorts for long. "But . . . ?"

"Well . . . yes. I didn't see much of a future running around waving a saber at a bunch of half-naked natives.''

He twisted in the saddle to speak to her more directly. ''We fought our second and last war with your country in 1814. Now we'll probably fight Mexico. This little episode of ours may turn out to be the first salvo.'' He rubbed his jaw, fingering the scar tissue of his wound.

''My father thinks we will yet have a war among ourselves, as well. The southern plantation owners against the northern industrialists. I think he hopes I'll be ready to help the South. It'll be a tough choice if it comes to that. Fighting with my state goes against everything I've lived for . . . the Point, the nation's Constitution. Huh!''

''Do you really think it will come to that?''

He scarcely heard her through the depth of his own thoughts. ''There's some truth in the idea, I suppose. The reason I became a topo officer was because we need to define the sources and tributaries of our river systems, study the Indians, check out the minerals, and the like.''

He was changing the subject, and he knew it. ''America will need to know what its got to work with.'' He slapped his thigh, bringing a twinge of recollection of his wound. ''It just made more sense than fighting Indians.''

Her horse took her a few yards ahead, and he spurred to catch up with her so he could finish. ''Trouble is, Captain Andrew Jackson Drumm, once an engineering officer of sorts, now a dragoon, can't seem find the world he wants to live in.''

They rode through the moon's light and shadows for some minutes before either spoke. Ahead of them through the dark, Drumm could see the command's rearguard, riding drag as some described the position.

Finally Drumm spoke. ''Right now and until I deliver you and your brother into safe hands and complete my mission I'm a dragoon, as my father was before me. And that's not all that bad, you know. I respect and love my old dad. As for my responsibility to you and Lord Parton, nothing can change that.''

He leaned over, pulled her toward his arms in an awkward embrace from horseback. He kissed her and she responded, surrendering herself to his strong arms.

It was another magic moment. Her horse moved away, breaking their hug, leaving them both gasping for breath. She pulled up, but before they could repeat, a voice knifed out of the dark, breaking into their reverie.

"Andy! It's me. Hard Winter." He held up a hand. "Nothing wrong back there . . . much. True to your figgerin', Morella's gang is coyotin' along back there, but a long way to the rear. Better join the command, hey? Ridin' alone back here unprotected ain't exactly healthy if them tamale-eatin' scouts decide on a little moonlight strike."

Diana and Andy laughed. "There is no one in the world I'd rather have than you, Mr. Davis, guarding me from scoundrels like our Mr. Andrew Jackson Drumm," she said.

Chapter Twenty-Four

"The hosses and mules is pretty well used up?' intoned Farrier Sergeant Rawson. "They could use a hoss holiday, beggin' your pardon, sir."

Davis, seated beside Drumm, told him that the trail was still clear behind them. Morella was back there, still moving for another attack, but slowed by his lack of supplies and favoring his wounded. Drumm's command had forded the Medicine Bow River two days back, and crossed a rushing stream. Davis said Bochey called it "'e Roche" because of the many rocks and boulders there.

Despite its rocky bed, Blanchard and his crew had taken out a big catch of firm mountain trout. They were at the moment sizzling in Blanchard's big dutch ovens. In other big cast iron pots with lids rimmed to hold embers, bread was baking and stew was simmering.

Drumm balanced his alternatives, making a mental checklist. "All right. We declare a horse holiday August 21 at Rock Creek. First, post your sentries. Now!"

A worm of worry wiggled through Drumm's head. It kept him from sleep, even after a fish, stew, and fresh bread supper.

The others were dark lumps under thick bedrolls around several small campfires. Wrapped in his thoughts, and a long way from sleep, Drumm wandered up to Newman on sentry duty. Drumm needed someone to chat with, to let his worries settle out. Then he could sleep.

"Just me, Newman. Captain Drumm."

"Yes, sir. But ain't it a beautiful night. Too gorgeous to waste it sleepin'."

The moon was low in the east, being born almost out of the mountains separating them from Fort Laramie. At first it was yellow as tallow and large, turning silver as it rose higher.

Drumm had often pondered the moon. It loomed large when it rose, and as night progressed, it grew smaller. His astronomy courses at the Point had taught him that the moon was always the same distance from Earth; still there were times in its cycle when it looked closer. He'd figured he'd have to ask Augie Von Holder—a scientist, even if he were a botanist, surely would know.

Drumm and Newman silently regarded the moon and its bath of light on the Earth for several minutes before Drumm spoke.

"Where are you from, Newman?"

"Filmore, sir. Not that far from your home place at Pamlico."

"I remember now."

"Yes, sir. My family fishes and digs clams. Always have, ever since I was a small boy."

"You're practically a neighbor, Newman. What brought you to the Dragoons?"

"Your pappy, beggin' the Cap'n's pardon. Colonel Drumm himself gave me a job exercisin' his hosses when I was a lad. You were away at the Point. Your dad said I rode good enough to be a dragoon. I respect your father, Cap'n, though sometimes he's a tough old bone, beggin' the Cap'n's pardon."

Drumm nodded. "I agree. And I've known him longer than you."

Newman allowed their common background to overcome his sensitivities about rank. "I pure didn't care for fishin' and such. So, your dad, the Colonel, wrote a letter to Colonel Kearny. You were still away at the Point when I joined up."

Drumm was silent for a moment realizing how his father would always affect his life, no matter where he was or who he encountered. He was jolted back to the present by the earnestness of Newman's voice.

"You going to put us deserters in chains once we hit Leavenworth, sir?"

"Who told you that?"

"By your leave, sir, was Cap'n Irons. Said we'd all do time in a military prison and be drummed out of the service."

Drumm spoke slowly. "Do you believe I should do what Captain Irons said I would do, Newman?"

"After we watched you fight Cap'n Irons, sir, none of us who panned for gold believed you'd ever do what Cap'n Irons said."

"What's your given name, Newman?"

"Private Jesse Newman, sir."

"Well, Jesse, you and the others keep your noses clean, do your duty, and I doubt I'll even remember the day you caught gold fever. By the way, how much did you find?"

Newman turned bashful. "Not enough to make the risk worth the while, Cap'n. But I got somethin' better than gold. I learnt somethin' out of it. Somethin' good . . . somethin' to last. Duty. Greed does terrible things to a man. But duty, doin' what you've obliged yourself to do, does good things. Duty comes first. And I'm a better man for the knowing of it."

Newman cleared his throat. His thoughts were coming from somewhere deep. "Cap'n, me and the men have done a sight of talking since then. We're all of a mind. Ain't none of us going to do anything but our best from here on in, sir, and God bless you!"

Drumm stood up. He'd be ready for sleep now. He looked at Jesse Newman, a private in Drumm's Devils. "We North Carolinians got to stick together, Jesse," he said. He walked back to his bedroll leaving a very happy Jesse Newman. I feel good, too, he thought.

But sleep still had to be held off. Hard Winter and Bochey were waiting for him. "Bad news, Andy."

"*Lamenter* . . . terrible," Bochey added.

"Me and Clauday calc'lated we had Brother Morella figured to where we could slip in and steal his hosses anytime we wanted 'fore he know'd we was in his camp. 'Stead o' that, we let him plumb outfox us. Damn!"

Hard Winter fingered his lips, finding the proper words for his report.

"Lost him like a whisper in a high wind. He's rode around us,

Andy, and ol' Clauday here spotted him eight, ten miles ahead of your line of march." Davis rubbed the same hand across his bristle of whiskers, making a sandpaper sound.

Drumm rubbed his left leg, and somehow the pain had suddenly grown strong again. "Well, now. No time to cry over spilled milk. It's done. The next step is to rationally figure our next moves. Bochey, go wake Peagram, Ives, and Von Holder. But quiet. No need to alarm the others. They'll need all the rest they can get."

As Davis was explaining their position to the others, who had come fully awake by now, Parton showed up at their ring around the campfire.

"I say, jolly old Morella between you and safety, eh?" Blanchard had also been aroused and as if by magic, had produced a huge enameled pot full of steaming coffee. Parton buried his upper lip in a mug of the stout stuff.

"Black as sin and twice as tough," Hard Winter observed, for a moment taking their minds off the hazardous turn of events.

"What Lord Parton says pretty well sums up our position," Drumm said, fully awake now and sidelining concern in favor of clear thinking of the moves he'd have to make.

"My hunch is Morella will shift to the right or the left to block us out of the Sybille Canyon which gives fairly easy passage through the Laramie Mountains," Drumm said.

"Checkmate," Parton enthused, relishing the challenge of logistics, despite the personal threat.

Peagram broke the silence that ensued. "Well, sir. I ain't no sojer loaded down with technical learnin', ain't read that many of the tactics books and such. But I remember a situation once in Florida we could mebbe mull over with your permission, sir."

"By all means, First," Drumm said. "I'm stumped." Drumm scratched his head.

Well, sir, what's the hurry?" Peagram again blew through his yellowed mustache. He squinted as his eyes roved the faces around the fire, letting his words sink in.

"We got the best cook in the world here," Peagram continued, pointing at the beefy Blanchard standing with his immense blackened coffee pot, ready to refill any empty cup.

"Morella's chewing leather fringes and boilin' boot soles he's so hungry, and him armed with them smooth-bore musketoons. I figure we're the ones that's got hold of him nearby where the sun don't much shine."

Drumm began to brighten; Peagram was making sense. He waved at Peagram to continue.

"Mr. Davis and Mr. Bochey can keep us supplied with venison, elk, antelope, and buff'lo, and now and then fish." He waved eastward. "Old Morella is in a sight of trouble. His men are hungry, it's a long way to Mexico, and here we are blocking his road with a couple howitzers he's come 'round to respect. He's the one got his tit shoved in the wolf's mouth, not us."

Drumm's eyes beamed on Peagram with a depth of respect he'd felt for few men. "I follow your line of reasoning, First."

"By your leave, Cap'n Drumm. Let's us jus' sit here. If we have to fight, let's study out the battleground and learn how to use it to our advantage." He huffed again through his handlebars. Feeling good about his plan, Peagram carved off a wad of Mickey Twist and wedged it into his cheek as he waited for others to respond.

"I say, First Sergeant, did this plan work in Florida?" It was Parton who broke the silence.

"Well, your Lordship, we never did use the idea. But I always did think it was a good one."

Suddenly, Von Holder brought their attention to the east where lightning stuttered as it pounded the ground while an anvil-shaped cloud carried the rumble of thunder inside. "Besides," said the scientist, "the weather might turn out to be our friend. If it comes to a spell of wind and rain, we can make do with our Indian rubber cloths for a roof and enough to eat. I daresay Morella's men are geared for Taos-type and weather hadn't packed for Wyoming gullywashers."

Drumm spoke up. "How far to Fort Laramie, Hard Winter?"

Davis and Bochey mumbled a few words together. Then Davis looked up, himself studying the faces at the fire. "As the crow flies, me and old Clauday here figure five or six days hard ridin'."

Drumm looked at Davis. "Well, you're lookin' fat and sassy after these rich days of Blanchard's chow. Take your pick of the horses, with two replacements. Get to Laramie like the devil was after you. You know our situation. Tell them we are trying like hell to get there, and the odds are running against us.''

Drumm, too, let his eyes rove the expectant faces around the fire. ''A relief expedition would sure be a big help, because I think now that Morella's mad enough to fight us to the last man.''

He saw Davis off with dawn only a thin band of grey along the distant eastern peaks. He handed him a message he'd dashed off with Von Holder's quill and ink to point out his desperate situation.

The camp was now alerted, and Diana appeared to offer Davis her slim hand. ''Godspeed, Mr. Davis. Our hearts ride with you.''

''Nothin' to fret about, little lady,'' Davis responded bashfully. ''I've rode this oountry a sight of seasons. I could nigh do it blindfolded. I'm comin' back, you can set store on that.''

Hard Winter stepped to his horse, holding the reins of his extra mounts. Blanchard stepped olose, handing Davis a large leather packet. ''My best for you, Davis,'' Blanchard said.

Davis's eyes squinted on Blanchard and the others. ''Don't take no chances,'' he said, levering into the saddle. ''Bear sharp and light sleep.''

With Davis having booted his horses into the gathering dawn, Drumm, Ives, Peagram, and Bochey rode out of camp seeking a likely place to face Morella.

In camp, Diana wandered over to see if she could be any help to Blanchard. The big cook grinned as he related that he'd seen choke cherries and buffalo berries growing along the stream. Irons, now standing and gaining strength every day, offered to go along on a berry-picking expedition when Blanchard said he could bake some grand delicacies, if only he had some of those berries.

Diana looked at Irons; the man had lost a dozen pounds since his near-fatal wound. Some of the anger and meanness seemed to have drained out of him.

He smiled, but weakly. ''I'm strong enough now, ma'am. I need the exercise. At least I figure I'd ought to be doing something useful.''

By nine, the unlikely trio was busy filling Ives' canvas artillery buckets with berries. As they harvested the succulent reddish-purple gems, they stayed alert to possible apprehension by agents of Morella's force, though they didn't expect them. Neither of the men had thought to carry a gun.

They hadn't anticipated, however, the enemy they encountered; they hadn't guessed they'd be poaching berries from a local resident whose passion for berries was huge at this time of year.

"Lordy, Miss Diana," Blanchard called out. "Come see what I found!"

"What, Mr. Blanchard?"

"Goose berries, right here in this thicket . . . Judas Priest!"

Blanchard reacted with lightning speed after he parted the deep foliage to come face-to-face with a huge yellow and brown grizzly bear.

Fast on his feet for a man his size, Blanchard sprinted toward Diana; the bear lunged after him, a huge paw batting him to the ground. Blanchard was paralyzed by fear, but Diana cut loose an ear-splitting scream that stunned the bear and brought Irons to her side.

"Go get help," he yelled at her. "Get a gun!" Irons commanded as he picked up a long piece of thick timber to jab at the growling bear as it proceeded to its intended attack on Blanchard.

"Get up, Blanchard," Irons yelled. "Run for your life." Irons backed up, still fencing and parrying with the bear's great paws. The monster bear was confused by the stick punching at him, and he batted at it while standing on his hind legs.

Blanchard was no coward. Once on his feet, he found large stones to hurl at the menacing bear, as it batted the offending branch from Irons' hands. As the grizzly prepared to envelope Irons, Blanchard hit the beast in the face with the fist-sized boulder. Weighing at least two pounds and hurled by a three-hundred-pound man, the rock stunned the bear as it collided with its snout and bounced into one eye.

Blanchard and Irons stood transfixed as the bear looked at them stupidly for a long moment, apparently sizing up the uncommon situation. At length, it dropped to all fours and lumbered back into the bushes.

Irons sat down, exhausted. Blanchard stumbled to him and flopped down.

"Drumm is always right, Blanchard," Irons said. "You're the best damned cook in America's army. But now I've got him one better. You're the world's best at scaring off a grizzly."

"Out here they call him Old Caleb," Blanchard said.

The two had a good laugh, and Blanchard began to feel that Irons was going to be a much less painful thorn in Drumm's side. They were weak with the laughter of relief when Diana, Harrigan One, Rawson, and Parton showed up, percussion rifles at the ready. When Blanchard related Irons military parry and thrust with the stick, they all had another good laugh. Blanchard still had them fill the four buckets as they followed the stream back to camp.

Drumm's scouting party rode in at dusk to find a fine meal awaiting them. It was topped off by slices of delicious fresh bread, each liberally sprinkled with choice berries.

When Parton remarked that the dessert was the *"piece de résistance"* to a beautiful repast, Claude Bochey caught Parton's eye and winked knowingly.

Chapter Twenty-Five

The next day, with some apprehension, the command left later than usual. They planned on a four-mile march to the area Drumm, Peagram, and Ives had chosen as defendable. Drumm had determined the day before that the only avenue from which Morella could attack was from the right flank and he committed the strength of his small force accordingly.

"That's what Morella tried to do the first time, " Drumm said. "Strike us from the flank, cut us in two, and mop up the column's separate pieces. Now we're ready for that. He must have gotten that from some Spanish tactics manual."

Peagram was watching him.

"Let's invite him to try his luck twice, eh, First?" Drumm thumped Peagram on the back.

"Sure be somethin' were we to hammer Morella from the rear." Peagram commented.

Ives puckered his lips and blew a tuneless whistle as he looked over the terrain. Neither Drumm nor Peagram spoke as they watched Ives figure his fields of fire, gun positions and the like. Finally Ives spoke.

"I believe we can surprise Colonel Morella one more time."

He pointed at a long gulley veering off the flat terrain Drumm hoped would tempt Morella into a charge on the American column.

"I know Doyle, Quinn, Rawson, and Ehler can handle Betsy. I'll position her tonight." He pointed to a dip in the flat meadow. "I'll place her there. Morella won't see the gun until he is at least 500 yards from that position. I'll assign Getter to aim Betsy and depress the tube as Morella rides closer."

Ives grinned. "That's ought to do it. Once Morella has committed his troops to an all-out charge, he'll know when only one gun shoots at him that he's fallen into another trap. Then, when he tries to halt his men, I'll push Lou from that ledge of rock, and we'll have Mr. Morella in a cross fire."

Drumm listened intently. "Do you really want to split the guns? If Morella decides to ride down Betsy, I believe we can handle him with the rifles from 200 yards to our main line of defense."

Drumm tossed a stone into a deep draw beside them. "We won't have more than five rifles to stop a charge. And I'm going to be honest with you, Guns. Morella is no novice at open-field charging. We caught him in the open last time, and surprised him with your guns."

Drumm paused for effect as the midmorning breeze toyed with his hat brim. "And you were aiming and firing Betsy and Lou, not rookie artillerymen."

Ives bit his lower lip in thought. Peagram was silent; he knew Drumm was right.

"They'll be scouting back this way. Why not leave the column picketed at noon, a juicy target. Leave enough people to make it look real. Tonight we move both guns into that dip where you can command the pair."

The details of the trap were built in Drumm's head. "Let Irons take the sharpshooter crew out tonight, two-man teams, two guns to each team, one man to load, the other to fire. And they can take turns shooting." He cleared his throat. "First Sergeant Peagram and I will take the remaining men down into the ravine below this rocky ledge. It's a good screen, and we can be in motion for a charge before they even know where we're coming from. We'll keep watch on Morella's movements and at the right moment, we'll hit his left flank and blister him, God willing."

Ives's blue eyes gleamed in admiration. "I like your plan, Cap'n. That's why I'm artillery and you're horse."

"Get out your notebook, Ives," Drumm commanded. Ives pawed in his jacket for the small pad and dabbed the tip of a stub pencil to his tongue. "Here's how we do it. Tonight all able men will turn to setting up Betsy and Lou. Ives and his men—Ehler, Quinn, Smith, Getter, Doyle, and Jones—will bed down with the guns until the action begins. Put seven down for the guns."

Drumm pulled a blade of grass and nibbled and sucked the juice out of its pulpy stem. "Bochey will take Biltmore, Von Holder, Brady and Bonnett with him. That leaves Irons, Parton, Diana, Blanchard, Killdare, and Collier with rifles and holding down the picket line."

He watched Ives draw in the numbers. "Right. Five for Bochey's team, and six for Irons and his gang."

Drumm grinned at Peagram. "Here we go again, First. Thirteen of us trying to behave like a whole platoon."

He watched Ives write in the names as he called them out. "Drumm, Peagram, Miller, Rawson, Kilmer, Attix, the three Harrigans, Newman, G. Smith, Upton, and Kincaid."

The three huddled together, their backs to the brisk morning breeze. Each looked over the terrain again, their eyes following an imaginary cavalry charge.

Drumm jumped up abruptly. "All right. Let's head back to camp. We'll move slowly today. Each of you get your men together. Explain our plan. We can't allow any slip-ups. This one may well be for keeps. Either we send Morella skallyhootin' back to Santa Fe with his tail between his legs or tomorrow the buzzards will have what Hard Winter calls prime fixin's."

Drumm got to Irons with his orders. "You still aren't strong enough for a charge." Irons tried to cut in, but Drumm motioned toward Diana. "I know that you reopened your wounds helping save Lady Diana and Blanchard today. I've noted your courageous act in my log. You're up for a citation, my friend. For now, though, your job is to hold this line, don't let Morella scatter our mules and horses."

Drumm gave his group a wry smile. "Lord Parton can shoot a rifle; Diana can load for him. Irons, I suggest you train Blanchard to do the same for Collier, and Killdare can load for you. I'll leave you six of Davis's percussion rifles, and plenty of powder, lead, and tins of caps."

He looked the group over. "I can't tell you all how important it is to guard our stock behind those picket ropes. They are our ride out of here, as you well know."

Drumm walked into Peagram's meeting. "They all know the plan for tomorrow?"

Yes, sir," the First Sergeant said crisply. "All notified and ready for a night's work on Betsy and Lou."

Bochey grinned; the little black man was in his element. Here, Drumm thought, was a man ready to die standing up, but better prepared to render a few others that way and come out of it with his own scalp intact—what there was left of it.

"*Mon ami, le Capitaine*, I have myself trained all of these men. They are fine sharpshooters."

Drumm looked at Von Holder. "This is more than you or your men reckoned on, Augie."

Von Holder walked closer to Drumm with a steaming mug of Blanchard's old reliable coffee. "You are so right, Andy, my friend. None of us figured on Diana and her brother being here either. They are here and all of us, every last living son of us, is ready to fight his way through so they can tell their story in Washington and in London."

He tipped his hat to a rakish angle, emphasizing his guts and his eagerness. Augie Von Holder also had unmeasured reserves of grit. "Besides, all of my men are having the adventure of their lives."

"Yeah," Drumm said matter-of-factly, "and I only hope it isn't the last adventure of their lives."

Von Holder's eyes bored into Drumm's. "There isn't a one of my men who isn't prepared to survive to write his memoirs. This is too precious an experience for them to take a chance on dying and lose it."

Later that night, while racing clouds passed across the brilliant face of the moon, Drumm's Devils and Von Holder's Bug Catchers were a lively lot.

Ives and Drumm looked over the plain they wanted Morella to

use. Gazing to the southwest, Ives commented, "You can see forever. The plains look flat as a tabletop. In reality, there are all sorts of depressions and likely hiding places."

It was a night of back-breaking labor, dismounting the guns, the panniers of ammunition, piling the powder and cannister between the two brass cannon. Ives continued to fuss over his guns. With the only tools they had, their sabers, they hacked piles of willow and sagebrush which Ives piled over the guns and along the terrain ahead of Betsy and Lou.

Ives waved Drumm and Peagram goodbye as he and his crew added a touch here and there to make certain their position would not give Morella a hint that he was about to be led into a snare for the third time.

"All right," Ives said to himself, leaning against Betsy's breech. "What have I forgotten?" He peered through the gray moonlight at his crews.

Ives paused before continuing. "We will have to wait on our Mexican friends to find out." Getter translated for Smith and Jones. "We will see them a long time before they drive into our effective range. That means we commence firing at seven hundred yards."

Again he paused as the Austrian relayed the words to the Germans with the American names.

"Once Morella spots us, he'll turn and ride pell-mell at us." He distinctly heard Getter use the word "schnell," about all the German he knew. "We want him to veer in his charge because that will allow Captain Drumm to roll up his left flank while Bochey and his marksmen pick off stragglers on the right flank."

Ives wiped his face with a handkerchief.

"Captain Drumm figures Morella lost twenty men at the hot springs. If Bochey and Davis count Morella's strength right, they've somewhere between forty and forty-five men." Getter continued his guttural German while Doyle, Ehler, and Quinn listened closely.

"Our objective is to mangle Morella's first and second ranks. We have to unhorse at least fifteen to twenty men and properly harass the rest of the Mexicans. That'll take some doing. Bochey will account for six to ten men, leaving Morella with less than half his strength. If we do that, we'll turn Mr. Morella and we can be on our way to Fort Laramie unperturbed.''

Getter's translation finished, Ives saw broad and eager grins on the faces of Smith and Jones.

Chapter Twenty-Six

From the effective cover of trees and rocks, Drumm and Peagram watched the skyline of the Laramie Mountains rear up in relief as the morning sun peeked over the ragged peaks. Long streaks of sunlight played across the plains. As they watched, the sun began its ascent across the face of a cloudless, azure sky.

Drumm shivered along with his men in the early dawn and welcomed the sun's growing warmth as it climbed higher in the sky. Peagram moved to a better vantage point twenty yards away, scanning the horizon for any signs of movement. Neither man spoke. The ground was warm and the sun began to heat their backsides. After an exhausting night of tension, work, and worry, Drumm began to feel his excitement and his zest growing.

Peagram hissed at Drumm. "Them antelope, sir"—he pointed at a distant herd turning skittish from something they heard, saw, or smelled. Some of the antelope began bouncing for cover, like fall-crisp leaves dancing before a winter wind setting tolerable fair—"jumpy as hell."

Drumm came to his knees for a better view through the screen of scrub growth. "What do you make of it, First?" His eyes saw several dark shapes rising and falling.

"Something's aroused those antelope. Hell, it's Morella's troopers trying to turn us around and hit our flank."

Drumm called to Miller. "Ride to Ives, but keep low and out of sight. He's got to square Betsy and Lou to face Morella as he

comes out of that draw yonder.'' He saw Miller mount his horse
screened by the land's depression behind him. "Keep right on until
you find Bochey. Tell him to fall back to Captain Irons. Defend
that line. Now! Off you go!''

Peagram was up, heading for his horse, ready to mount. "He
signalled the rest of the dragoons to follow. "Morella is dumb like
a fox,'' he told Drumm. "With all respect to our artillery officer,
if we'd listened to Ives, we'd be knee deep in trouble.''

"All right,'' Drumm called quietly as he threw a leg over the
saddle. "Follow me.''

Drumm led the small column of grim dragoons up the draw until
he was certain Morella would turn his force, trying to blindside
Ives and rip the horses and mules at the rear where Morella would
be certain the Englishman and his sister were.

"Damn!'' Drumm thought as he rode silently out of the ravine's
shallow mouth. "Morella's plan nearly worked. A herd of skittish antelope gave him away!''

From their position, the gun crews pulled, wrestled, and turned
the brass cannon a full quarter. Their round snouts now pointed
at the draw from which Morella hoped to produce a real surprise.

Miller found Bochey and relayed Drumm's command. All of
them, including Miller, ran doubled over, taking advantage of small
depressions and draws and what modest cover they could find.

Irons was cool and confident. His force had swelled to thirteen,
all of them with rifles. He had Killdare, Blanchard, and Miller
set up a new picket line for the mounts a hundred yards to the rear
behind the cover of a small hill. They drove picket pins deep into
the ground, and ran new lines to restrain the horses and mules.

Parton called, sweat glistening on his handsomely furrowed
brow. "I say, Captain Irons. I believe Morella is headed our way.''

"That's what Drumm wanted,'' Irons called back. He squinted
to see Morella's men trotting confidently up a long ravine. Irons
placed his riflemen where he thought they'd have clear fields for
a raking zone of fire.

From his vantage point some distance away, Ives peered through
the brush piled around his guns. He caught his breath as the Mexicans burst out of the ravine Miller had indicated. His men saw
the enemy, too. "Hold!'' Ives called cautiously to them. "We have

to let them clear the draw. That's where they'll form two ranks, ready to charge the column.''

Ives watched until he sensed the timing was right. ''All right, men. Get this brush out of the way. Time to start taking the tallies on Mr. Morella.''

The guns' muzzles cleared, Ives continued his commands. ''They're in range, and we're deflected right on target. I'm ready to fire Betsy at the count of ten and at twenty, Lou. We'll try to run them in and out and fire as fast as we can . . . four, five, six . . .''

Morella was in the lead of his troops, but drew off to one side and was in the midst of a shouted command when the first cannister burst forth from Betsy as his last trooper cleared the draw.

The Mexican troop was caught unawares and slammed broadside. Three or four horses fell as their riders were either hit or dismounted. Confusion reigned in the Mexican ranks as they peered through the dust or tried to listen for a command to attack or withdraw. Panicked horses milled, their riders powerless to control them.

A second round exploded in their ranks, maiming more men and horses and further scattering Morella's force.

Drumm saw it all happening. Morella, he thought, for whatever he was, knew how to hold his men together. They quickly regrouped, closing ranks around the holes wrought by the exploding cannister. Morella darted among them, slapping bewildered riders and horses with the flat of his saber and yelling.

He had discovered Ives's position and, rallying his remaining troopers, began an all-out gallop directly toward the death-dealing howitzers. They were all of five hundred yards away.

Betsy and Lou, right on course, sent shrapnel and grape slicing through the hard-charging Mexicans. Morella appeared oblivious to the bursting shells and the throaty roar of Ives's battery.

A third report of both Betsy and Lou at two hundred yards drove more holes in the enemy ranks. Morella swerved as if to pass the guns. Once more Ives laid a pair of howitzer shells bursting with deadly accuracy on the Mexican's explosed right flank.

The battlefield filled with the screams of shells and the thunder of their distant explosions, and the cries of wounded and dying

148

men and horses. Still Morella charged on and, to his surprise, Drumm and Peagram boiled out of the draw on Morella's left flank, placing themselves between Irons' position and the galloping Mexican horsemen. The Mexican officer turned his force to meet Drumm's onrushing charge. The two-hundred-yard gap was closed to one hundred. Drumm's voice joined those of his men, most of them Southern, in an ear-splitting Southern cry, the kind of long, piercing, shrill shriek given in the forests and hills to signal a companion, the grandfather of the infamous Rebel Yell.

Another explosion and then another trimmed the Mexicans' ranks. The cavalry lines slammed together, sabers thrusting and slashing. Over the screams and bellows of rage and combat, Drumm was aware of the popping of rifles. Morella was taking a hammering from three sides.

Drumm parried the thrust of a swathy Mexican's saber, seeing white teeth bared beneath a black mustache. When the Mexican reared up in his saddle, his saber arced high, Drumm thrust his sword deep into the man. He slid lifeless to the ground.

It was a good feeling to Drumm, this zest of combat; it let out a lot of buried anger. The thought was jarred out of him by Peagram's shout. "Ha, Captain!" Peagram yanked back on his saber from the body of Drumm's adversary, another dark Mexican taking a wild swing at him; he had just impaled the man above the belt buckle. Peagram, ever the fastidious soldier, ran the blade between thumb and forefinger to cleanse it of blood. He shook the blood off his hands.

"You all right, sir?"

"Yeah, thanks," Drumm yelled, hastily surveying the enemy threat in midfield.

Above the arena of close combat, Ives and Doyle peered over the breeches of Betsy and Lou. They saw Drumm unhorse one opponent, only to see Peagram's saber run through a trooper whose main intent was to finish off the dragoon captain.

Drumm's charge further scattered Morella's men as the dragoons fought bravely against three-to-one odds. "Damn!" Ives cursed as he saw Harrigan Three run through by a beefy Mexican. Three didn't fall, but leaned forward, hugging his horse's neck as the animal tore back to the column.

Harrigan's brothers broke out of the cluster of Mexican fighters, dismounting one and wounding another as they rode to halt their brother's horse and help him slowly sag to the ground.

Two Mexicans stuck the spurs to their mounts, charging the two dismounted Harrigans waving their sabers in glistening circles at the prospect of two more gringo kills.

As they leaned forward to deliver the death blows, Harrigan One and Two calmly drew their .54 caliber horse pistols, and blew the attackers off their horses. Harrigan One made certain they were dead by shoving his saber into each.

Ives then saw Harrigan Two jam a Mexican saber into the ground to mark where their brother fell. As a team, the brothers Harrigan leaped back into their saddles and disappeared back into the melee of battling combatants.

Chapter Twenty-Seven

Irons and Parton, standing side by side, watched with astonishment as Drumm's brave challenge to Morella broke up into small, individual combats, while at least half of Morella's force continued its charge on their position, now three-hundred yards away.

Decisively, Irons called for Bochey and his riflemen; his quick orders were obeyed as he placed his ten rifles in two ranks.

As Morella's men broke through the dragoons, Irons steadied his front rank. "First rank!" Irons commanded, "Present arms! Fire!" The rear rank stepped forward. "Second rank! Present arms! Fire!" As the five rifles cracked in unison, the first rank was ready and Irons repeated the command.

He saw four figures melt from their saddles, dropped by the sure shooting of his first two volleys.

Irons grunted to himself in grim satisfaction; he was laying an almost perfect zone of fire. Morella's men hadn't expected this kind of reception; they withered and wavered in the face of pinpoint gunfire. As they milled indecisively, another volley killed a trooper and wounded a horse. Now another volley sang through their disorderly ranks; a pair of Mexican horsemen fell.

Morella was black with fury as he managed to keep seven or eight of his men speeding at Irons. The next volley took another man, and it seemed to Irons that the Mexican leader was immortal as he thundered straight at him, his saber swinging in a deadly circle over his head.

As he rode the American down, his saber smashed into the officer's husky neck. Irons died instantly.

Morella passed the riflemen and by twos and threes; his force gathered its equilibrium and regrouped for another foray at the small command. Yelling and spurring their horses into a mad gallop, Morella and about twenty cavalrymen rode through the now disorganized Americans.

Morella spotted Ives and his unprotected guns and with a shouted command, rode straight for Betsy and Lou.

Ives and Drumm though remote from each other, knew in an instant what was on Morella's mind. Ives's men instantly sprang to action, maneuvering Lou into position. Inch by inch, with Ives throwing his shoulder behind a wheel, they slowly brought Lou to bear on the charging Morella.

Drumm had lost two Harrigans, Smith, and Upton, but he, Peagram, Rawson, Kilmer, Newmann, and Harrigan One rode shoulder-to-shoulder screaming like banshees as they tried to divert the Morella force.

As the only one with command experience left, Parton used the time to regroup the remaining riflemen. He checked for casualties, first noting that Biltmore was down, bleeding from a bad slash across his nose and face.

Diana was in the midst of them, frantically trying to do what she could to stem the flow of Biltmore's blood. Bonnett and Bradley were dead. Parton drew his small unit together, and had them take positions as they watched Morella's desperate charge on the howitzer squad.

Parton made sure all rifles were ready to fire, and he spoke reassuringly to the men of his small command, calming them. All eyes were on the Mexicans bearing down on the unprotected guns. Ives and his crew calmly sponged out Lou, rammed powder home and fed the gun the shell destined for the charging rank.

At two hundred yards, Ives depressed Lou's barrel, touched the slow-burning match to the vent. The rest of Ives' crew—Getter, Ehler, Quinn, and Doyle—were hard at work, inching Betsy around.

A massive explosion and flash of flame erupted at Lou's breech as the tube blew up, the fire and powder and fragmented carriage flying in all directions. Smith died instantly; Jones, his jacket singed and glowing, staggered away from the scene of the explosion, blood beading and flowing against his powder-blackened chest and face. Jones walked only a few feet before falling dead.

Ives was hurled ten feet from the death and destruction. Groggily he crawled over to Ehler who had turned Betsy and readied the second gun for firing.

Morella's troops were not slowed by the explosion. They rode into the smoke and debris as Doyle fired Betsy point-blank, the round tearing at horses and men, leaving a ten-foot gap and causing Morella to swerve around him.

Again Morella rallied his force to regroup for a charge and at last destroy the undefended gun crew. Seemingly out of nowhere, Drumm and Peagram and their four remaining horsemen leaped their horses past the surprised force manning the remaining howitzer.

They charged into Morella's men, stalled while their leader screamed commands attempting to reorganize them.

For Drumm, it was a reprise of minutes before as he cut the first man he met out of the saddle. He heard Peagram roaring and cursing as he slashed and stabbed right and left, emptying two saddles. Rawson and Harrigan One were like men possessed, yelling and swinging their sabers in deadly arcs.

Drumm spurred to Kilmer's side to parry the blow a Mexican sergeant was about to deliver; he pulled his pistol and squeezed the trigger at a close target. As his horse tore past, Drumm took small note as Kilmer's assailant pitched from the saddle clutching his face.

With that brief scrap of action, the fight was over. An eerie, almost deafening silence hung shroudlike over the field of combat. Drumm stood in the stirrups alongside Peagram, harking to the only sound, that of retreating hooves as they watched Morella's totally whipped and panicked troops gallop off into the distance to be swallowed up by the Laramie Mountains.

Peagram's vague, unblinking eyes surveyed the field. "Sixteen, seventeen, eighteen, uh . . . uh, twenty-one or -two." Peagram rumped down into his saddle, his hands and arms locked as he clutched the saddle horn for support.

Drumm spoke slowly. His right arm ached from wielding the saber, and he was drained of energy. He, too, slumped in the saddle with a kind of trembling relief.

"We know he had forty-two men this morning." He glanced at the sun. "It's still morning." He knew he was mumbling; the need for command caught up with him at last. He found strong voice. "Take charge, First Sergeant. Full report at Parton's position with the riflemen!"

He trotted his horse over to the grimy, blood-soaked Ives. "What happened, Guns?"

"Lou blew up!" Ives sat down, gasping for breath. "She was too old. She took Smith and Jones with her. Damn! They were good men."

Drumm was thoughtful. "Hard Winter says a man's bravery is measured by the size of a hole he leaves when he's gone."

Ives's bloodshot eyes bore into Drumm's. "Then we got a hell of a cavity in our ranks, Andy."

Doyle stepped up. "We lost Quinn, too, sir. A piece of that flying brass cut his windpipe."

Doyle, Getter, and Ehler collapsed on the ground beside Ives. "The brass, *Herr Hauptman*," Getter said. "Too old . . . she quit . . . poof! *Ja*. Poof goes our gun!"

Drumm still clutched his saber, dangling at his side, the blade awash with blood that dripped from the tip. "It was a big price to pay," he said. "But once more, Ives, you and your guns saved us." He frowned in thought. "How's Betsy?"

"I believe she'll be r'aring to go, sir," Doyle said. Ives nodded, still trying to clear his mind of the shock of the explosion and the deaths of good comrades-in-arms.

Drumm wheeled his horse and rode to Parton and Diana among the riflemen. "Where's Captain Irons?"

Bochey pointed. "*Mon ami*, he is there." The bodies of several dead riflemen had already been gathered and arranged in respectful positions. Drumm reacted with shock as he stepped off his horse; Miller caught the reins. Drumm staggered slightly, waving off a concerned Diana. "Just a bit weary, Diana," he said.

Irons was laid out beside Bonnett and Brady. From the corner of his eye, Drumm saw someone coming with an Indian-rubber cloth to cover the three dead of the rifle corps.

A wounded Biltmore peered at him past a bandage which left only one eye uncovered. Drumm knelt. "How bad, Biltmore?"

"Miss Diana says it's only a flesh wound. I can see out of both eyes. She tells me it will leave an honorable scar." Drumm chuckled at the man's guts, despite his grief. He laid a hand on Biltmore's shoulder. "Get well soon, soldier."

Von Holder, Drumm, and Diana walked to where Parton stood, rock-firm and glowing in victory. "Irons was a good soldier," the Englishman told Drumm. "He skillfully handled the riflemen, and fell to the thrust of a Mexican trooper. He died well, if there is such a thing, Andy."

Augie spoke up. "True. Irons did a soldier's work. But I must add that Lord Parton stepped into the void left when Captain Irons fell."

Drumm cocked an eyebrow at Parton. "But Lord Parton, you are a neutral."

"I say, old boy. Never been called a neuter or a neutral when some dirty beggar is trying to claim my life." He grinned as he looped an arm over Diana's shoulder. "Or that of my sister!"

Drumm looked at the sky again. "Augie," he said, "what time of day is it?" Drumm turned, leaning on his saber, as he again surveyed the battle ground.

"Ten-thirty a.m."

"Lord," Drumm sighed. "I'm so tired, I thought we must have fought all day!"

Chapter Twenty-Eight

Three hours of back-breaking labor was needed to bury the dead of Drumm's Devils. Their only shovels were three small ones Ives used to settle his carriage wheels.

The Mexican dead that Morella was forced to abandon on the field were treated with the respect one good soldier has for another, regardless of sides. The Mexican dead were decently placed in a giant fissure in the sandstone ledges.

Ives contrived a bomb which, when exploded, loosened tons of dirt and rock to bury the bodies forever. A Mexican saber was jammed into the ground above the rock- and dirt-filled drift.

Ten sabers marked the graves of Drumm's Devils. Drumm spoke a few simple sentences as Miller lifted the clear tones of taps to signal the end of the burial ceremony. Time, Drumm knew, was still running against him. The sad task of the funerals over, he slipped immediately into a businesslike posture.

"Morella isn't finished with us. He's a tough soldier dedicated to carrying out an order. We also know that Morella stands between us and Fort Laramie." He pointed to the pine-covered range to the east. "After we eat, we'll fall into a column of twos, and march until late tonight. Mr. Von Holder tells me it is four in the afternoon of August 24, Sunday; a proper day to bury our comrades."

Drumm turned, saluted the graves and told Peagram, "Have Betsy loaded, and all the gear. Be prepared to march as soon as the troops are fed.''

He walked away from Peagram, who stood silently with his soldier's grief, watching Drumm pick his way across the plain that had held so much death and terror that day.

Diana watched as well. She mounted her horse and slowly walked him after Drumm. For a moment the entire command watched the two until Peagram, like a man coming out of a trance, roared at them.

''Come on, lads. Let the Cap'n have a few private moments. By damn, he earned it.''

Hearing approaching hoofbeats, Drumm turned to watch Diana ride to him and stop. He leaned against her horse, his dirt- and blood-stained hands resting on the pommel. Neither spoke, their eyes intent on each other. Without a word, Diana slid back off the saddle to the horse's rump, and Drumm wearily lifted himself into the saddle.

Together they rode to the wrecked carriage and tube of the gun called Lou. Diana tightened her grip around Drumm's waist as he urged the horse to the draw where Morella tried to gain an advantage during the ferocious struggle.

''I wonder . . . '' he finally said, as they turned and slowly rode back to camp. His words trailed off without finishing the statement.

''No one questioned you, did they?''

He shook his head.

''Brother said you and your men were magnificent against three to one odds.'' She squeezed him affectionately. ''Besides all that, Captain Andrew Jackson Drumm, I love you.'' Drumm tried to turn in the saddle, but found it impossible. Diana hugged him forcefully, holding on until they arrived where Parton and Blanchard stood talking. She slid off the horse while Drumm dismounted to accept a steaming cup of coffee.

As the march began, Drumm waved Bochey over to him. ''Morella is out there, my friend. Remember, one of his men killed today was an Apache. Probably a scout. Morella may have more Apaches.''

Drumm gripped Bochey's shoulder. ''Be damned careful''—he slapped the little black man on the back—''be my eyes and ears.''

Bochey grinned, eyes a-twinkle. The little fellow had guts,

Drumm mused.

"*Oui, mon ami,*" Bochey said softly. "I am, as you say, one jump ahead." He patted his scarred head. "This hair—what is left—will never hang from Apache belt!" With a jaunty wave, Bochey rode off ahead of the column to scout Morella's moves.

After a day of battle the long ride was tough on those who were well, but pure torture for the wounded. Drumm's head was full of concern as Von Holder eased up beside him.

"Newman, I understand, is from Pamlico?"

"Right," Drumm said. "A good horseman, too. That's why he's keeping watch on our rear. Morella has tested us every way he can. I've sent Doyle and Rawson to scout our left and right flanks."

Drumm regarded the scientist riding beside him with an intensity.

"But every time, we've sent Morella off yipping, tail between his legs. But he'll keep hammering as long as he has a man who can stand to saddle. It's now become an affair of honor for him. The mission to eliminate Parton and Diana is his main driving force, but now there's something more to it. We're close to whipped ourselves, but the final confrontation with Morella is still out there waiting for us."

Augie Von Holder nodded in sober agreement. He changed the subject. "I never thought I'd find myself standing to load, kneeling to fire, commanded by a member of the British House of Lords."

"At least a fine addition to your memoirs, Augie."

"Captain Irons gave a first-class account of himself."

"He was as trouble-maker, but in the end, he proved his mettle."

"Diana tried so hard to stop the flow of blood. But I had a feeling he did what he had to do; die a soldier's death. He wiped the slate clean in the end."

A sudden tic of grief twisted Drumm's face. "Yup. A good man. And a better officer."

Peagram materialized out of the mass of riders and dust. "By your leave, sir, there's a fine campground about a mile ahead. Good water, some shelter, good grass, and we can defend it if necessary."

"All right, First. I'll take the first guard with Sergeant Ehler.

You figure out the rest of the guard roster."

Bochey slipped into camp at dawn as Drumm was rolling out of his blankets. The little black man's face was pinched with fatigue and the hunger that cramped his gut. He drank his coffee, ate some fresh bread, and chewed some jerky.

"The devil Morella," Bochey said through a mouthful, "he is always in advance of you, say four to six miles."

He washed his food down with the last of the coffee and offered the mug to Blanchard for more. He gripped the full, hot cup, warming his hands against the chill of dawn.

Bochey licked his teeth with his mouth closed. "Morella will be in Sybille Canyon before we are there. Once in, there is no escape." His black eyes gleamed as the morning sun revealed the concern stamped in his eyes and firm-set jaw.

Peagram and Drumm heard Bochey out. Drumm motioned Ives to join them.

"Let Mr. Bochey rest. This afternoon, Ives, I want you to ride with him to see if you can determine where Morella will be waiting for us in those mountains." Drumm knelt, smoothing the ground.

"If Morella is at X here," he said to the others, pointing with a short stick, "is there a back door, say another way around him so Guns can set up Betsy and hit him from the rear?" Bochey's face lit up. "Maybe Mr. Bochey, we can bait the trap one more time. While our Mr. Morella prepares to charge, perhaps Mr. Ives can help him along with a goose from the rear."

Bochey grinned eagerly as Drumm signalled that the meeting was concluded. Drumm asked Peagram to stand by.

"Sir!"

"First, we are half of what we were just sixty days ago."

"Correct, sir."

"It looks like we're going to have to fight Morella again. Frankly, the men are spent—bone-weary and they need rest." Drumm surveyed his tattered command. After the hot springs, most of them had quit shaving. He grinned at the stalwart First Sergeant whose scarred visage was also crusty with dirty stubble.

"Let's camp here two days. Recruit the horses and ourselves. Everybody gets shaved, clothes washed, boots cleaned. That meet with your approval, First?"

Peagram was jubilant. "Yes, sir! Then we face the enemy rested and like a crack military outfit!" His face spread into a wonderful skin-stretched smile, his scars blending with the grin.

"All right, then. Work out your duty roster. Let the men sleep, bathe, and sew up their clothes. Just so we are ready to march on Saturday, August 29. That's two mornings from now."

Once again the men held India-rubber tarps for Diana by a deep pool as she bathed and washed her clothes. When she was finished, Drumm's Devils took over the pool, splashing and cavorting and shouting like kids out of school.

By dark they were shaved, washed, and with Blanchard's cooking, were already well on their way to storing much-needed energy for the gruelling test that lay ahead of them. The tragedies of past battles slipped into the dark recesses of Drumm's mind, and he sensed growing satisfaction and optimism for the days ahead.

He'd lose more of them, of that he was certain. There were charts and statistics for this sort of thing in the tactics books he'd studied at the Point. He grunted mentally. Command was never easy and it was doubly tough on a compassionate man. And, Captain Andrew Jackson Drumm knew, he was long on compassion where the men of his command were concerned.

At dawn the next day, Ives and Bochey slipped back to him. After a hot cup of coffee, Ives told Drumm that "Morella has only two choices open to him. If he takes what Mr. Bochey and I called Number One, then we just have to fight him on his terrain."

Ives bit his lip. "There's just no way we can slip around him unless he picks Number Two. It is a broad valley, perhaps four hundred yards wide, and it makes an S curve around this mountain." Ives sketched a map in the dirt.

"Now, if Morella goes for Number Two, we can take off around this mountain, follow this narrow valley and join the main valley about six hundred yards out of sight and below the Mexicans."

Drumm and Peagram asked questions and got answers. There were several valleys and Bochey could blaze a trail into the right one. "How will I know if you're set up and ready, Guns? I can't commit what few troops we have left unless I'm dead certain you're behind Morella."

Ives' eyes gleamed with inspiration. "Miss Diana, don't you

have a hand mirror?''

Parton's face lit up. "I say, old boy, heliograph and all that. Magnificent thinking, Ives! The chaps in India used to send messages, in the code Morse invented nine years ago. Splendid chap, Morse. Came to England and wanted to send messages by electricity. Ha! Our chaps in India used his dots and dashes with the sun and mirrors.''

Ives explained how he and Parton could communicate with the flashing mirrors. "Have to smash Diana's mirror. Supposed to be bad luck and all that—don't believe it.'' Parton personally saw to the fracturing of the tiny pocket mirror in half.

Ives counted the surviving force. "Fourteen men including Lord Parton. If I'm to load a gun and reassemble it, fire it, swab out, ram and fire again, I'll need Corporal Doyle, Getter, Sergeant Ehler, and Kilmer and Bochey. Still, that's cutting the cheese pretty thin.''

Drumm was thoughtful. "That leaves me with Peagram, Sergeant Rawson, Harrigan One, Miller, Newman, Blanchard, Killdare, Von Holder, Collier, and Miller. I'll leave Blanchard, Lord Parton, and his sister to hold our line. By God, you're right, Ives, the cheese will be sliced so thin even a blind man could see through it!''

Drumm stood up abruptly. "Well, I suppose we could sit here till hell freezes over. Eventually Morella or our force would win.''

"I say, old man,'' Parton said. "Aren't you forgetting Mr. Hard Winter and the arrival of the relief column?''

Drumm's eyes bored into Parton's. "That was a calculated risk. Davis had to ride through an area where Morella has Apache scouts. Even if Hard Winter made it past that point, a million things could happen before he found help. Lame horse, weather, any number of hostile elements. I'm hopeful, but not counting on it.''

For the benefit of the officers and men grouped around him, Drumm gestured at Lord Parton and Diana. "We've got to get them to safety, and that means one more fight.'' He looked at Peagram. "Do you think we can trick our friend Captain Morella and his Seventh Regular Mexican Regiment just one more time?''

"Yes, sir!,'' Peagram hallooed in assent. "And I personally am looking forward to it!'' Peagram emphasized his enthusiasm by nearly drowning a creeping stink bug with a squirt of tobacco juice he'd saved for just this moment.

Drumm grinned and noted that others around him were smiling too. "First Sergeant," he said in his most military tone. "When this is all over, I shall remedy your crude manners. If we get through this, remind me to have you transferred to any company I command!" Peagram punctuated his glee by again drenching the struggling stink bug.

"Yes, sir."

Chapter Twenty-Nine

Lieutenant Merry Christmas Ives, commanding the twelve-pound brass howitzer called Betsy, moved his gunnery crew into the Laramie Mountains under the convenient cover of a moonless night, led by a cautious, probing Claude Bochey.

Bochey slid ahead, fifty yards in advance of the quietly moving cannon, his knife hilt clutched in his palm, ready to evade or eternally silence any enemy sentry he might encounter. Bochey grinned into the darkness; this was the kind of work he relished. He had trained for it for years.

Behind him, Ives felt his way gently in the dark, leading the team and its ordnance-laden mules. Gunny sacks muffled the mules' hoofbeats, and the cannon gear had been tightly lashed to the packsaddles to avoid any giveaway squeaks or clatter.

Ives could feel the half-mirror buttoned safely inside his shirt. It seemed like hours before Bochey took form out of the dark ahead of him and moved in close to press his mouth to Ives' ear.

"This is the place, *mon ami*," the husky whisper told Ives.

It took all the men to hoist Betsy's barrel off the tired mule. Little by little, and with the least possible noise, Ives assembled and positioned Betsy.

If Morella made a charge at Drumm's column, Betsy would be within a three-hundred yard range of Morella's rear. "Ought to be able to punch Morella with five, maybe seven, good tastes of grape," he mused to himself in the dark as he polished off last-minute details.

Ives hummed to himself as he worked. His only doubt was Betsy herself; would she hold up or blow up as Lou had? He and Doyle and Getter had checked Betsy over, inch-by-inch. They found lines of metal fatigue around the breech, but the vent hole looked fine.

Ives had seen these barely imperceptible stress-marks on cannons before, and had seen ordnance engineers go ahead and qualify them for service. Many had withstood months of intense combat; he also knew of other apparently battle-worthy cannon tubes that had ruptured with devastating results for crewmen in their very first ordeal of combat.

By dawn Ives was in position. He hissed a "stay alert" command to the crew and began the arduous crawl up the backside of the sharp incline of the granite mountain. His mirror lay in his lap as his eyes searched through the gray half-light at the knifelike mountain Bochey had climbed. He detected a faint movement as he swept the mountain with Von Holder's telescope; it was Bochey.

Bochey's sharp eyes had spotted Ives and he waved to let Ives know he could see the valley Drumm would march through, and the branch off the main course where Morella and his troopers waited under cover of rocky ravines and abundant trees.

Finally the sun hung bright enough in a crisp morning sky for Ives to signal Parton that everything was in place. Parton's response, "Success, by jove," sent a thrill rippling though Ives's frame. Ives grinned as he carefully made his way down the mountain, recalling Parton's joviality in anticipation of this final brush with Morella.

Betsy was well hidden in a willow thicket; it afforded room for the crew to perform its work while still remaining reasonably shielded from stray gunfire. Horses and mules were picketed securely at the rear.

In full daylight, Ives now could see the promise of his position. "All we do now is wait for Morella to come pouring out that draw," he told the crewmen. "When he comes wheeling out to the valley floor, Betsy is going to say hello to El Capitano Francisco Morella late of the Seventh Regular Mexican Cavalry." He leaned down to kiss Betsy's breech for luck.

Farrier Sergeant Ehler witnessed the affectionate display. "By your permission, sir, I always did think gunners were a queer bunch. Now I stand convinced, especially when I see you kiss a howitzer. My suspicion is right.''

None of the others responded to Ehler's attempt at humor. Each man was caught up in his own private thoughts; would the gun hold up? Would Morella turn and charge the gun, hoping to knock it out, as he'd done before? Then Drumm's pitiful command would be fair game.

Doyle whispered to Ehler, "It's times like these I wish I was a coward. I'm tired of bein' a hero, ain't you, Ehler?''

Ehler was jumpy, and this made him cranky. "Why don't you shut up, Doyle, and help me load these rifles.'' Ehler and Kilmer were loading a half-dozen of the percussion rifles Drumm had told them to take along.

"You never know,'' Drumm had cautioned Ives. "Could be they'll come in handy.''

Now that Ives had communicated with Parton, Bochey eased downslope to a point about two hundred yards from Morella's soldiers. His keen vision poked into every nook and cranny, seeking any place a sentry might be hidden. If he could knock out some of Morella's "eyes,'' it might give Drumm the advantage of surprise.

Bochey's reward wasn't long in coming. "There!'' he hissed under his breath. The sentinel sat on a table rock, his horse cached fifty yards behind him. Bochey's gaze expertly probed the mouth of the canyon. Again his sharp eyes spied a second sentry. He estimated the man to be two hundred yards away, his back against a square block of granite as large as a house.

For long minute, Bochey studied the scene before him, gauging his moves. He figured the nearest sentry was to pass the word to the other of any enemy movement in the valley. Easing up, Bochey went into a crouch and a gentle glide around and through cover to the sentry's horse. He quickly sliced the reins close to the bit and slapped the animal's rump. He dropped to the ground, knife in hand.

The horse's getaway alerted the sentry, who dropped off his rock and sprinted toward Bochey's position. *"Ho! Caballo! Ho, caballo!"* the man shouted.

Suddenly the sentry halted, seeing the sliced reins dangling from the limb where he had secured his horse. In the instant he had brought his cavalry musketoon to the ready, Bochey was on him, cat-quick, sinking the fourteen-inch blade into the man's chest.

Bochey caught the man as he fell, making certain he was dead. He substituted his hat for the black, flat-crowned Mexican hat, slung the white crossed saber belt over his shoulder and ran to occupy the dead man's sentry post. He studied the guard opposite him for a time but saw nothing to alarm him.

"*Mon ami*, Bochey," he breathed to himself. "This horse run to join his brothers. I must do this *rapidement*." Carefully he stoked his mountain rifle, measuring the powder, seating the patched ball, and securing the reddish copper cap on the percussion tube. He lay flat, drawing a keen bead on the enemy, just then in the act of yawning.

Bochey's rifle spoke, its belch of muzzle blast caroming along the ravine walls. His intended victim spun backward, the second Mexican soldier of the day to fall victim to Claude Bochey's prowess at stalking and killing his prey.

Agile as a cat, Bochey leaped from the rock, grabbed his hat and ran like the devil was at his heels. He knew the riderless horse and the rifle fire would draw a scouting party. He didn't want to give away Ives's position, so he crawled into a fissure between two rocks, and hid out as a party of six troopers, mounted and alert, sabers at the ready, scoured the mouth of the box canyon, finding only their two dead companions.

They were furious as they rode back and forth, their saber blades reflecting the sun which by now had moved even higher into a cloudless August morning.

Ives had heard the shot. "Old Claude is having him some fun," he allowed.

"Hope he don't draw no soldiers here," Ehler observed. "Not Bochey," Ives said. "Too slick for that. He scouted a sentry post, would be my bet. I'm thinking he bagged one, at least. Maybe two."

Ehler grinned. "That's a relief."

"Bochey's only drawing them out so we can take them on about the time Captain Drumm is in position. Prepare to fire on my command."

Drumm's party had climbed the low profile of Sybille's Pass and were on the forward slope when the winking glitter of Ives's mirror held them, almost in a trance, as they waited for Lord Parton to receive the message.

"Proceed." Parton whooped jubilantly. "All is right on schedule." He pronounced the last word as "shed-jual," amusing Drumm. "What's he mean, sir?" Peagram asked.

"Betsy is in position," Drumm interpreted. "Bochey is out scouting. Morella is just where we hoped he would be." Drumm drew a fine draft of crisp, clean air into his lungs and sighed it out. "And if he turned the wrong way, Betsy will tell him so!"

Drumm held up a hand. "Augie, you and your men do not, I repeat, do not have to ride with us today. No one expects you to volunteer for what may well be suicide action."

In response, and to a man, Von Holder, Blanchard, and Collier kneed their horses forward and into line. They each had strapped holstered percussion pistols onto their saddles. Each gripped a dragoon saber.

"We've talked it over," Von Holder said. "Blanchard and Collier and I. If you will allow us to join you, Captain Drumm, it would be our honor." Augie Von Holder sat straight in his saddle. Drumm's lips were set in a grim line as he studied the middle-aged scientist, his hat rakishly slanted across his forehead, his hands resting easily on the pommel. Drumm's eyes took in Blanchard, whose big frame was no longer a product of fancy eating. He was almost slim. "Well, Blanchard," Drumm said, "I hate to use a fine cook in any fighting cause, no matter how honorable."

Blanchard responded by expertly whirling his saber over his head, made several lunges and slashes with it, and deftly dropped it with a slithering clang into its metal scabbard.

"Once, a long time ago," Blanchard said, "I went to Paris to study cooking and baking. Because I was an American, a large one at that, I was much abused as being stupid and clumsy. So I took lessons in sword play. I'll take my chances with you, Cap'n."

Blanchard sat his saddle proudly. He looked, all six foot, six inches of him, a soldier.

"Your accomplishments . . . ahem . . . continue to amaze me, Mr. Blanchard."

"But you, Collier. You're a mineralogist, not a soldier."

"Ever sinoe I got jabbed in the buttocks by Morella's men when we were panning gold, I've sought revenge, Captain," Collier said. His black eyes snapped. "Don't deny me that revenge."

"I sha'n't," Drumm responded.

Drumm eased his horse over to speaking distance of Biltmore, whose face was still a giant scab across his forehead and the bridge of his nose and left cheek. Biltmore's blue eyes held Drumm's in a grim stare.

"You looking for revenge too, Biltmore?"

"No, sir. A man does what he has to do when his honor is at stake. I'm not one to stand by and let someone else risk his life to save my bacon. I'm no master at fencing like Blanchard. But I'm considered pretty good with dueling pieces. These pistols here aren't what I'm best at, but I'd venture to say I'm better than anyone here."

Drumm shook his head. "All right. You all are now graduates from Von Holder's Bug Catchers to Drumm's Devils." He rose in the stirrups. "Lord Parton, sir. You know the drill!"

"Daresay I do, old boy," Parton whooped back. "Once the action is joined, our Monsieur Bochey will seek out Sis and me, and we'll ride for cover, just in case Morella breaks through. Am I correct, sir?"

"Correct."

"But damn it, man, I can swing a saber with the best of them." Parton raised up in his saddle, but quickly slumped down as pain wrenched his injured shoulder, and he recognized his incapacity to fight.

Drumm ached for him. An old soldier dislikes nothing more than to be left out when the clash and crunch of battle resounds all around him.

Diana rode to support her brother. "It isn't right," she said, "All these men fighting and being hurt for Hardy and me." Her brother threw his good arm around her shoulder to console her.

"I don't care," she said. "It just isn't fair."

Von Holder broke the silence that followed.

"It isn't a case of fair or not fair, Lady Diana. Every one of us volunteered for this duty." He looked at Drumm. "Do we pass muster, Captain Drumm?"

Drumm inspected his ragged, tiny command; if guts had any bearing in a battle, they'd win the day, he mused.

Witnout a word, he tossed them a crisp, soldierly salute, straight out of his training at West Point.

Chapter Thirty

Swelled from seven soldiers to eleven with the addition of the four scientists, Drumm's Devils descended the little freshet called the Sybille as it began its wide turns in the valleys ahead. Growing larger as it was joined by springs until three miles into the Laramie Mountains, the Sybille became a pretty mountain stream.

These mountains rose rapidly along each side of the Sybille. As the creek rushed along, it passed through a broad pleasant valley. Many of the ridges exposed rock strata that stretched like a granite backbone from the crown of the hill to the valley floor. The beautiful valley was populated with ponderosa pine, juniper, willow, and aspen.

Drumm brought his command to a halt where the broad bottomland appeared. Miller rode up. "All clear ahead, Cap'n."

The sound of a single distant shot poked a hole in the silence around them. Drumm strained to hear more; only the soft breeze, toying with evergreen needles, filled the air.

"All right, Miller. Newman!"

"Sir!"

"You and Miller take the lead. Be alert, men. Be alert!"

Both men jogged their horses into the valley, closing the gap to the next turn, and were quickly hidden from sight.

As they did, Morella made his play. His troops streamed in single file out of a box canyon six hundred yards from where Miller and Newman had disappeared; they wheeled into two columns of twelve men each with Morella at their head.

Miller waited no longer. The silver notes of his familiar warning call, "To Arms, To Arms!" echoed and re-echoed down the valley.

Drumm ordered, "Walk." His pitifully thin ranks eased their horses out into the sun-drenched valley to join Miller and Newman.

"Bugler!" Drumm called.

"Sir?"

"Blow me a tune!"

"Trot, Bugler. Blow me that tune!" Miller tilted his bugle and blew Drumm's order as the men, side by side, stared at the distant enemy.

Drumm's eyes narrowed as he realized that Morella still outnumbered him at least two to one. He felt hot under the collar, pulling his hat brim down for relief from the stern morning sun.

"A fine mornin', sir!" Drumm looked to his left at Peagram, big as life, his teeth showing a chacteristic spunk beneath his orange-colored walrus mustache.

Drumm felt better. He grinned at Peagram and shouted, "Bugler!"

"Sir!"

"Gallop, Miller. Play me that tune!" With Miller's notes again resounding through the canyons, the rollicking sounds of the gallop picked up the cadence. Somewhere, down the valley, a huge explosion blossomed in Morella's ranks and two or three horses fell like stalks of grain before a keen scythe. Clearly, Drumm thought, nothing would stop Morella. His force galloped too, heedless of the death and destruction that lay ahead.

Another round from Betsy splayed one side of Morella's two charging lines. Miraculously, only one horse fell, the rider alive and running for one of the dazed horses whose rider had fallen with the first round. Bochey, holed up in the rocks, was too far for a shot at Morella, but his big-bore rifle bowled over the running soldier. Reloading as he ran to his horse, Bochey knew he had to find Parton and his sister.

Ives's men worked like slaves, the sweat pouring off them as they fired Betsy a third time. "Hellfire and damnation," Ives cursed as they worked furiously to ready Betsy for a fourth round.

Morella peeled six men from his main charge and directed them with a wave of saber point at the howitzer emplacement. They rode bent over their saddles, lazily swinging their sabers as Ives made the choice of aiming for Morella rather than depressing the tube for the close-in round at the six charging Mexicans. Betsy belched her explosive contempt for Morella's force.

"Good for you!," Ehler sang jubilantly as they watched their fourth round knock two more of Morella's men from the saddle.

"Quickly," Ives yelled as they scurried to reload Betsy for a point-blank round. The charging horsemen were closer than a hundred yards as Ives touched his smoking match to the vent. Cutting the fuse to explode that close was dangerous, but Ives taught his crew what to expect. They came up with the loaded rifles for close-in combat.

"If they ride past us," Ives called frantically, "wait until they turn. Then nail them. It's our only hope!"

As Betsy spoke, the Mexicans veered so only two riders took the devastating explosion. Those two were simply blown away. Where they had been was a mound of smoking and squirming horse and human flesh.

The four survivors, still leaning foward, rode directly at Ives. They thrust their heavy sabers at the gunners, one slicing the rammer staff in two as Ives tried to joust with the Mexican with his great rod of rammer and sponge.

Then they were past, and the four wheeled to gallop back to complete their assignment. Kilmer and Getter had been badly slashed as the horsemen thundered past. Ehler ripped off his shirt, and wound it around Kilmer's badly cut arm. Getter received a fatal saber thrust into his neck and died almost instantly.

Ives and Doyle crouched amid the smoke and dust beside Betsy, rifle stocks kissing their cheeks, waiting for the horsemen to pull up and turn in preparation for another charge at Betsy's crew.

Ives called to Ehler, "Keep loading the rifles fast as you can." The rider he was following over his sights turned, presenting his chest for a broad target. Ives squeezed the trigger and watched the man, arms flailing as he dropped the reins, slide sidewise off his galloping horse to thump brutally into the dirt.

Doyle's shot took its target as well, but the man remained in the saddle to join the two remaining.

The three came at them unchecked, only one sagging slightly in the saddle. Ives and Doyle were handed two loaded rifles. At 50 yards, Ives scored again, but Doyle's gun misfired. He stood, trying to parry the sword thrust with the rifle's long barrel. The odds were against him as the Mexican rode him down and thrust his saber deep into Doyle's gut.

Ives thumbed back the hammer of the fresh rifle handed him and, leaning against Betsy's breech, took a quick sight and slammed Doyle's killer with a round at no more than a few feet.

The man swayed, grabbed at the saddle horn but missed, and leaned to his right; his boot caught in the stirrup as he fell and his hysterical horse bolted, dragging and bumping the dead man over the rough ground and out of sight.

Ehler pointed. "Got all of 'em, Lieutenant!" Doyle's wounded man slowly got off his horse. He started toward Betsy, brandishing his saber, his eyes red and determined. Blood stained and the front of his tunic.

The man staggered, took a few groggy steps, dropped his saber and crumpled, forty yards from Betsy's position.

Ives spoke softly to Ehler. "Get the horses. We've got to help Captain Drumm." Naked to waist, his body glistening with sweat and the ebony mottling of burned powder, Ehler ran down the canyon and appeared with three horses.

Ives leaped into the saddle, gripping a bloodstained Mexican saber. "At the gallop!"

Chapter Thirty-One

His own force at the gallop now, Drumm saw two more rounds deplete Morella's troop. As he rode, he watched several Mexicans swerve out of line, turn, and ride to the rear.

"After Ives," Peagram yelled. Drumm agreed, but nothing would stop their momentum now as they faced the Mexicans at two hundred yards and closing fast. Drumm yelled at Miller. "Sound the Charge!" Miller produced the quick staccato cavalry command. Drumm's force now stood in the stirrups, leaning forward, each saber held at the attack while Von Holder and Collier brandished pistols.

The distance continued to close, but slowly, Drumm felt as he counted nearly even odds. He felt a warm glow for Ives, who was responsible in several ways for evening the odds this August morning. Or was it September? Drumm wished he could remember as the lines merged, slashing and twisting with the distinct bang! bang! of Auggie's and Collier's pistols.

Drumm was aware of at least one Mexican lurching from the saddle with a direct hit from a pistol ball.

Then he was past Morella's ranks. Reeling his horse around, he brought his saber, whack!, deep into the exposed dark neck of a foe who fell abruptly from the saddle. Out the tail of his eye, he was aware of Bugler Miller struggling on the ground as an enormous adversary drew back to thrust his saber into the boy. Von Holder rode close and shot the startled Mexican in the face.

Harrigan One finished him off as Von Holder guarded Miller until he could retrieve his sword and horse.

All around him, Drumm was aware of the clash of battle, the curses of men mad with fury and pain, squealing horses, and the rasp and ring of sharp steel sabers. The choking dust rose all around them. The hot, dry August air captured the dust and held it over the milling, yelling crowd.

To Drumm's left, a sudden surge of motion caused him to duck involuntarily as a wiry Mexican engaged him in sword play. The man was good, Drumm thought, as the grimacing soldier parried Drumm's thrust and slapped Drumm a deep slash on his left arm. The Mexican quickly gained the advantage again and, leaning inside Drumm's guard, thrust his saber into Drumm's left side. As the man reared back for better leverage, Drumm, nearly out of the fight, mustered the strength to slam his saber to the hilt in the center of the crossed white belts over the breast of the Mexican's tunic. As the man fell, Drumm's gory saber slid out of the fatal wound and blood pumped out to turn the snowy belts crimson.

Through a break in the dust, Drumm saw Morella and one of his men turn their horses, gesturing with their sabers at Parton and Diana back on the crest overlooking the valley.

His mouth baked dry with dust and heat, Drumm's voice came out as only a weak croak as he tried to yell for help: he rammed spurs to his horse to take out after the charging Morella and his trooper.

At an angle to Drumm's left, he saw the diminutive Bochey emerge out of the dust in an attempt to distract the charging Morella. Drumm stared helplessly from rushing horseback as the two sabered Bochey off his horse. The little black man's courageous act gave Drumm valuable time as his horse labored up the valley.

Morella was not aware of Drumm quickly closing the gap between them, his horse leaning into the wind at the urging of its rider. Drumm saw Parton accept a rifle from Diana. The valiant Englishman leaned against a horse, propped the rifle on the horse's neck, aimed, and fired to kill Morella's companion.

Then, as Parton turned to take another rifle from Diana, Morella charged around the horse and, bending low from the saddle, delivered a vicious cut at Parton with his gleaming saber.

Parton quickly ducked under the picket line, taking Diana with him. Morella drew up, and rode slowly down the picket line cutting each horse or mule free and in doing so, narrowing Parton and Diana's chance to escape.

When Morella reached the end, he looked at the defenseless Parton and Diana, and stepped stiffly from his horse, his heavy curved saber pointed menacingly.

Morella appeared oblivious to everything but the completion of his mission to kill the two before him. Drumm wheeled up, swaying in the saddle from two serious saber wounds, the loss of blood already turning him feeble and trembling.

Still he drove his horse at Morella, knocking the Mexican officer to all fours while he slid from his horse and stood spread-legged to keep his balance.

Drumm croaked against the dryness and weakness in his throat. "Me, Morella. Me!"

"Aha!," Morella shrieked, turning to confront Drumm. "The gallant *capitano*." His black eyes measured Drumm who was fighting his own body, trying to keep his defensive stance; slowly Drumm sank to his knees, his saber jammed into the ground helping to hold his torso erect.

"*Si, si,*" Morella growled. "The Second Dragoon *capitano*. Now! Die!"

Morella raised the curved saber with both hands, ready to bring it slamming down into the hated gringo.

As he started the downward arc, Diana charged him from behind, flinging one arm around his thick neck, her free hand scratching at his face and eyes. Her eyes were furious, her face blanched in outrage.

"Not if I get you first, you Mexican swine!" she shrieked.

As the beleaugered Mexican tried to shake the wildcat off his back, Drumm fought to get to his feet, but he was too weak and could only watch helplessly as Morella peeled Diana from his neck and back, hurling her away.

Turning, Morella found Parton trying to level the rifle, and he parried the barrel, spitting out his words. "No, *Englez*. First the *capitano* and then you and your sister." Parton fell heavily on his bound left arm, while Diana crawled to his side. The rifle fell

176

harmlessly away.

Satisfied he had the situation in hand, Morella waved the saber at the vulnerable Drumm, scribing with the tip an imaginary rectangle where he would deliver the fatal thrust.

Drumm pushed off with his saber, falling to one side as Morella made his killing thrust. Drumm rolled several times to come to rest against the body of a dead horse.

"Now, *gringo*, die!" Morella had become a madman as he leaned into his death-dealing saber arc to bring it crashing down on Drumm.

An arrow appeared to grow under Morella's jaw, severing an artery. Blood spurted in a crimson fountain around the quivering shaft, which had nearly penetrated his neck. The Mexican died instantly.

Drumm wedged himself painfully into a sitting position, watching in amazement as Morella crumpled. The whiskery visage of Hard Winter Davis appeared like a wraith over him. Drumm noted only two things about Davis; the long Hawken rifle he clutched in his right hand and the grin that was spreading over his face like soft butter.

Drumm reached out a hand to Davis and slid deep into a swirling vortex filled with the sounds of cannon fire, the ringing clang of saber against saber, and the sight of Diana.

Drumm came to as hot coffee was forced into his mouth. He sat up, wincing from the wounds in his side and arm. He slowly opened his eyes to a busy camp.

Blanchard, wielding thread and needle was stitching up Harrigan One's nearly severed ear. He turned to see Peagram beside him, a snowy white bandage circling his head creating a stark contrast against the grime and drying blood of his face. The First Sergeant nudged Drumm. "Drink?"

Drumm accepted with his good right hand the mug of hot coffee well laced with something stronger than sugar. He coughed as the drink hit bottom and started back up. He winced it down again.

"Hurt much, sir?" Peagram's face looked lopsided; it had to be a big chew of tobacco.

"Like sin," Drumm grunted, feeling his body filled with puckering pain that throbbed around the edges. "Blanchard sew me up too?"

Peagram nodded. "While you was off visitin' with the angels. Just like a jolly seamstress, he is, sir. By god! The man's a wonder. Cook, swordsman, doctor. It's a wonder some female ain't marched him down the aisle and lived the life of ease with a man like him to look after 'er.''

Augie Von Holder clumped up, flanked by Hard Winter and a man dressed in a strange outfit. Drumm blinked in disbelief. "Can it be?" he grunted, taking another look. Memory swirled back; Long Lance, the Cheyenne war chief he had dueled with for Hard Winter's life. He struggled up, remembering vividly the arrow piercing Morella's neck.

"Then it was you, Long Lance . . . the arrow?" Drumm struggled to his feet, supported by Peagram.

Long Lance, his face still carrying black, red, and yellow bars of war paint, cocked his head at Davis who translated Drumm's question.

The Indian grinned in understanding and thumped his chest in pride. He tilted his head back to yelp a victory chant. *"Ehiyeo Ehiyeo . . . Yu he!"*

Long Lance began a ritual dance around Drumm. He snatched out his huge scalping knife and drew the keen edge along his thumb, blood welling behind the bite of the blade.

Peagram started to protect Drumm, but Davis waved him away. Long Lance grabbed Drumm's right arm rudely and peeled back the bandage covering the saber slash. He pricked the raw sutured line. When blood appeared along the thread, he stuck his bleeding thumb to the wound.

The tall Indian looked into Drumm's eyes, speaking as Davis translated.

"You gave me my life four winters past. Today I gave you back yours." Long Lance held up Drumm's bleeding arm and his own bloody thumb. "We are now blood brothers, and all Cheyenne shall know you as War Drumm!"

Caught up now in the ceremony, Drumm spied his sheathed saber leaning against a bedroll. He snatched it up, and drawing the gory blade with a rasp and clang, he held out his belt, scabbard and blade to the Indian.

"In all ways we are brothers," he proclaimed. "Accept my weapon fit for a war chief of the Cheyenne. From this day forward, let all know your new name, Long Knife, as my brother."

It was a good speech, and the Cheyenne chief's pleasure was evident in the beam of pride that spread across his dark, painted face. He punched Drumm affectionately in the chest. Long Knife turned and, agile as a squirrel, leaped to his barebacked Indian pony to ride off with some of his warriors.

Hard Winter Davis's face knotted in glee. "They showed up in the nick of time, Andy. I never got to Laramie. They heard they was army in the neighborhood and was coming in to scout you. When I told him it was you, they wa'n't no way but Long Lance was goin' back with me join in the fracas. And then you went and made him the proudest Indian in these parts today. Damn, I'm so tickled I'm goin' to have to stay up nights to laugh!"

"Where'd he go? He sure left in a hurry."

"He sent his boys out chasin' Meskins. When they get tired and have lifted a few of them chili-pepper scalps, they'll be back by 'n by. I suspect that's where Long Knife went too. Wantin' to see if that saber is all it's s'posed to be. They know that long knife's got a heap of medicine; ownin' one's goin' to make Long Knife the next thing to a Cheyenne king."

Drumm eased down and tried to make himself comfortable against a bedroll. He had assured himself of Diana's well-being and saw Blanchard inspect Parton's reinjured shoulder. He called Peagram to his side.

"What's the butcher's bill, First?"

Peagram tongued his chew farther back in his cheek and accepted a soiled paper from Von Holder.

"Sir!" he croaked, his throat still dry from the dust-choked battlefield. He took a sip of his whiskey-laced coffee. "Fit for duty is Lieutenant Ives, Farrier Sergeant Ehler, Mr. Blanchard, Mr. Von Holder, and Bugler Miller." He took another sip.

"The wounded?"

"Besides the Cap'n—yourself, sir—and me, there's Kilmer, Harrigan One, Newman, Mr. Biltmore, and Mr. Bochey."

"And . . . ?"

" 'Tis a sad duty, sir, to report the loss of Farrier Sergeant Rawson, Co'pral Doyle, Private Getter, and Mr. Killdare. They was all good dragoons, sir!"

"Carry on, First. Organize a burial party for a morning service. We head for Fort Laramie immediately thereafter." He stood again, Peagram helping him. "We are quit of this place. Drumm's Devils march for home tomorrow."

Drumm mustered the strength to stroll with Von Holder to a huge flat rock overlooking the valley entrance to Sybille Canyon. They watched as Ives and his crew returned with Betsy.

"There ought to be a national monument wherever Ives set up Betsy and Lou," Drumm said, chewing on the sweet, juicy pulp of a grass stem.

"I agree, Andy. Ives saved our bacon all through this rather uncommon campaign."

"That's right, Augie. And won't a court-martial board make mincemeat of me. Told to lead a civilian reconnaissance probe into Mexico with specific orders for no fighting" He leaned back and chuckled. "I fought all right. Seems like every inch of the way. Let's see. First at the crossing of the Green. Number two near the Yampa, and three at the gold strike." He counted on his fingers. "Four at the hot springs, five was the Rock Creek battle, and today was number six."

Von Holder thoughtfully fired a cheroot as Drumm continued.

Just six lines on a page of history, Augie. Six skirmishes. I lost five of your nine men, and I lost twelve dragoons. I'm left with sixteen out of thirty-two if you count Bochey, Ives, Parton, and Diana."

Von Holder spoke slowly. "We're lucky to be alive, Andy. A tribute to your leadership. You really never once lost sight of your mission." He flicked a long ash off his cigar. "No one is going to be court-martialled. More likely the President will want to visit with you, and later on you'll meet the impulsive Secretary of State and the Secretary of War."

Chapter Thirty-Two

It was an elegant coach drawn by four fine grays that drew up before the palatial mansion of James Buchanan, Secretary of State. Inside, Drumm, Ives, and Peagram nearly sparkled as their crisp uniforms proclaimed the arm of the military they served.

Drumm and Peagram's piping on cuff and blouse was the orange of the dragoons. Ives's uniform carried the scarlet piping of the artillery. Dr. August Von Holder, resplendent in a new mouse-colored suit of tailormade clothes and a tall beaver hat to match, was the fourth man in the coach.

"You are the guests of honor," Von Holder proclaimed. "And Lord Parton insisted a certain First Sergeant Enoch Peagram was to be invited along with Drumm and Ives."

Peagram blushed. "Augie, I ain't never been to one of these two-fork and three-knife affairs. I'm more at home in the enlisted man's mess. I'll just embarrass you."

Von Holder leaned forward tapping the big soldier's thigh with the stiff brim of his top-hat. "Stick by me, First. Stick by me. Your own character will soon take care of the social graces and your cherished fears." He flipped his cigar out the window.

"Well, gentlemen," Augie said grandly. "We have arrived." He stepped out, followed by Peagram Ives followed them, leaning briefly on the coach door to survey the magnificence of the Secretary's portico.

"Huh," he grunted. "I'm like Peagram. I'd rather face Morella than the sit-down dinner in there.'' He jerked a thumb at the stately Buchanan mansion.

"This is the place where careers are made, Guns,'' Drumm said, gritting his teeth in momentary pain. "In drawing rooms with bright people. Not on the fields of battle whose aftermaths are always judged by pukes the likes of Captain Willfred Goggle.''

His wounds had pained him greatly on the trip East; by the time he reached Washington was running a fever. Ives and Von Holder could clearly see the perspiration above his straight black eyebrows.

"You all right, Andy?'' Von Holder asked as Drumm swiped at his forehead with his crisp, white dress gloves.

Drumm stepped out. "Don't worry, Augie. If they can stand me, I can stand them.''

But Drumm was still nursing emotional wounds over the treatment he and Ives had been given at the end of the patrol at Jefferson Barracks in St. Louis.

He caught Von Holder's eye and quipped, "You're sure the erstwhile Captain Goggle isn't being honored in there, too, Augie?''

Peagram spoke up. "Cap'n, sir, don't get me started on that again. It's all behind us now.''

That's right, Drumm thought. Good old Peagram saved Ives and me from a nightmare of indignities. He remembered the day they all parted company . . .

When the patrol reached Jefferson Barracks, Augie took the daily log book with him, even his own orders and warrant as a dragoon captain.

"I'm going to hightail it to Washington, Andy. I'll do up a report for Buchanan and Marcy. I'm going to see to it that they really understand and truly appreciate what went on out there.'' With that, Von Holder took his surviving Bug Catchers, requisitioned an express coach and debarked from St. Louis the very day he arrived.

Parton and Diana lingered a day, and then a military escort whisked them to the British Embassy in Washington. Drumm hardly had a chance to catch a grip of Diana's hand, let alone hear her whisper, "I love you, Andy.''

Then she was gone. Drumm's only consolation was that he'd

see her in Washington soon.

But it wasn't to work out quite that way. The few dragoons left behind were swept up in the draft of soldiers heading for Fort Jesup near New Orleans. It seemed, some Jefferson barracks soldiers said there might be a war with Mexico on the horizon.

Suddenly it was just two dirty men in tattered clothing claiming to be Captain Drumm of the Second Dragoons and a Lieutenant Ives of the artillery.

The officious Captain Willfred Goggle, Quartermaster Commandant at Jefferson knew bad actors when he saw them. He told his aide, Corporal Jeremy Millet, that the unseemly pair were not only impostors but thieves as well.

He had sent the Officer of the Day with two sentries to the quarters occupied by Drumm and Ives. Under house arrest, they were brought to Goggle's office and interrogated.

Goggle demanded to know the disposition of two twelve-pound howitzers charged out to Drumm, and where were assorted grape, powder, and the mules used to haul the guns? Ives explained, but Goggle was unimpressed. "Pure fantasy, soldier. Pure fantasy."

He also called Drumm to account for percussion pistols, rifles, sabers, saddles, wagons, and horses. He had the damning sheaf of consignment sheets before him.

"Colonel Kearny gave us a list of everything he left with you at South Pass," Goggle said accusingly. His round spectacles slipped down the bridge of his nose and he repeatedly punched them back in place. Behind the glasses, his milky blue eyes measured Drumm and Ives with contempt.

Goggle was a bureaucrat, a desk soldier. He even made certain the creases in his trousers were knife-sharp when he crossed one leg over the other as he sat at his desk.

"Come, come Captain Drumm. All we have is twenty horses, no mules, and one badly used howitzer. Where is the rest of the material on this list?"

Drumm's arm was swollen and ached like a sore tooth; he was woefully lacking in stamina and spirit as he tried to explain the patrol to Goggle. Goggle filled a pipe and used innumerable matches to keep it going, repeatedly tamping the ash with a blackened and callused thumb-tip. Even that grated on Drumm's nerves. He could see from Goggle's expression that he thought Drumm's report was fantasy, too.

"Oh, hell. The report, the full report, will be out in a matter of days. My lieutenant and I haven't even had a chance to shave and bathe and find fresh clothing." He touched his arm. "I need to see a doctor. My wounds are not in the best of . . ."

"No doctor until you confess. You and your cohort are under arrest. Willful disregard for military property. I'll furnish you with ink and paper. When I see your report, then you'll see a doctor."

He had Drumm and Ives thrown into separate cells. In Drumm's cell a table, chair, and paper and ink were provided. Straw-filled sacks served as a bed, and each had a bucket of water.

Ten days later in Washington, Parton called on Buchanan and related the remarkable odyssey he and his sister had survived. If the Secretary of State were to have a small sit-down party, Parton suggested, he would very much like to impart good news for the United States. He added that he would make his official report only if Captain Drumm, Lieutenant Ives, and First Sergeant Peagram were the guests of honor.

Once Parton left, Buchanan sent a note to Secretary of War William Marcy. He was elated and congratulated Marcy, suggesting he round up the three soldiers for a proper Washington recognition.

Inside the hour, Marcy found Dr. August Von Holder deep within the rabbit warren offices of the War Department where he was drawing up the full report of Drumm's reconnaissance patrol. After conferring with Marcy for twenty minutes, Von Holder sought out First Sergeant Peagram. Neither had heard a word of just what had happened to Drumm and Ives.

Together they reported to Marcy who personally penned a "To Whom It May Concern" memo and by four p.m. Peagram was booting a good horse to St. Louis. He rode as far as he could, exchanging horse after horse at taverns, livery stables, stage stops, or wherever he could wheedle a fresh mount.

He slept in haystacks, farmhouses, and stage stops. Finally, after riding 150 miles a day, he arrived at Jefferson Barracks.

Peagram's old-soldier savvy told him something was amiss. "If I didn't see Cap'n Drumm and Mr. Ives on the trail, then somethin's gosh-awful wrong."

As he entered the post, one with which he was entirely familiar, he headed for the permanent Sergeant Major of the post. After greeting his old friend Sergeant Brian O'Malley, Peagram inquired after Drumm and Ives.

O'Malley spewed out the whole sordid affair. "Goggle's got 'em dead to rights, or so he thinks. Ain't no way they can get away with losin' all that gear, Enoch." O'Malley smiled a huge, ruddy smile, his green eyes never leaving Peagram's face. "Tell me, Enoch, old sock. This patrol story is like Goggle says, a fantasy, eh?"

When Peagram finished outlining the patrol and showed O'Malley his "To Whom It May Concern" document, the big Irishman laughed until tears coursed down his leathery jowls. "'Twould do me heart good, Enoch, to visit Captain Goggle with you. But, my presence would tip that puke off. I been waiting a long time to see our dear Captain Goggle crawl."

By noon, Peagram was shaved, his uniform dusted and pressed. ue marched up the steps of Goggle's office and went in with as much stiff military bearing as he could muster. Ramrod-straight, he strode to a clerk wearing corporal stripes.

"Co'pral," Peagram said. "I carry orders to release Captain Drumm and Lieutenant Ives."

The bespectacled clerk peered at Peagram out of a pinched face with a snotty, superior look. He lazily reached out. "Let's have a look at those orders, soldier."

As a First Sergeant, Peagram had little use for rear-echelon clerks, and this one suddenly bobbed to the top of his list. The pipsqueak's use of the word "soldier" he considered the worst kind of insult to the uniform and the rank he had earned.

He leaned down, his nose a mere six inches from the clerk's face. He was so close, his angry breath fogged the man's glasses. "Hark, and hark well, Co'pral. You got them magnifiers on your face for something." He tapped his sleeve. "See these stripes and see if you can't remember your insignia of rank. Address me as First Sergeant!"

Instantly intimidated, the clerk shot out of his chair and came to attention beside it.

"Son, don't get the idea I'm grinnin', because I ain't. That's a saber scar, and I earned it in a bloody battle. The man did that to me is dead, and I had fun killin' him. Do you follow my line of reasonin', Co'pral?"

Before he got an answer, Peagram said, "Show me to your commanding officer and do it at the double-step." He looked around. "This goddamned place stinks."

Peagram moved directly to the closed office door at the end of the room, the clerk barely beating him to it. Peagram stormed past, striding halfway across the room before coming to a heel-clicking ramrod figure of attention. He whipped out a smart salute to Captain Goggle.

Before Goggle could open his mouth, Peagram barked again, this time his voice ringing with full military protocol.

"First Sergeant Enoch Peagram, Second Dragoons, reporting, Captain. I am here at the orders of Himself, Sir!" Peagram paused, waiting for a reaction frcm Goggle. The captain was speechless from Peagram's crashing entrance.

"I am here to escort Captain Andrew Jackson Drumm and First Lieutenant Merry Christmas Ives to Washington, Sir!"

Goggle recovered from his astonishment. "Who sent you on this fool's errand, First Sergeant?" Goggle looked Peagram over, checking his spotless uniform, his saber, his huge red face, orange mustache, and the ugly gash from his ear to his mouth.

"It was Himself, Sir!"

Goggle ran a well-manicured hand over his face. He sized Peagram up for exactly what he was—a field and line first sergeant unskilled in the politics and protocol of garrison life.

"'Himself'? What kind of idiotic answer is that?"

Without a word, Peagram dug in his blouse for Marcy's memo and handed it to Goggle. Goggle took his time, running his clean half-moon nails along the crisp folds of the unopened document. "First Sergeant, I have been in the army fifteen years and I have never heard anyone referred to by that absurd title, Himself."

"Sir . . ."

"All I know, First Sergeant, is that both officers in question have not satisfactorily answered me about the loss of stock and weapons while carrying out a topographical expedition. Their case is presently pending the disposition of a court martial and they are being detained.''

"But, Sir . . . "

"By God, Sergeant, that's what's going to happen, and the sooner we get on with the court martial, the better.''

Goggle carefully unfolded Peagram's orders and smoothed the paper flat against his desk. He read the words intently.

Peagram turned to watch the clerk staring at him with a certain fascination. Peagram gave him his widest, most wicked grin displaying his scar and lots of teeth. The clerk quickly looked away, obviously intimidated by the fierce-looking, scarred First Sergeant. Peagram studied the ceiling, rocking slowly back and forth on his heels.

Goggle's chair skidded across the wood floor with a sharp rasping sound. "Millett!" Goggle looked up to see the clerk still near the door. "At the double step, Millett. Have the Officer of the Day and a detail bring Captain Drumm and Lieutenant Ives to this office immediately!''

Obviously shaken and humbled, Goggle came around in front of his desk and, leaning against it, said, ''Tell me again, First Sergeant. Who do you think 'Himself' is?''

Peagram fancied himself the cat tormenting the mouse. "By your leave, Sir." Peagram wrinkled his forehead. "Last year 'Himself' for me, at least, was the Secretary of State, Mr. Buchanan."

Goggle's face mirrored the question. "I mean this year."

"Oh, Sir," Peagram intoned in mock apology. "Mr. Marcy, himself. He's the Secretary of War, y'know."

Goggle swallowed his Adam's apple twice as his brain reeled. He hustled around his desk again, scratched busily with pen and ink on some paper. He sanded the paper and offered it to Peagram "That's the release for Captain Drumm and Lieutenant Ives. I'll want you to sign this release, too." He couldn't resist a dig at Peagram. "You can write, can't you?''

Unperturbed, Peagram drew up a chair, laid his heavy saber across the desk, scattering Goggle's mementos and papers, and accepted the inked quill. ''Sir, I'll remind the Cap'n that I am a First Sergeant in the Second Dragoons. I can write.'' He stared cooly at Goggle. "I can read, too.''

"Do you have transportation, First Sergeant?"

"I'm sure Captain Drumm will be obliged were you to requisition a fine coach for his journey to Washington, sir!" Damn you for a puke, Peagram thought.

When he told O'Malley, Drumm, and Ives about the scene, they laughed with him.

"Well, Sir," Peagram said with a smile. "Just seein' the face of Cap'n Goggle was better'n a drink of the best Kaintuck sour mash!"

Chapter Thirty-Three

Drumm surrendered his hat at Buchanan's door, and turned to see himself in a full-length mirror staring back at a more slender, weaker verson of the Drumm he once know. He brushed an errant lock of hair from his pale forehead. God how I've aged, he thought.

"My forehead is just as pale," Von Holder reminded him. "A common thing, you know. It tells the field soldier from the desk soldier; their's is a bleached look." Von Holder looked at the three and found no smiles. "Or so they say."

Von Holder probed in his grey coat for a cigar, but thought better of it. "Well, come on. Let's get this maneuver started." He was doing his best to brighten dour spirits. He marched the three into the salon where he introduced First Sergeant Peagram, Lieutenant Ives, and then Captain Drumm to Mr. Buchanan and his wife.

Buchanan gripped each of their hands strongly and noted warmly, "You have successfully completed a dangerous mission with honor." Marcy agreed, praising them for their "forthright action and valor."

The quartet drifted off into the crowd of strange faces and brilliant uniforms of other countries before seeing two familiar faces, burnished and gleaming, looking oddly out of place in this cultured surrounding. The knew each other from other places, other times, other intensities.

Lord Parton and Lady Diana moved through the crowd toward them, but had to stop on the way to greet old friends. Their eyes ever returned to the four near the entrance as they tried to make their way to across the room.

Neither Ives nor Drumm had seen them in well over a month since they left Jefferson Barracks.

Ives tugged at Drumm's sleeve. "Parton's wearing the uniform of a General." He was stunned. Peagram merely stood at attention as Parton strode up.

In time, the six were clustered together, the three soldiers saluting Parton, whose right arm rested in a black silk sling. They bowed to Lady Diana who returned the honor with a stylish curtsy. She rammed her arm through Drumm's, murmuring "Where *have* you been?" Before he could respond, Lord Parton stunned the guests with, "You bounders! Ha! Buchanan, these are the three I told you about. Ha! A rum lot, I say, top soldiers."

Parton's enthusiasm knew no bounds. The Americans looked at Parton with eyes gleaming with pride. This was the sorely wounded Briton who threw a rifle at Morella; the Englishman who bore his wounds without complaint. This man, his ways foreign to them, had become their comrade-in-arms. Now, in this unlikely setting, he was heaping praises on them among men of national prominence, men whose names were familiar but who, in their wildest dreams, they had never hoped to meet.

Buchanan countered, "Yes, Lord Parton. I do believe you've had occasion to meet these three American soldiers."

Drumm thought, "Oh, yes, and a hell of a lot more."

"Meet them?," Parton whooped. "If these three men were English soliders, I'd see they were made members of the Household Guards, and that the Order of the British Empire was pinned to their tunics!" He drew in a breath. "And then, by cheeky, I'd ask Her Majesty to knight them . . . and still they deserve more!"

He beamed as he stood in front of them. His eyes bore into Buchanan's and Marcy's. "In this country you treat your heroes in strange ways." He let the statement lay in the stunned silence of the opulent ballroom. "My people tell me you actually were under arrest with a court martial staring at you. That is, until the valiant First Sergeant Peagram saved you."

Buchanan acknowledged the error. "Both Mr. Marcy and I were to blame for that, Lord Parton."

Marcy's expression was one of seeking help as he stared at Von Holder who could only raise his shoulders and shrug.

"Yes, a grave mistake, Lord Parton," Marcy said. "We value these three men and we admire their courageous and meritorious action in carrying out a difficult and dangerous mission."

"Ha!" Parton said throwing an arm about Diana's ivory shoulders. "We saw them, eh, Diana? These three men led fewer than nineteen at times, time and again, against a whole squadron of the Mexican cavalry. Ha! Saved our lives three"—he paused, pulling at his lip—"no, by gad, it was four times."

Buchanan smiled benevolently. "We are all well aware how you and your lovely sister were the . . . ah, shall we call it, the bait laid by the Mexican government."

"Duped," Parton said. "Duped by those scoundrels."

Buchanan also saw that it was time to change the subject. He offered his arm to Diana. "Will you be my dinner partner, Lady Diana?" She smiled in acknowledgement and they led the way into the spacious dining room.

By now Peagram was in the grasp of a powdered, wrinkled dowager who seemed completely enchanted by the huge trunk of a man whose face carried the honorable scars of combat. Peagram was equally intent on helping her to her chair. Von Holder followed Peagram, and Drumm and Ives sat separated by Lord Parton.

Drumm queried Parton. "I didn't know you were still in the cavalry, er, the Household Guards."

"The Tins, my boy, the Tins. Name comes from those blasted chest plates. It really is a sort of honorary rank, don't you know." Parton winked at Drumm.

"If the Household Guards were called into action," Ives asked, "would you go?"

"Emphatically yes!" Parton pounded the table. "I am their commanding general. Where they go, I go!"

Buchanan let the large table of guests eat their way through an elegant and lengthy supper. Both Drumm and Ives heard Peagram speak, and laughter followed. They smiled at each other, giving the thumbs-up sign over the way their reluctant comrade-in-arms had adjusted to what he had earlier described as "choppin' in tall cotton."

Finally, Buchanan rose, holding his wine goblet in a toast.

"Ladies and gentlemen, distinguished guests, Lord Parton, Sir Hardwig Abney, General of Queen Victoria's Household Cavalry, and Envoy to Washington '' Buchanan paused for effect. "That same Lord Parton bent my ear earlier this evening." His eyes centered on the three representatives of Drumm's Devils.

"Our good English gentleman, diplomat, and general badgered me, saying that if First Sergeant Peagram, Lieutenant Ives, and Captain Drumm were Englishmen he would see they had medals pinned on their jackets and would arrange to have them knighted by the Queen herself."

He peered at Lord Parton. "Am I correct, sir?"

Lord Parton rose, ready to raise his own wine glass in Buchanan's toast.

"I say, old chap, do proceed with the toast. My claret is losing its color!" Buchanan led the entire group in laughter.

Buchanan collected himself and spoke. "I rise to salute First Sergeant Enoch Peagram whose duty and honor to his country we hail!"

The entire company rose and drank to Peagram's health while the huge fighting man sat and burned with embarrassment.

"Next, I raise my glass to salute First Lieutenant Merry Christmas Ives whose ability as an artillerist was paramount to the success of this recently concluded dangerous mission."

Again the assembly raised their glasses, their eyes all on Ives. Buchanan waited until the goblets were again filled.

"In every successful battle scenario there appears a standout leader, a man who takes command. He makes decisions, the right ones, and stands by them, never wavering. The role of the commanding officer of this valiant unit belonged to Captain Andrew Jackson Drumm. I salute Captain Drumm!"

Secretary Marcy followed. "Lord Parton, we have no gracious Queen to knight our soldiers or pin medals on them for a job well done. But we do step each man ahead in rank, and give them each six months leave with full pay!"

A general acclaim arose, led by the flamboyant and vocal Parton. "Hear! Hear!"

Marcy picked up a large roll of parchments that had been beside his plate throughout the meal, and unfurled one to read: "By personal order of James Polk, President of these United States, Enoch Persiper Peagram, First Sergeant, United States Second Dragoons, will assume the warrant officer rank as Regimental Sergeant Major."

He motioned Peagram to come forward to receive the warrant. After saluting and a warm handshake from Marcy and Buchanan, Peagram found his way back to his seat accompanied by a round of applause.

Then it was Ives's turn, and he received a commission as Captain of Artillery while his cheeks burned red with embarrassment.

After Marcy handed Drumm his warrant, he restrained him with a hand on his good arm. "Major Drumm, I only wish your father could have been here tonight." His voice raised slightly. "Drumm's father is Colonel Toyal Drumm, a legendary hero of the War of 1812—the last time we will ever cross the swords of war with our British cousins."

Back at his chair, Drumm remained standing and raised his glass, shaking with a strange exhaustion as he did it. "It was our pleasure—Regimental Sergeant Peagram, Captain Ives and myself—to spend time in our recent excursion with Lord Parton and Lady Diana. Their courage and valor were the equal of any in the command, including its officers."

He staggered slightly, using his napkin to erase a shadow of perspiration from his forehead.

"How can I say how much our entire command admired 'Hardy and Diana', as we called them, except to quote from their own William Shakespeare."

Drumm turned slowly toward Buchanan. "With your permission, sir."

A curious Buchanan signalled Drumm to continue.

"Then from *King Richard II*, Act II, these words tell us why you are who you are, and why we regard you with our deepest affection: England—This fortress built by Nature for herself against infection and hand of war. This happy breed of Englishmen, this little world, this precious stone set in the silver sea. This blessed plot, this earth, this realm, This England . . ."

Drumm stopped, raised his glass, and again wiped his face. His legs trembled under him, and a faint odor told him his wounds, refusing to heal, were suppurating. Drumm knew his eyelids were flickering and felt heavy; his muscles sagged in spite of himself and he was weakening by the minute. He felt Ives tuck a handkerchief in his left hand to prevent the drain from the wound from leaking on the tablecloth. Still, he finished.

"Here too, in our beloved country, we have a poet who wrote these lines not so long ago:

"Cannon balls may aid the truth,

"But thought's a weapon stronger.

"And, of all, will win our battles by its aid."

Everyone toasted Parton and his sister. Diana watched horrified as Drumm slumped at his chair while Ives and Von Holder rushed to him, whispering behind him. Those at the table watched with growing concern.

Appropriately, it was Lord Parton who broke the tension. "By God, Mister Secretary, you'd better send this Major straight to Buckin'ham Palace as an envoy. He's got more diplomacy in his little finger than you or I have crammed in our entire hides!"

Von Holder nudged a weakening Drumm. "Cover your left arm, Andy. You're losing blood." He handed Drumm a clean napkin while Ives bent over, cleaning Drumm's wrist and hand while Drumm leaned back in his chair, eyes closed on drawn cheeks.

Buchanan's keen eyes sensed Drumm's predicament. He motioned to Von Holder to his side. "You and Ives take Major Drumm into the kitchen. I'll follow."

In a moment, Peagram deserted his dining companion as he and Ives helped Drumm from the table, led by Von Holder. Inside the spacious kitchen, a squat naval officer strode up to Drumm, taking charge.

"Captain Nathaniel Edwards, Naval Surgeon," he said crisply, peeling off Drumm's jacket, its sleeve sodden with bright blood. He handed the jacket to a maid and stripped off the blood-soaked shirt as Diana entered the kitchen.

The wounds, taken at Sybille Pass nearly six weeks before, were ugly and purple, oozing blood and yellow matter around the black thread stitches put there by Blanchard. Drumm was only semiconscious, his temperature on the rise, and faint from infection and loss of blood.

The doctor hummed. "Saber, eh, Major?"

Drumm nodded, his eyes steadying on Diana. "Our cook . . . Mr. Blanchard." He was rambling now, his thoughts refusing to stabilize. "Could make the best damned coffee I ever tasted . . ."

He fought against a blackness seeping in his mental vision and, like a drowning man, tried to keep his eyes and mouth open. He held out his right hand to Diana in supplication; she took it and held it to her breast. Buchanan and Marcy appeared to lean into the circle around the sick man.

"Get this man immediately to Hampstead Hospital," Edwards commanded, rolling down his sleeves. "I'll be along as soon as I take Mrs. Edwards home." His marble-blue eyes bored into Buchanan's, and then into Marcy's.

"Who the hell is responsible for this utterly filthy, dirty way to treat an officer in our Army?! By God, in the Navy we take care of our wounded. This man could lose his life. Or his arm. Or both!"

Edwards walked behind Ives and Peagram, who had formed a basket with their arms, lifting Drumm and walking past the startled and staring guests as Diana followed with Drumm's jacket.

Edwards strode away, still angry.

"The Godawful stupidity of the medical treatment of this man is worthy of a butcher in a slaughterhouse!"

Chapter Thirty-Four

It was May 15, 1846, before Drumm was judged by Dr. Edwards and his family doctor at Pamlico Landing to be strong enough to rejoin his regiment.

"By gad, boy," Drumm's father thundered. "When you came here from Hampstead Hospital, none of us figured you would live. Praise the Lord!"

Colonel Toyal Drumm's right leg was gone. "Carried away by a British bullet . . . cannonball, I guess," he had often said. Drumm thought his father looked like a falcon. His hawk nose curved down to his mouth, supported by a long jaw line. Wisps and tufts of white hair fell over his forehead, buffeted by a soft onshore breeze.

He pointed with his crutch. "Only one here said you were going to live and that was our friend Peagram." He smacked his lips, studying his old orderly, now thickening with age. "Mr. Peagram. I like that sound and if ever a lad earned R.S.M., you surely fill the bill, Enoch."

Drumm hitched his body into a more comfortable position. "Huh, dad, that's remarkable. Years ago—or so you told me—he was the only one who said you would live."

The elder Drumm leaned against the garden's birdbath. "Well, that's what Regimental Sergeant Majors are for; to lean on, to listen to, and to learn from."

"Yes, sir," Peagram allowed sheepishly. "I knowed I'd be needing Major Drumm. We both've got to get down to Matamoras and join up with our regiment."

Drumm remembered. "Ives is chasing all over Mexico with Ringgold, Bragg, and Lord's artillery units."

The father watched his son stand, stretch, and run a few steps to get his circulation going. He thought he looked all right. In the days that followed, Drumm and Peagram practiced every day with their sabers, rode before breakfast, and again in the afternoon. Drumm's wound knit good as new; he could feel his arm becoming limber again as he went through his saber drill from horseback.

"General Taylor is on the move now," he told his father one afternoon, "along with the Second Dragoons, and his artillery. He has Brown and the Seventh Infantry, and Hardin and the Fourth Infantry."

He held out a message to his father. "Enoch and I leave tomorrow. We sail to New Orleans, then it's overland to Jesup and Taylor in Mexico."

"Damn me!," the elder Drumm growled. "Go on. Win the war." He aimed his crutch at his son. "Just as soon as it's over, we sail for England to get you properly married."

His son beamed with the thought. An almost royal wedding. They would be good times; something to cling to and hang on to in the rough weeks and months ahead.

His father cackled at Peagram. "And you'll go with us to England. We'd get lost, both of us, without you, hey?!"

At dawn the two climbed into a buggy. Colonel Drumm folded his son into his arms. "Andy, go with God." He smiled. "And with Enoch!"

He shouted at them as the buggy dusted out the circular drive in front of the Drumm home's portico. "You whipped them Mexicans once, and by all that's holy, you can get the job done again!"

Next day, Major Andrew Jackson Drumm with his right arm strong again—and with his other strong right arm, Regimental Sergeant Major Enoch Peagram—boarded a coastal steamer. In a short time they were on horses headed for their regiment at Matamoras.

They fell in with a military convoy heading for the Rio Grande. News of the great May 9 victory at the Battle of Resaca de la Paloma was on the lips of returning teamsters and the wounded they carried.

The two men listened eagerly, picturing Captain May of the Second Dragoons, a well-known and splendid horseman with a full beard to his chest and his hair falling to his shoulders, leading a classic cavalry charge ordered by General Zachary Taylor at Resaca de la Paloma.

The week after July 4, they reported to Colonel David Twiggs, only recently made a Brigadier General.

"Ha!" the immaculate Twiggs thundered. He stood, rearing up to his six feet, six inches of height, measuring Drumm and Peagram. "I know you, Enoch Peagram. Knew you when you were a boy bugler and orderly with this man's father at New Orleans in 1814. Toy Drumm!" He smacked his lips savoring the words. "There was a soldier!" He looked keenly at the younger Drumm. "And from what Kearny says, you were a holy terror when it came to the Seventh Regular Mexican Cavalry."

His bright blue eyes held Drumm. "Glad to have you and Enoch in our regiment." He motioned to his orderly. "We have mail for you, Major Drumm." He handed over the heavily stamped and sealed envelope.

"Hope it's good news. Came all the way from Surrey, England. It carries a diplomatic seal on it." He spoke to his orderly. "See to it my new Regimental Sergeant Major finds his quarters nearby, and set up a tent for my new aide-de-camp, Major Drumm." He cut a piece of tobacco, offered the plug of Mickey Twist around as he saw the orderly still standing at the tent entrance.

"Now!" he growled, and the orderly disappeared. He grinned past his mutton-chop whiskers. "Now, the both of you, git! Report right after morning call, both of you!"

Drumm went into the orderly tent, consumed with curiosity over his letter. His clasp knife's keen blade quickly did justice to the envelope, and he unfolded the letter. The corporal ducked outside where Peagram engaged him in a few inquiries about the regiment while Drumm read his letter in private.

Peagram waited a long time and finally, hearing nothing, slapped the tent's front canvas. "Sir? Major Drumm? Are you all right?"

"Come in, Mr. Peagram." Drumm's voice had a hollow note

198

that alarmed Peagram. He stepped into the dull sunlight of the tent; it had a new, but familiar smell of fresh, waterproofed canvas. He found Drumm seated at the orderly desk, a letter crumpled in his hand while he stared at the tent's wall.

"Beggin' your pardon, sir. Bad news?"

"The very worst. Dad will be devastated." He held it out with a soft sighing sob. "Read it for yourself."

Peagram smoothed the wrinkled parchment and read:

Parton House, Surrey
April 15, 1846.

Dear Andrew,

It is with a heavy heart that I inform you that Diana lost her life just as our ship entered a fog bank near the mouth of the Thames River. God forbid, but a lugger loaded to the gunnels with hogsheads of beef and pork rammed our ship on the larboard side, exactly where Diana's cabin was located. The only consolation we have is that death was instantaneous.

I write you this extremely difficult letter because of your troth and the great love you had for each other. My heart is rent almost beyond repair, dear Andrew, but even in the dark depths of despair I offer you, your valiant father, and the magnificent R.S.M. Peagram the courtesy, love, and hospitality of Parton House.

Win your war, Andrew. Then come visit us. You know, old man, that I have two more sisters.

God go with you, as my friendship and affection travels with you always.

Hardy

Peagram slowly read the title. "Sir Abney Hardwig, Lord Parton, M.P., General of the Household Guard, O.B.E., K.G.B." His eyes blurred and he pulled a huge handkerchief out, wiped his eyes, and blew his nose. He handed the letter back to Drumm who carefully folded it and slid it into his jacket. He looked up at Peagram with moist eyes.

"Well, Enoch?"

"What's best all around, sir. Drumm's going to war again, right after mornin' report!"

GLOUCESTER COUNTY LIBRARY

3 2928 00079 5371

FIC
BRAGG   Bragg, William
            Frederick

         Drumm's war

DUE DATE   **BRODART   03/93   16.95**

4-93

GLOUCESTER
COUNTY LIBRARY